Witness Protection 2
The Return of Whiskey Tango Foxtrot

Holly Copella

ISBN: 1947694006
ISBN-13: 978-1-947694-00-2

To my great friend, Daniela
From one dreamer to another…welcome to your dream!

ACKNOWLEDGMENTS

Copella Books: First Paperback Edition 2016
Cover Artist: Daniela Owergoor
Dani-owergoor.deviantart.com
Printed by CreateSpace, An Amazon.com Company

PUBLISHER'S NOTE

Chapter One

Salvatore Romano's office building was located in an industrial park on the outskirts of Chicago. The impressive building was twenty-one stories of commercial offices, which housed medical professionals, real estate moguls, and many other businesses. It was already late afternoon on a beautiful Friday, promising a warm and sunny weekend. An investment firm, one of Romano's many businesses, was located on the nineteenth floor. An attractive woman in her mid-twenties, who was dressed business casual, entered the receptionist area. Leeann Whitley attempted to contain her wild, dark hair in a business-style bun, but stray locks made daring escapes only adding to what most would describe as a country girl appearance. She crossed the elegant reception area decorated in fine antique furnishings while on her way to her boss's office. A large floor to ceiling window revealed the distant city skyline, a sight she'd grown accustomed to seeing daily.

Lee approached the perky, blonde receptionist seated behind her desk. She seemingly guarded the boss's office from any unwanted visitors. The attractive woman in her mid-twenties appeared bored as she flipped through a magazine. Tonya Rhodes was the first friend Lee had made when she moved to Chicago and started working for Salvatore Romano. Despite only working for the company a little over seven months, she and Tonya became close friends. Lee stopped before Tonya's desk just outside the boss's office. Tonya jumped slightly when she saw her then relaxed. She grabbed a business card from her desk and placed it between the pages to mark her place. She pushed the magazine aside and focused her attention on her friend.

3

"Thank God it's Friday," Tonya announced while groaning. "I have to get out of this place for a few days."

Lee sat on the edge of Tonya's desk facing her and smiled sympathetically. "Yeah, you're not kidding," she remarked. "It's been a long week."

"At least you get to hide in your office," Tonya remarked.

"Yeah, but they always find me," Lee teased.

The office door opened with a little more vigor than necessary, startling Lee. Lee quickly sprang up from the edge of the desk and looked toward the boss's door. A tall, moderately muscular man stepped out of the office. Jericho was a ruggedly handsome man who dressed more like a hitman for the mob than a businessman. Despite his rugged good looks, he wore a serious look on his face and came across as moderately intimidating. His hair was in a military buzz cut that seemed to extend into a stubbly beard of sorts. Lee was sure he had his share of women fawning over him because of his outward appearance, but she knew he was more brawn than brains, making him less than attractive to her.

Jericho eyed both women, gave an impolite nod, and continued from the receptionist area. Lee wasn't sure why she always felt as if he was on his way to 'bump off' someone. He almost never spoke, at least not that she'd ever heard.

"Well," Tonya announced with a sigh as she watched the man leave. "He was friendlier than usual."

Lee chuckled softly, forcing Tonya to grin at her own joke. Lee returned to the edge of the desk facing Tonya and studied her perky friend.

"How are the plans coming for the boss's birthday bash?" Lee finally inquired, changing the subject.

"Looks to be quite the gathering," Tonya replied. "No big surprise there."

"Considering he's had you planning it for nearly a month, I should hope so," Lee teased her friend. "I've never seen his house before. Have you? I hear it's pretty impressive."

"I was there for that one Christmas party. I suppose impressive would be the correct term," Tonya announced then appeared distracted. Her smile turned into a frown. "If you need something from *the man*, I suggest you talk to him now, because I'm about to put him in a bad mood."

"Oh?"

Tonya shifted in her chair and appeared sympathetic. "His daughter sent her regrets about the party," she informed Lee while making a pouting face.

Lee groaned softly and immediately felt her heart sink. "Yeah, you're right, that's going to kill him," she replied gently. "How long has it been since she moved away?"

"Nearly two years."

"Before my time," Lee responded then gave her friend a curious look. "What happened anyway?"

Tonya shrugged. "Beats me," she responded while leaning her elbows on her desk. "But she hasn't returned his phone calls since she moved out of the house. I think it involved some guy he didn't want her seeing."

"I find it hard to believe Sal doesn't like someone," Lee announced. "He likes everyone."

"Well, she's his little girl," Tonya remarked. "I know my father didn't like any of the boys I brought home." She appeared to consider something then tilted her head. "You know, I had heard some strange rumors around the time she'd left. Something about his daughter hacking into his computer. They had a big fight right after that. I thought he was mad about her snooping in his computer. But when I spoke to her after she'd moved out, she mentioned something about being upset with what she found on his computer."

"Huh, I wonder what she found that would upset her like that," Lee remarked.

"She didn't elaborate, and I didn't press," Tonya replied. "I try to stay out of the boss's personal business, especially where his daughter is concerned." Tonya straightened in her chair and swiftly changed the subject. "We're going out tonight, right?"

"If I get out on time, I can meet you at 'The Roadside' for dinner," Lee replied.

Her friend made a face. "You have to get out of the rut you're in," Tonya announced while groaning softly. "We eat there every Friday night."

"And afterward, we go to that club you like so much," Lee reminded, almost feeling offended. "If you're going to throw me to the wolves at that dance club of yours, I'd at least like to go with a full belly."

"You're a strange girl, Lee," Tonya announced while laughing at her friend's expense. "I'm going to have a hard time finding you a suitable mate."

Lee rolled her eyes and looked away. "I'd rather you didn't. Thanks."

"What do you have against the male population?" Tonya demanded. "For nearly six months I've been trying to find you a nice man. You shoot every one of them down."

5

"There are two types of men," Lee announced firmly while indicating the count on her fingers. "The rich guys with overinflated egos, and the not-so-rich guys wishing they could be the rich guys. And do you know what they both have in common?"

Tonya eyed her friend but refused to respond, because she seemed to know where the conversation was going.

"They both want women with all boobs and no brains," Lee replied.

"Now, you know that's not true," Tonya scolded.

"Guys want Barbie dolls and princesses," Lee dramatically informed her friend. "They want women who'll dress up, wear high heels, and paint their face with a layer of make-up. I don't want to be that woman." Lee sank into her own fantasies and smiled dreamily. "I want some cowboy," she gleefully announced. "I want a man who isn't afraid to get dirty, and who doesn't mind if I wear jeans to dinner."

"We live in the middle of Chicago," Tonya replied dryly. "Good luck finding a cowboy."

"He doesn't have to be a cowboy in the literal sense," Lee scoffed and glared at her friend. "You know what I mean."

"I'm all for playing a cowboy," a man with a Southern accent announced from across the reception area.

Both looked toward the reception doorway and saw Finn casually leaning against the doorframe while grinning at Lee. Finn was a moderately creepy looking man with thinning dark hair and beady eyes. The man in his mid-thirties was Southern born with a backwoods accent that only added to his psycho killer charm. When he smiled at Lee, she felt as if he were sizing her up for his next meal. Tonya immediately frowned and pretended to be working.

"Your stalker is back," she muttered softly to Lee.

"Be nice," Lee whispered as she stood then returned her attention to the man in the doorway while attempting to remain pleasant.

Lee always feared turning her back on Sal's right hand-man. Something told her Finn might very well hump her if she didn't keep close watch on him. He was a sharp dressed man, always smelled shower fresh, and attempted to maintain a gentlemanly appearance, but his actions, tone, and the way he stared with his beady eyes always set her on edge.

"It's not polite to eavesdrop," Lee informed him.

Finn straightened and approached them at the desk with an overly confident swagger. His creepy smile and fixed gaze upon her sent a chill down her spine.

"Yes, I know," he replied in his slow, Southern drawl. "But I hear your voice, and I'm drawn to it like a bee to pollen."

"Kind of romantic," Tonya muttered while keeping her nose in her magazine, pretending she wasn't listening.

Lee wanted to smack her friend, but she doubted Finn heard the comment. He stopped a few feet before her and sat on the edge of Tonya's desk. Tonya shot a glare at him, although he was too busy casting sweeping looks over Lee.

"I got me a pair of snakeskin cowboy boots and a jacket to match," he informed Lee while grinning. "I could wear them tonight. There's this country bar just outside of town I'm sure you'd love, if you'd permit me to take you out."

"I've already made plans for tonight," she informed him and refrained from flinching at his invitation even though she felt her body shiver slightly.

He glanced at Tonya behind him then back at Lee. "You two going out to that club? Maybe I could meet you there. First round is on me."

The office door opened, alerting all three to the boss's presence. Finn jumped up from where he sat on the edge of Tonya's desk and turned toward the office. Salvatore Romano was a robust man, although not necessarily overweight. He held his weight well. Despite being in his mid-forties, his face had a youthful appearance and almost cherub in nature. His baby face and moderately balding head gave him an innocent appeal. No woman over sixty could refuse his charm. Thankfully, he was wealthy and could lure in young, attractive women with the size of his bank account. He was the first to admit it and joke about the type of women he attracted. Lee and Tonya couldn't deny they were lucky to have such a pleasant boss. He gave Finn a stern look, almost as if sensing he was pestering the women.

"Would you wait for me downstairs in the lobby, Finn?" Sal asked although it seemed more of a command.

"Certainly, boss," Finn replied then smiled slyly at Lee before leaving the reception area.

Once he was gone, Sal focused his attention on Lee. "You'll have to forgive Finn, my dear. He has a tendency to lay the charm on a little thick," he announced cheerfully and smiled in a way that would melt any grandmother's heart.

"I suppose he's harmless," Lee remarked.

Sal smirked and shrugged his shoulders as if unable to agree with her statement. "The jury's still out on that one." His cheerful mood immediately returned. "You must have been working hard this morning. I didn't see you in the break room. There's a plateful of pastries going to waste."

"Yes, I saw them," she replied and hid her smile, "which is why I've been avoiding the break room."

"You should have known what you were getting into when you agreed to work for an Italian," Salvatore announced cheerfully. "I have all my grandmother's recipes stored in my head, and I love cooking for others. I should have been a chef."

"He is a wonderful cook," Tonya informed Lee. "He's cooking some of the food for his party."

"Just the best dishes. I have a team of caterers for the rest." Sal grinned proudly then looked at Tonya. "Anymore replies on my party invites?"

Tonya immediately shifted in her chair. "Ten more said they'll be attending. Only one regret."

Sal stared at Tonya a moment as his grin slowly faded. "Was it my daughter?" he asked timidly.

Tonya slowly nodded as if it pained her to inform him of the bad news. Sal frowned as his shoulders sagged. He attempted a polite wave and walked away from the desk, cutting his pleasant mood short. Tonya shook her head as she watched him walk away like a lost puppy.

"Breaks my heart."

"Where does his daughter live now?"

"Somewhere in Colorado," Tonya replied and glanced back at her friend. "I heard rumor she's a lounge singer or something. Changed her name and everything. She's using her mother's maiden name. Pinto, I believe."

Lee sighed deeply and shrugged as she sank into thought. "Maybe she's just looking for her cowboy too."

Chapter Two

*J*t was an hour later and only two hours from the end of the day. Lee poked her head into the accountant's office and saw him staring at the computer with his chin in his hand. Wiley seemed to be off in his own little world. He had been under a lot of stress the last few weeks in both his personal and professional life. She knew his wife had left him, but no one seemed to know the reason why. Wiley came across as a decent guy. He was slightly nerdy looking and a little round in the mid-section, but his broad shoulders balanced out his frame.

"Wiley?" she announced, uncertain whether she wanted to disturb him or not.

He lifted his head as if she had startled him. Wiley was an average looking man with a head of thick, dark hair that would make most men envious. He managed a smile, although it was clearly for show.

"Hey, Lee," he replied and squirmed in his chair while attempting to look casually relaxed. It was obvious he was uncomfortable. "What can I do for you?"

"I had to make an adjustment to Samuel's paycheck, and I got some weird message from my check writing program that the account is in use," Lee informed him. "I couldn't make the correction. Are you working on something in the bank accounts?"

"Uh, oh, yeah," he replied and straightened. "I'm attempting to locate a discrepancy I found earlier. I'll log out for the next twenty minutes, so that you can make your adjustment."

"Great," she replied. "I appreciate that."

Lee was about to turn and leave then hesitated and reconsidered. She entered the office, leaned against the desk edge, and offered a sympathetic look.

"Is there anything I can help you with?" she asked then hesitated and considered her next question carefully. "Or something you want to talk about?"

He glanced at her, fidgeted, and appeared hesitant to respond. "I appreciate that, but I'm sure I'll find the problem," Wiley replied then offered a tiny smile.

She glanced at the picture of his wife and children on his desk and immediately felt bad for the man. Lee then saw a gold tube of lipstick setting near the picture and became curious.

"What's with the lipstick?"

He eyed the gold tube then looked back at her and grinned. "I'm a cross-dresser on the weekends."

Lee stared at him with some surprise. Wiley suddenly laughed at the look on her face.

"That's how rumors get started," he teased. "I found it in the hallway earlier. I think it belongs to one of Sal's clients. She'll be back on Monday."

Lee hid her embarrassed smile. "I'll buy that."

"You'd better get back to your computer and make that adjustment while you can."

"Yes, I should," she announced and straightened from where she had leaned against his desk. "Samuel will hover over my desk until he gets his check."

Lee turned and left the office. Wiley stared after her and appeared deep in thought while strumming his fingers on the desktop. He glanced at a gold tube of lipstick, picked it up, and removed the back to reveal a USB drive. He again glanced at the doorway then inserted the USB into the computer port and transferred several files onto the fancy thumb drive. Once he was finished, he removed the lipstick flash drive and replaced the cap. He set the faux lipstick back on his desk and removed a standard USB flash drive from his drawer. He stared at it a moment and then stuck it in his pants pocket. Wiley inhaled deeply, leaned back in his chair, and stared blankly at the computer screen.

†

*L*ee sat behind the desk in her cozy office. She handed the revised paycheck to the man standing before her desk. Samuel nodded his appreciation and left. Lee returned to her computer and logged off the banking program. The computer suddenly flickered and the screen went blank. She stared at the screen with surprise and pressed the space bar several times. Nothing happened.

"What the hell--?"

She attempted to turn the computer off and then on again, but nothing happened. Lee groaned then stood and headed into the corridor. She walked along the hallway toward the computer closet. As she opened the door, Wiley straightened and looked back at her. He attempted a smile.

"I'm already working on the problem," he informed her. "Just one more glitch for a Friday afternoon."

"Should I notify Tonya so she can call ComServe for tech support?"

"Why bother?" he replied. "They'll give us the runaround and refuse to come out until Monday anyway." He fiddled with the computer system then frowned. "I'm sure I can figure out what's wrong. And if I can't," he glanced at her and smiled, "it'll give you an excuse to leave early."

"Wouldn't that be nice," she teased then left the computer closet.

✝

*I*t was a little after five o'clock that afternoon. Lee walked along the corridor on the nineteenth floor while rooting through her purse. She was frustrated. Once again, she was unable to find her car keys. She passed by Wiley's office, noting that he still sat behind his desk.

"Lee," he called to her.

She paused within the corridor then returned to his office and stepped into the doorway.

"It's Friday, Wiley," she reminded him and added a teasing smile. "Don't you know you're supposed to be packing it in for the weekend?"

"You know me," he replied. "I'm a workaholic. Now that I'm a recently *single* workaholic, I have more time to spend on my addiction." He fidgeted slightly. "Are, uh, you and Tonya going out tonight?" he asked almost timidly then forced a tiny smile. "God that sounded desperate."

Lee hid her smile as she approached his desk. "You're always welcome to come out with us, Wiley," she boldly informed him. "I couldn't live with myself if they found your rotting, cobweb covered corpse in that chair Monday morning."

"Are you sure you don't mind my tagging along? There's a good chance I'll just ruin your good time," he replied while leaning back in his chair. "I'll probably spend the entire evening crying in my beer and telling you how much better things were before that shrew, Polly, cleaned out my bank account and left me."

"And I'll tell you how all men are pigs," she announced cheerfully. "It'll be fun. Now, come on."

Wiley laughed softly and straightened, his mood miraculously improving. "How about I meet you there in an hour? The computers just came back online, and I have to figure out what the hell I did wrong."

Lee cast her purse on the vacant chair before his desk and joined him behind the desk. His computer screen was blank. Lee appeared puzzled then glanced at him.

"I thought you said the computers were up and running?" she remarked.

"Well, they are," he announced. "I just have to reboot first. This thing isn't as young as it used to be."

"So what's the big problem this time?" she asked in a teasing tone. "Did you lose another fifty cents?"

"Sort of," he replied and raised his brows in suggestion. "But you'd have to move the decimal point another eight spots."

She stared at him with surprise as her mouth fell open. "Are you telling me that you lost fifty million dollars?" Lee gasped, almost unable to fathom such a large amount.

"Not lost," he replied simply. "Just *misplaced*. I mean, it's still--" Wiley indicated the screen before him and tapped it. "--in there somewhere. I just need to find out where it's hiding and put it back where it belongs."

"I don't think you're going to get much done tonight," Lee announced while reclaiming her purse and set it on the edge of his desk. "It looks like the server is still down, and I don't think it's coming back on until Monday." She laughed softly, although she didn't find it that funny. "Which probably explains why I'm actually going home on time myself." Lee again routed through her bag for her keys and no longer paid attention to him. "I'll look for you at 'The Roadside' in an hour." She cast a glare at him. "But no excuses or I'll come back and roll you and your chair out of here and down to the parking garage."

While Lee routed through her purse, Wiley secretly nudged his desk blotter, jolting her purse from its perch on the edge of the desk.

It dumped onto the floor, spilling more than a dozen items alongside Wiley's chair.

"What the hell is wrong with me?" Lee exclaimed. "I'm such a klutz lately!"

Wiley sprang from his chair to his knees and helped her pick up the discarded items, returning them to her purse. She reached for her keys just beneath the desk and groaned while staring at the small assortment of keys on the ring.

"There they are," she muttered. "I need to get a smaller purse. This is ridiculous carrying this much crap around."

Wiley slipped the gold lipstick flash drive into her purse along with her sunglasses. He returned to his chair and offered a pleasant smile as she stood. She placed her car keys in her jacket pocket, so she wouldn't misplace them again.

"I'll be sure to be there in an hour," he announced with an odd cheeriness to his words.

"Talk about switching gears," she remarked while eyeing him. "Are you admitting defeat in the battle of man versus machine?" Her eyes suddenly narrowed. "Or are you lying so I'll get out of your hair?"

He laughed softly and rocked in his chair. "Yes," Wiley replied and appeared amused by the stray look she gave him.

"Don't worry, I wasn't planning on staying," she remarked. "Your office is like a sauna."

Lee removed her jacket and immediately felt relief from the intense heat. Apparently, Wiley wasn't a fan of air-conditioning.

"Actually, I had a small revelation," Wiley announced. "I think I solved the fifty million dollar dilemma."

"Oh," Lee replied with surprise, although it was a relief. "I'm glad to hear. We'll expect you in an hour."

Lee gathered her purse and left the accountant's office. Wiley watched her leave then returned his attention to his desk. He sank into thought while rapping his fingers on the desktop then looked at the picture of his wife and two boys. He picked up the framed picture, stared at it a moment, and then removed the back. He pulled out a business card hidden behind the frame and removed his cell phone. Wiley's fingers trembled as he entered the phone number. He waited a moment and again rapped his fingers on the desktop as the phone on the other end rang. He jumped with surprise to the responding voice.

"Hey, it's Wiley." There was a brief pause. "I found what you were hoping I'd find, although it wasn't easy." He listened a moment then looked at his watch. "No, I'd rather you didn't.

Things have been very tense around here. I feel like I'm being watched. I know I'm probably just being paranoid. Can you meet me in an hour at a local dive called 'The Roadside'?" Wiley hesitated and listened to the person on the other end. "Yeah, I have the flash drive. I'll see you in an hour."

He disconnected the call with a trembling finger and again stared at the framed photo of his wife and kids. He sighed deeply and frowned.

"When this is all over, I hope you'll understand why I had to do this," he muttered.

The office door closed, causing Wiley to look up from the photo. His expression dropped slightly, and he appeared surprised as his visitor approached his desk.

"What are you doing here so late?" he asked.

Chapter Three

*O*nly a few minutes later, Lee exited the elevator and approached the security guard at the front desk within the first floor lobby. Jenner, the moderately out of shape security guard, greeted her with an electronic tablet in his hand. She set her jacket and purse down on the counter and didn't notice her jacket slipping from the counter to the other side. She accepted the tablet and signed her name on it.

"You're leaving late again on a Friday, Miss Whitley" he announced while attempting to sound cheerful. "You're always the last to leave."

She eyed him with surprise by the comment. "Everyone else left?"

"Well, except Wiley in accounting, but he's always here late since his wife, well, you know. Want me to walk you to your car?" he asked as he reached for her purse on the counter, apparently not seeing her jacket fall to the floor behind the desk either. He handed the purse to her.

"No, I'll be fine," she replied while accepting her bag.

"It's creepy in the garage when most of the cars have gone," Jenner announced. "Lots of perverts out there. Never know when one might slip into the garage."

"Maybe," she announced and hid her smile, "but I'm from the country. I have one hell of a right hook." Lee fumbled around inside her purse, removed a silver tube of lipstick, and proudly displayed it. "And this."

"Lipstick?" he announced with a look of doubt.

"Not lipstick," she announced and removed the cap to reveal a spray nozzle. "Mace."

Jenner grinned with approval. "Nice." He again turned serious and almost fatherly. "Still, I'd feel better if I walked you at least as far as the parking garage door."

"Deal."

Lee and the security guard walked in virtual silence on their hike to the parking garage entrance. They passed another elevator not far from the rear entrance. Lee glanced at the lit penthouse button. The lightly used elevator was Salvatore's private elevator to his penthouse accommodations. Despite having a grand mansion in the suburbs, he had a lavish penthouse suite in the office building, which he used mostly during the week to avoid the city traffic. The lit button indicated he was upstairs. His private elevator was the only one that went as high as the penthouse on the twenty-first floor, and its access was restricted to those with an access card. Beyond his private elevator was access to his reserved parking spot next to the door. Jenner walked with her to another set of doors further down, which was the quicker route to the main parking structure. He paused before the main parking garage exit door and punched a code into the panel, indicating he'd already set the building's alarm system from the main desk. He held the door open for her.

"Good night, ma'am," he announced cheerfully.

"Night."

Lee walked along the empty, enclosed parking garage. The sound of her dress shoes clomping echoed throughout the entire level. She hated the sound her shoes made and the way it echoed. It always sounded as if there were multiple people surrounding her. Having Jenner walk her to her car would have been appreciated, but she didn't want to trouble him. He had a lot of building to secure as the only guard on the night shift. Despite her overactive imagination, she knew she was safe in the building's parking garage. She paused before her car and rummaged through her purse. Her expression dropped when she once again couldn't locate her keys.

"You've got to be kidding," she muttered with disgust. "I just had my keys--"

Her thoughts strayed to her jacket. She looked around then groaned softly.

"Great."

Lee turned and headed back for the parking garage entrance. If she wasn't losing her keys, she was losing her purse. If not her purse, her jacket. She never understood how she could be so forgetful. Lee approached the rear entrance and pressed the security call button. She waited several minutes, but the guard didn't respond. She looked at the security pad, inhaled deeply, and then pressed in a code. To her surprise, the light changed from red to green. She opened the door and entered the building without fear of setting off the alarm, because that would be all she'd need to increase her embarrassment. Lee walked the long corridor and eventually entered the lobby. Jenner wasn't at the front desk. She looked around but didn't see her jacket anywhere. She then realized she must have left it in her office, although she'd have sworn she'd put it on before she left. She approached the nearby elevator and pressed the button. It arrived almost immediately, which never happened during normal work hours. It was the only perk to staying late or arriving early.

✝

*L*ee walked along the hallway on the nineteenth floor and suddenly stopped as a realization hit her. She hadn't left her jacket in her office. She distinctly remembered having it in Wiley's office on her way out, so she had to have left it there. Lee switched direction and headed for the accountant's office. Their floor was always eerily silent after hours, lending a unique creepiness that tended to set her on edge. Her overactive imagination always made things worse. She entered Wiley's office and saw him leaning back in his chair, staring at nothing in particular.

"I must've left my jacket in your office," Lee announced as she approached. "Since I had to come all the way back here, I guess that means I'm dragging you along with me. So let's go."

She stopped a few feet from his desk while staring at his moderately pale face and the vacant look in his eyes. She then noticed his black suit jacket appeared shiny as if wet. Lee suddenly realized he wasn't blinking and his expression was more than just vacant.

"Wiley?" she gasped and reached for him.

As she touched his shoulder, his head dropped to the side, revealing a large puncture wound on the side of his neck, which bled freely.

"My God, Wiley!"

She pulled his jacket away from his chest and saw his white shirt beneath was soaked in fresh blood. Lee suddenly gasped and jumped back with horror. She couldn't take her eyes off what was almost certainly a bullet wound to his jugular vein. She wasn't sure how long she stood staring at her dead co-worker before finally lunging for

17

the desk phone. Lee stopped short of touching the phone when she realized she was standing at a crime scene. Wiley was murdered! Then a terrifying thought hit her. It was possible his killer was somewhere nearby! Lee wildly shot looks around the office then hurried to the open door while fumbling in her purse for her cell phone. She grabbed her cell phone as she entered the hallway. From the corner of her eye, she saw someone dart into one of the nearby offices. Lee gasped while gripping her cell phone and ran down the hall for the elevator. She entered 911 into her phone and cast several looks around the corridor while awaiting a response.

The elevator door opened as if on command. Lee saw a shadow from the nearby office. Fearing it was the killer; she suppressed her scream and jumped into the elevator, colliding with someone. Lee suddenly screamed and looked at the guard, whom she'd just run into. Jenner was possibly more startled by her scream than she was by his presence. He held his chest and panted heavily.

"How did you get back into the building?" Jenner suddenly demanded.

She could only stare at him, unable to speak.

Chapter Four

*L*ee sat quietly huddled in one of the plush lobby chairs with a fire blanket over her shoulders and a cup of water in her hand. She'd finally managed to stop her body from trembling after her ordeal. She couldn't believe Wiley was dead. She couldn't believe he'd been murdered. Several police officers milled around the lobby and talked with the security guard. A police detective in a tired, old suit with a matching face approached her and flipped through his equally worn tablet.

"You're Leeann Whitley?" he asked while briefly glancing over her.

She nodded in response.

"I'm Sgt. Grimm, Homicide," he announced with little emotion, which didn't help put her at ease any. "I know you've been through a lot, so I'll try to be brief."

"Thank you," she replied weakly.

"According to what you told the security guard when you ran into him on the nineteenth floor, you found the victim murdered in his office."

She nodded.

"You claim you saw someone sneaking around one of the nearby offices," he announced then looked at her overtop his small tablet. His tired eyes conveyed his distrust toward her and her story. "Ma'am, there's no one up there, and according to the security guard, the elevators would have brought our killer here into the lobby."

As the words registered, Lee stared at the detective with disbelief. Did he just accuse her of murder?

"You were the last person to see the victim alive," he stated then suspiciously raised his brows. "The guard walked you to the parking garage, yet you turned up only ten minutes later outside the dead man's office."

His moderately accusing tone was almost more than she could handle. "I didn't kill him," she blurted out in panic while resisting the urge to leap up from her chair. She could feel her body trembling once again.

"I didn't say you did," he remarked matter-of-factly while eyeing her with that same doubtful look.

Despite his words, she was almost certain he was toying with the idea that she had been involved in Wiley's murder. She wanted to be helpful, but her head was already swimming with the horrifying images of Wiley murdered in his chair and someone stalking her from another office, possibly intending to kill her as well. She didn't know how to respond to the detective's line of question or even rationally think what her rights were in a murder investigation. The detective was already suspicious of her, and she didn't want to add to it by asking for a lawyer. She needed someone who was thinking clearly to come to her rescue, but she found herself without a friend in the world. She needed Tonya or Sal to stop the detective's snide insinuations.

"Detective, give it a rest," a male voice announced from behind the tired looking detective.

Sgt. Grimm turned and stared at a tall, well-built man in his mid-thirties. The man was neatly dressed in a suit that screamed federal agent. If Lee had been capable of rational thinking, she probably would have thought this newcomer a handsome man, but it was the furthest thing from her mind.

"I'm sorry," Grimm announced in a stern tone as his eyes narrowed at the stranger. "You are--?"

"Special Agent Holden Falcone with the FBI," he announced firmly while flipping his badge open. The badge disappeared as quickly as it had appeared. "I'm the one taking over this murder investigation." His badge was back in his pocket before Lee even saw it. "I think, detective, your time would be better spent accompanying the guard to the security office and having a look at the surveillance video around the time of the murder. If we're lucky, maybe you'll have this case solved before I've finished interviewing the young lady."

Sgt. Grimm opened his mouth to speak, thought better of it, and smirked his displeasure. He indicated Lee in the nearby chair.

"She's all yours. Be my guest."

Lee watched the detective walk away then looked at Agent Holden Falcone. Now that she finally took in an eyeful of her white knight, she realized he was a surprisingly handsome man with dark, neatly trimmed hair and the darkest eyes she'd ever seen. He sat on the arm of a chair across from where she sat and studied her a moment.

"You were the last person to see the accountant alive, correct?" Holden asked politely, although it was more of a statement than an actual question.

At least he used a less accusing tone than the detective, which helped ease some of her tension. Lee nodded her response and then watched him suspiciously. She'd never actually met a federal agent before and wasn't sure if he too was attempting to trick her into admitting something that wasn't true.

"You didn't touch anything in his office?" he questioned. "You left it exactly as it was?"

"The moment I saw the blood, I got out of there," she informed him then leaned forward. "I swear, Agent--?" Lee held her pounding head and attempted to recall his name. She couldn't even think straight anymore. "I'm sorry--"

"It's Agent Falcone," he offered.

"Yes, Agent Falcone," she replied and met his gaze with a serious yet frightened look. "I saw someone enter one of the offices. Whoever killed Wiley was still on the nineteenth floor when I found his body."

"The responding officers didn't find anyone on any of the other floors and neither the front nor back door alarms were tripped," he announced. "The fire stairs or the elevator would be the only way off that floor."

"There's the penthouse elevator, but that requires a special access card," she informed him. She wasn't even sure why she mentioned that.

Agent Falcone stared at her a moment and appeared to be thinking about her comment. "So someone coming from the penthouse within the private elevator could arrive on the nineteenth floor and return to the penthouse unnoticed?"

"Well, yes, I suppose," she began, "but the only one in the penthouse is my boss."

"Salvatore Romano?"

As Lee stared at the handsome federal agent, a thousand thoughts raced through her mind. Was he accusing her boss of killing Wiley? She knew that wasn't possible. Sal wasn't a killer. Everyone knew he was a sweet man.

"That elevator has access to the parking garage on ground level," she informed him matter-of-factly. She finally felt her head clearing and rational thought returned to her. "If someone illegally obtained an access key and the security code--"

"They could have left through the parking garage undetected," he remarked. "We'll check the security cameras and see what they reveal."

"It's private access, Agent Falcone," she informed him. "Private in the sense that no one records those coming and going from the penthouse."

"Does Mr. Romano have something to hide, Miss Whitley?" he suddenly asked.

"No, he's just rich," she blurted out and immediately regretted it. She hesitated then shifted uncomfortably in her chair. "That makes him paranoid about his privacy."

Agent Falcone nodded without offering much emotion, although she could tell there was something more beyond his expression. Certainly, he wasn't suggesting her boss was in any way a bad man, because she knew him well enough to know he was just a lonely rich guy. Mostly everyone knew him to be a gentle, kind man, who treated his employees like family. Holden extended a business card and stared directly into her eyes.

"If you think of anything, don't hesitate to call me," he announced.

She uncertainly accepted the card while maintaining eye contact with him. That he continued to stare at her made her uncomfortable. She wanted to know what was hiding behind that look. He seemed to know more than he was willing to offer.

"Should I call you a cab?"

"Uh, no," she replied softly and stood with some difficulty. Her legs felt shaky beneath her. "My car is in the garage." Lee then hesitated, remembered her missing jacket with her car keys, and looked around. "I, uh, came back in for my jacket. I left my car keys in the pocket."

Holden now stood as well, looked back at one of the officers, and indicated the jacket lying on the counter. The officer brought it to him. Holden showed it to Lee.

"Is this it?"

"Yes," she replied and accepted her jacket with a trembling hand, almost certain Agent Falcone noticed.

"The security guard found it on the desk behind the counter," Holden announced.

"I, uh, guess it fell behind the desk when I was signing out," she replied timidly.

Lee removed her car keys and attempted to hold them in her trembling hands. Agent Falcone seemed to be watching her every movement, possibly searching for something that would tell him more about her. She felt almost intimidated by his actions.

"I'll walk you to your car," he announced a little too eagerly for her comfort.

It didn't seem as if she really had a choice. She couldn't help but feel the federal agent was up to something, but she didn't know what. She nodded and walked along the corridor with him.

✝

*L*ee walked alongside Agent Falcone across the parking garage in silence, listening to the horrendous sound her shoes made while clopping along the concrete floor. The echoing sound of her high heels with every step was nearly deafening. She cast a glance at the federal agent's profile, knowing something was going through his mind, but she doubted he'd be willing to share his thoughts or theories. She just hoped he wasn't trying to figure out how *she* killed Wiley.

"How well do you know Salvatore Romano?" he finally asked, breaking the silence.

She cast a quick glance at him. "Well enough to know he's not a killer."

"So you've dispelled any rumors that he's connected," Holden announced.

"Connected?" she asked with surprise, realizing she stared at him longer than she should have. "You think Sal's a mobster?" Lee laughed for the first time, although it seemed forced. "The guy's a teddy bear. You've got the wrong guy."

Lee paused before her car and fumbled with her car keys. As she pressed the automatic unlock button, the beeping of the car nearly caused her to jump out of her shoes.

"Did your co-worker seem upset by anything tonight? Was he acting strangely?"

As she turned to look at the well-dressed federal agent, her nerves were already shot by everything she'd been through. She

23

wanted to respond irrationally and curse him out, but something made her stop and reevaluate her situation.

"Wiley was going through a nasty divorce," she replied gently. "He'd been nothing but doom and gloom since his wife left him, which is understandable.   He planned to come out with me and another co-worker tonight."   She then remembered Tonya was waiting for her.

"At 'The Roadside'," Holden replied.

She stared at him with some surprise, allowing her mouth to fall open. "H-how did you know?"

"Because he was meeting me there tonight as well," he replied but offered nothing else, leaving her moderately stunned. "You have my card. If you think of *anything* at all, call me."

Agent Falcone politely opened her car door for her. She stared at him a moment longer while a thousand thoughts raced through her mind.   Her mind had been cluttered enough already.   She didn't know what to do with this new information suddenly thrust upon her. Why had Wiley contacted a federal agent?   Why had he made plans to meet with him on such short notice?   Agent Falcone obviously knew more about what happened than he led on.   When it became apparent he wasn't going to explain his relationship with Wiley, she decided to let it go.   As Lee climbed into the driver's seat of the car, he casually closed the door behind her.   She started the car then glanced at the federal agent standing just a few feet from her window. He was still watching her.   Lee couldn't wait to get home, hide under the covers for the entire weekend, and try to forget everything she'd been through tonight.

Chapter Five

*L*ee entered her sparsely decorated, studio apartment and bolted the door behind her. She leaned her forehead against the door a moment and drew a shaken breath. Now that her adrenalin rush had worn off, she was left feeling sluggish and exhausted. She finally straightened, tossed her keys into a decorative bowl on the table near the door, and slung her purse down. The contents scattered across the table. Lee groaned with disgust, held her head, and started to cry. She finally controlled her emotions and, with a trembling hand, stuffed the contents back into her bag. The silver tube resembling lipstick rolled behind the decorative bowl on the table just out of sight. Lee composed herself and carried her purse with her across the apartment and into her bedroom. She set her purse on a chair within her darkened bedroom then kicked off her shoes with added vigor and disgust. She wanted to cry, but she would save that for when she was in the shower. She tended to release a lot of emotion in the shower, which was ridiculous, since there was no one else living with her to see her weeping. She needed a glass of wine to calm her nerves before showering and crying herself silly.

As she headed back into the main apartment and toward the kitchen, there was a knock on the door. Lee jumped with surprise and stared at the door as if it were a monster prepared to attack. Her heart was pounding within her chest. She didn't know who would be at her door, being it was nearly eight o'clock. Her neighbors never bothered her, and she rarely received unannounced company. Lee slowly approached the door and looked through the peek hole. Her heart rate slowed and she allowed her body to relax when she saw Tonya outside her door. Lee unbolted and opened the door to reveal her friend. Tonya stared at her as if she'd seen a ghost then threw her arms around her, holding her for a long embrace. Lee returned the hug and felt her body shiver. She had to fight the urge to sob on her friend's shoulder there in the doorway. Tonya pulled away and joined her inside the apartment. Lee was quick to close and bolt the door.

"I heard what happened," Tonya gasped while watching her. "Are you okay?"

"Yeah, I'm fine," Lee replied softly. Physically, that was true. Emotionally, she was a wreck.

"Poor Wiley," Tonya whispered while holding her chest. "I feel so bad for avoiding him all week. You know, with the mood he'd been in lately, he was impossible to be around."

Lee headed for the kitchen, feeling she needed that drink more than ever. Without even asking, she poured a glass for her friend as well. Tonya followed her to the island counter separating the kitchen from the living room.

"I invited him to join us tonight before heading out," Lee announced and choked on her tears.

Lee forced a weak smile and handed Tonya the glass of wine, which she eagerly accepted.

"You saw him--?" Tonya hesitated then gently cleared her throat. "Before he, well, you know."

"Yeah," Lee replied softly and took a large swallow of wine. "I was the last person to see him alive, or so the detective and the fed were eager to point out."

Tonya stared at her with mild surprise. "They don't seriously think you--?"

"They hinted a little," Lee replied then drained the entire contents from the glass, which she immediately refilled.

"I think I should stay with you tonight." Lee was about to protest when Tonya interrupted her. "I insist," she announced boldly. "You shouldn't be alone."

Lee managed a smile and nodded while fighting her tears. "Thanks, I appreciate that."

"Hey, that's what friends are for," Tonya announced firmly and set her glass down on the counter. "I'm going to run you a nice, hot bubble bath. After you're finished de-stressing, we'll have a little more wine and you can get it all out."

Lee knew better than to argue with her friend.

t

*L*ee soaked in the deep garden tub filled with bubbles. She wore her long hair twisted in a bun on top of her head to keep it out of the water. She sobbed softly while recounting the evening's events repeatedly. She suddenly felt stupid, crying alone in her tub when she could be drinking wine and pouring her soul out to her friend in the next room. She heard a faint clunk from her bedroom. Lee tensed as she listened a moment then felt stupid for thinking the boogieman was out to get her. She'd had enough of her less than relaxing bubble bath and decided drinking herself silly was the better approach to relieving her stress. Lee dried off, wrapped the towel around her body, and entered her bedroom. She could hear her friend puttering around in the next room. She changed into a tank top and a pair of floppy shorts then released her damp hair from the messy bun.

As she approached her bedroom door, she saw her purse lying over on the chair with some of its contents spilled out. She groaned softly, set the purse upright, and tossed an escaped gold tube of lipstick and her sunglasses into the bag. She headed into the living room and saw her friend casually curled against the corner of the sofa while playing on her cell phone. Tonya looked up as Lee entered the living room and waved her cell phone.

"Can you believe I've received over twenty texts, voicemails, and emails from our co-workers already?" Tonya remarked as her eyes widened from the revelation.

"I don't intend to check my phone for messages," Lee announced with a dreary sigh and reclaimed her newly filled glass of wine from the coffee table.

"Yeah, that's why they're all contacting me," Tonya replied and scrolled down on her phone. She read from the list, "Tell Lee to call me. Lee's not answering her phone. Is Lee okay?" She looked back at her friend. "Should I respond?"

"Just tell them I'm fine," Lee announced without emotion. "Tell them I'm lying down."

Tonya nodded and did as instructed. Lee collapsed onto the sofa on the opposite end from her friend. She groaned and held her head while resisting the urge to cry.

"Those poor kids."

"What?" Tonya asked and glanced at her.

"Wiley's two little boys," Lee replied and avoided looking at her friend. "They're too young to lose their father like that. I can't imagine what they're going through."

"Don't," Tonya announced firmly and wiped a tear from the corner of her own eye. She attempted a tiny, nervous smile. "You're going to make me cry."

Lee stared silently into her wineglass while Tonya studied her mood.

"Did the police have any theories about what happened?" Tonya finally asked, breaking the nerve-racking silence.

"None that they offered to me," Lee replied without looking up from her glass. "Well, except that I make a fine suspect."

"They don't suspect you," Tonya scolded then shifted in her seat. "I mean, nothing was missing, right? Not a robbery gone bad or anything like that."

"Nothing was missing that I could tell." Lee remained in her own thoughts then looked at her friend. "Something the fed told me has me a little bothered though."

"Oh? What's that?"

"He said he was meeting Wiley tonight at 'The Roadside'," she announced. "That's really weird, because I had just invited Wiley to join us maybe fifteen minutes before he was killed."

"Are you saying you invited him to join us, and he calls this fed guy to meet us for dinner?" Tonya suddenly asked then cocked her head to one side in silent question. "I don't get it."

"Yeah, that's what I was thinking," Lee announced and sank into thought. "I think there's more to the story."

"Such as?"

"I don't know," she replied gently and again stared into her glass. "But Wiley mentioned something about not being able to find a large amount of money."

"How large?"

"Fifty million large."

Tonya nearly choked on her wine and immediately set her glass down on the coffee table. "That's a pretty good motive, don't you think?"

"Yes, it is." Lee tapped her fingernails against her wineglass while deep in thought. She finally looked at her friend. "What if Wiley found the money and called this federal agent."

"You think Sal--?"

"I don't know," Lee muttered and shook her head. "I can't believe Sal is involved with the mafia, but the fed suspects the killer used the penthouse elevator, which points right back at Sal." She shook the thoughts from her head. "I'd rather not think about it tonight."

Lee was about to drink her wine when there was a gentle knock on the door. Both women exchanged puzzled looks. Lee felt her heart pounding in her chest and attempted to keep her imagination in check.

"It's nearly ten o'clock," Tonya announced in a hushed whisper. "Who would that be?"

Lee was about to get up when Tonya leaped to her feet and hurried past her to the door. She looked through the peek hole. Panic filled her as she spun to face Lee, who now stood. Tonya's look frightened her.

"It's Sal," Tonya gasped softly. "What do I do?"

Lee relaxed slightly, although her body still trembled from the initial knock on the door. "It's okay, Tonya. Let him in," she replied. "He's not involved in any of this."

"I hope you're right."

Tonya took a deep breath, unbolted the door, and pulled it open. She smiled politely at Sal.

"Sal," she announced with a false cheerful tone. "What are you doing here?"

"I came to check on Lee," he announced with a look of concern on his face. "When I got back from my meeting, I'd heard what happened." He looked past Tonya to Lee and immediately turned sympathetic. "Are you okay, Lee?"

She attempted a smile and nodded. "Physically, I'm fine."

Sal crossed the room and extended his hands to her. She uncertainly accepted his hands. As he looked into her eyes, she couldn't see anything that indicated this man was a killer. Although, she supposed she wouldn't.

"Don't feel any pressure to return to work until you're ready," he announced gently. "If there's anything you need, you let me know. I'm here for you."

"Thank you, Sal," Lee replied. "I appreciate that."

He released her hands and glanced at both women. "I don't want to intrude. I know you're probably exhausted, so I'll leave you two. You know how to reach me, if you need me."

Lee nodded and watched her boss leave the apartment. Tonya appeared surprised and shut the door behind him.

"Well, that was--weird," Tanya remarked.

"He's just being thoughtful."

"That's one way of looking at it," her friend muttered then offered a smile. "One more glass of wine, and then I'm ready to call it a night."

Tonya returned to the sofa and picked up her empty wineglass from the coffee table. Lee collected her full glass and headed into the kitchen.

"I've had enough," Lee replied with a dreary sigh. "I'm going to hide under the covers and pretend this day never happened."

She dumped her wine into the sink and rinsed her glass. Tonya leaned on the counter, watched her friend, and then lifted the empty bottle of wine.

"Well, rather than open another bottle, I guess I'll fix the guest sofa for myself," Tonya announced.

"You don't have to stay, Tonya," Lee informed her. "I'll be fine, really. I don't want to inconvenience you."

"Don't be ridiculous," she announced and abruptly straightened. "I'm your friend. You'd do the same for me."

"I appreciate that," Lee remarked and smiled warmly. "See you in the morning. Good night."

"Night, Lee."

Lee headed into the bedroom and partially closed the door to reduce light from the living room while Tonya made up the sofa for her bed.

Chapter Six

$\mathcal{I}$t was nearly two in the morning when Lee woke from her light sleep for no apparent reason. She turned over in bed and, through the darkness, saw the outline of a man standing over her bedside. Lee jumped up in bed and attempted to scream, but the man already had his hand over her mouth and pushed her back onto the mattress with all his weight. His muscular body nearly crushed her, and his face was close to hers.

"You wouldn't want to alert your friend, now would you?" he whispered in a low, husky voice. "I wouldn't want to hurt her. Either you tell me what I want to know, or neither of you are making it out of here alive. Got that?"

Lee mechanically nodded out of fear. He removed his hand from her mouth but maintained his weight on her body, keeping her pinned to the bed.

"Where's the flash drive?" he demanded softly but in a threatening tone.

Her mind was racing, but his question made no sense. "What flash drive?" she gasped softly.

"The one Wiley intended to turn over to the fed. I know he was meeting you at the diner tonight," he growled. "The flash drive he had on him was blank, which means he gave you the real one." His tone was so matter-of-fact it frightened her. "Where is it? Give it to me, and I'll let you live."

Lee stared at the man's silhouette through the darkness. There was something almost familiar about him. She was certain he was someone she knew. A thousand scenarios raced through her mind, and every single one ended with him killing her. She didn't believe him when he said he wouldn't kill her or Tonya. For all she knew, Tonya was already dead. The thought sent chills down her spine.

His body against hers while keeping her pinned to the bed was almost enough to keep her paralyzed with fear. She raced for the response that would buy her the most time and possibly get him off her. Lee nodded across the dark room.

"It's in my purse," she lied softly.

He moved off her while keeping his hand securely on her wrist and, with great force, pulled her from the bed with him. She nearly fell to the floor from his strength, but he kept her from falling. She clutched his lower arm to catch her balance before he pulled her to the chair by the door. Her senses exploded to the feel of his skin and tight muscles on his bare, lower arm. She was convinced it was Jericho! Sal had sent his strong man to recover some flash drive that he believed Wiley gave her! She couldn't believe Agent Falcone had been right. It was true! Sal had Wiley killed! While clutching her wrist to keep her from escaping, he dumped the contents of her purse onto the chair. She had stupidly thought he'd either let her go to recover her purse or allow her to retrieve the flash drive she knew she didn't have. She attempted to pull away from him as he routed through the contents of her bag spread out across the chair. He yanked her by her wrist with force, causing her to fall to her knees near his feet, and stood over her without releasing her.

"Where is it?" he demanded in a slightly louder tone.

She struggled to free her hand from his grip. "It was in my purse, I swear," she easily lied, although the panic in her voice was real.

She saw the mace disguised as lipstick had fallen on the floor near the foot of the chair. It was only inches from her reach. Lee grabbed the tube in the darkness, even though she knew he would see her.

"Here it is," she announced and popped the lid casing as he violently pulled her to her feet.

Lee raised the tube to his face and plunged her index finger into the firm lipstick. She gasped with horror, realizing she'd grabbed an actual tube of lipstick instead of the one containing mace. Realizing that he'd been deceived, he nearly pulled her off her feet by her wrist and violently shook her.

"That was a mistake," he growled while nearly pulling her arm from its socket.

Lee screamed and thrust the tube of lipstick for his eye. Unfortunately, she missed her intended target, and instead struck him just beneath his eye. Although missing his eye, it had caused him enough pain to cry out and release her. Lee thrust her knee into his groin and bolted from the room as he clutched himself while dropping to his knees. As Lee ran across the living room, Tonya stepped out of the nearby bathroom and nearly collided with her. Both women screamed. Lee grabbed her friend's hand.

"We have to go! Now!"

Before Tonya could question her or protest, Lee was pulling her to the apartment door. Both women, in their bare feet, ran along the well-lit corridor.

"What's happening?" Tonya cried out with alarm.

Jericho stepped into the hallway outside the apartment and looked in their direction. Despite the pink lipstick caked beneath his left eye, he was a menacing sight. Tonya stared back at the large, intimidating man with a look of horror while Lee pulled her toward the stairs. Jericho charged down the hallway for them with his teeth gritted and a nasty scowl on his face. Tonya attempted to pull free from Lee's firm grip.

"Not the stairs," Tonya gasped with alarm. "We can't outrun him."

"We don't have to," Lee announced and stopped short of the stairs just before the fire pull station. Without hesitation, she pulled the fire alarm. As the alarm wailed, both looked back at Jericho with frightened anticipation. He stopped in the center of the corridor while looking around. Apartment doors quickly opened and residents began filtering into the corridor. Jericho sneered at both women then ran for the opposite fire stairs.

"We should lock ourselves in the apartment," Tonya announced and attempted to pull her back toward the apartment.

"No," Lee announced and pulled her friend toward the large group of people now heading for the fire stairs closest to them. "Safety in numbers."

†

*B*oth women sat in the bland police station interrogation room still dressed in their sleepwear and nothing to cover their bare feet. Tonya sat in the chair before the table with one leg neatly crossed over the other while bundled in a fire blanket. Her leg bounced around while she chewed on her fingernails, casting stray looks at her restless friend. Lee paced the interrogation room in her bare feet that were almost black from the dirty police station floor. She alternated wrenching her fingers together and running them through her mussed hair. Lee wore a borrowed policeman's jacket to conceal her mostly see-through tank top with no bra beneath it, leaving little to the imagination. The jacket nearly reached the bottom of her floppy shorts.

"Jericho," Tonya muttered with her fingernail in her mouth. "I can't believe it was Jericho." She vigorously shook her head while staring blankly at nothing. "And to think, I actually considered sleeping with him."

"Not all killers are hideously ugly with scars on their faces," Lee muttered.

"Yeah, but you have to admit, Finn looks more like a killer than Jericho."

"Just because Finn is creepy, that doesn't mean he's the killer type."

"If Jericho is a killer, it's because he's working for Sal," Tonya warned her. "If Sal wants us dead, we're completely screwed. We shouldn't be here. If what your fed said about Sal is true, he probably owns half the police force."

"We don't know that Sal is involved in organized crime or any of this for that matter," Lee informed her and increased the rate of her pacing. It was becoming more difficult to convince herself of Sal's innocence. "We don't know Jericho was acting on Sal's orders."

"Be serious, Lee," Tonya nearly exploded and stared at her friend. "Jericho isn't capable of being the brains. He's all brawn; you know that. Someone is pulling his strings, and that someone has to be Sal." Her look was demanding. "Do you honestly want to rat out the mob?"

"I'm pretty sure I don't want to die," Lee responded. "My chances of staying alive are better in a police station than they are out there."

Tonya rested her elbows on the table and allowed her head to fall into her hands. She groaned softly then threw her hands defensively in the air and glared at her friend.

"Why did you have to feel sorry for Wiley?" Tonya suddenly cried out, startling Lee. Tonya attempted to collect her emotions and spoke softer. "If you'd just left him alone in his misery, we wouldn't be in this mess."

Lee glared at her friend with an astonished look. She couldn't believe Tonya was blaming her for befriending a lonely man going through a tough time. She loved Tonya, but she wasn't happy with her right now. Wiley was dead! Murdered! No one deserved that. The door opened, causing both women to jump with alarm. Holden

Falcone entered the interrogation room, shut the door behind him, and stared at them.

"Who wants coffee?" he asked almost politely. "It's going to be a long night."

Lee took several quick steps toward Holden and stopped only a foot in front of him.

"Did you search my apartment?" she quickly asked with concern. "Did you find the flash drive Jericho was looking for?"

"We searched your entire apartment, but we didn't find any flash drive." He straightened proudly and drew a deep breath. "Look, I know you've been through a lot, but we're going to need to take your statements before we move you to a safe house. If we're lucky, we'll get this all straightened out and have Jericho in custody by morning."

"And if we're not lucky?" Tonya asked.

He frowned at the thought and folded his arms across his chest. "Then we'll be spending a lot of time together until we catch a break."

"Define a lot of time," Lee remarked gently.

"Anywhere from a few days to a few months," he replied.

Both women groaned. Tonya gently pounded her head against the table before her.

Chapter Seven

An abandoned, dilapidated warehouse boldly sat on a corner lot in the moderately undesirable area of the city's business district. It was just before sunrise and several unsavory characters stumbled along the sidewalks, possibly heading home after an all-night bender of substance abuse. A black SUV drove up to the abandoned warehouse through the severely bent although functional gate in the chain-link fence. A beat-up black sedan with a coating of dirt on its slightly dented finish followed behind as they stopped before the building. A plain-clothed officer got out of the sedan and surveyed the area. When all was clear, he nodded to the SUV. Agent Holden Falcone and both women got out of the vehicle. Lee and Tonya, who secured a change of clothes, looked across the dirty building. They shared similar distaste and followed Holden into the dilapidated warehouse. The plain clothed police officer followed them inside carrying a duffel bag for each woman.

"Not to complain, Agent Falcone," Tonya announced timidly while looking around at the cobweb-infested rattrap that looked worse on the inside. "But couldn't you come up with someplace a little less--"

"--like a roach motel," Lee muttered while grimacing at a large spider crawling across the floor.

Lee wasn't stuck-up, but she wasn't prepared to spend a few weeks or longer sharing a bunk with a bunch of crackheads. Somehow, eluding a killer seemed the lesser of two evils at the moment.

"Trust me," Holden announced while hiding his grin. "It's nicer on the inside."

"Uh, we are inside," Tonya remarked.

"Not exactly."

Holden lifted a rusted panel to expose a digital keypad. He pressed several numbers and an electronic hum followed, opening the door. He stood aside and allowed the women to enter first. They uncertainly entered the massive, studio apartment. The well-appointed, two-story apartment was roughly the size of a house with an open floor plan. There were at least four bedrooms upstairs. The first floor had a kitchen, living room, dining room, and game room combined all in one. The tastefully furnished room contained high-end electronic equipment and a large screen television. Tonya grinned her approval.

"Okay, now this is more like it," Tonya announced while scanning the large area. "Just tell me where the hot tub is, and we're in business."

"Sorry, there's no hot tub," he replied.

Lee stared at the large windows lining the backside of the room then looked at Holden with concern.

"I'm not comfortable with those large windows," Lee announced timidly.

"Think of those windows as large two-way mirrors," he informed them. "You can see out, but no one can see in. To anyone on the outside, they look like they're coated with dirt, and they're also bulletproof."

Holden gave a nod to the plain clothed officer, indicating that he could leave. He left their bags and headed out.

"All four bedrooms are essentially panic rooms," Holden informed them. "If the alarm sounds, you have ten seconds before the bedroom doors seal. Anything short of an atomic bomb isn't getting through."

Both women eyed the bedrooms on the second floor then exchanged looks.

"And if we're not in one of the four bedrooms?" Lee asked with concern. "Can I assume that's our only exit? If someone gets in, are we sitting ducks?"

"There's an emergency exit on the first and second floor," Holden replied then straightened proudly. "I've grown paranoid over the last few years. I'm not a fan of safe houses without emergency escape routes."

"Where's this emergency escape route?" Tonya asked. "I mean, if you're killed, I'd like to know the backup plan."

Holden indicated for them to follow him to the stairs leading to the second floor. He lifted a fake light switch plate to reveal a simple, red button.

"You press this and the wall opens up," he announced. "There's an identical one at the top of the stairs. Once this button is pressed, the alarm sounds and we're in lockdown. There's no escape through the main door, and the bedroom doors seal. The emergency exits become the only escape route. Once that emergency door closes behind you, there's no returning."

"And anyone not through that door is suddenly trapped with the bad guys breaking in?" Lee asked.

"Every security feature has its risks," he replied. "If things go south, we always have the option of tossing in a few canisters of knockout gas, and it's nighty night bad guys."

Lee let out a nervous laugh while rubbing her chilled arms. "Wow, you guys really thought of everything."

"I had a particularly difficult case once," Holden announced. "Motivated killers with a long reach and deep pockets; and a spirited witness, who was a bit of a flight risk and a major pain in the ass."

"How did that turn out?" Lee asked, feeling slightly insecure in her new prison home.

"Pretty much how you'd think," he replied casually and placed his hands in his pants pockets. "I married her."

Both looked at him with some surprise to the comment. He flashed a smile, allowing them to relax and laugh a little at their situation.

"When do we get our cell phones back, Agent Falcone?" Tonya asked.

"You don't," he replied. "We have an untraceable phone for your use at my discretion. If your boss is motivated enough to get to either of you, there's a good chance he'll find a way to wiretap those you might call. Although our phone can't be traced, there are other ways of deciphering someone's location. What you say can be used to locate you." Holden inhaled deeply and looked around. "But, for now, you're probably low risk. All we have is your testimony against your boss's right-hand man. Romano isn't going to risk his entire operation and freedom over one of his generals."

"So you didn't get anything off the security cameras back at the office?" Lee questioned.

"It was just as you said. There weren't any cameras for that private elevator or Romano's corner of the parking garage," he replied. "He can come and go as he pleases without anyone ever knowing."

"Then you also have no proof that Sal had anything to do with Wiley's murder either," Lee remarked firmly. "This could all be Jericho."

"To be honest, Jericho isn't a mastermind by any means," Holden bluntly informed her. "He's a soldier. He does what he's told."

"Told you so," Tonya muttered to Lee.

"That still doesn't mean Sal is pulling his strings," Lee informed her friend.

"Since you didn't actually witness Romano killing the accountant, it's not as if we need to keep you in custody until the trial," Holden announced. "We just need to keep you out of sight until we eliminate Romano's reason for wanting you both dead."

"So, basically, if you find the missing fifty million dollars, Jericho no longer has a reason to want us dead," Lee announced, uncertain if that made her feel any better.

Tonya sharply raised her brow and chimed in with her own comments. "And for some strange reason, he thinks we have that information."

"Basically, yes," he replied.

"Then I suppose we should make the best of it," Tonya announced with a reluctant sigh.

"Yes, because no matter the outcome, we're unemployed," Lee informed her friend.

"On that note, I'm going to bed," Tonya remarked and headed for the stairs.

Chapter Eight

*I*t was a little after seven o'clock in the morning. Lee lay on the bed in her official prison cell and stared at the bland, concrete walls. She wasn't going to sleep, so remaining in bed seemed pointless. Of course, getting up seemed equally pointless. She didn't want to be reminded that she was a prisoner for her own protection. She remained in bed another two hours, alternating between staring at the ceiling and staring at the walls. Around nine o'clock, she reluctantly got out of bed, dressed casually in a pair of jeans and a sweatshirt, and left her room. She heard voices as she walked down the steps. Agent Falcone stood near the door with an attractive, dark-haired woman in her mid-thirties. Both looked at her as she reached the bottom of the steps.

"Miss Whitley, I was just on my way out," Holden announced. "Your boss *requested* a meeting with me this morning in his penthouse."

"That's a good sign, right?"

"Well, it means he either wants to talk or put a bullet through my head," Holden remarked.

"What prompted the sudden meeting?" Lee asked, feeling oddly uneasy about the request.

"He heard through his *sources* that Jericho broke into your apartment last night," Holden announced, "and he wants to cooperate in any way he can."

"You're wrong about him," Lee announced and folded her arms across her chest. "Sal's a nice guy, I'm telling you. You've got the wrong guy."

"I've heard plenty of young trusting women tell me the same thing," he replied. "And those same conversations haunt me every time I'm forced to identify their bodies in the morgue."

Lee glanced at the woman standing alongside Holden. "Your husband is a ray of sunshine."

The women appeared surprised, glanced at Holden, and then burst out laughing. She looked back at Lee and could barely contain her grin.

"He's not my husband," the woman announced maintaining her humor. "Personally, if I had to live with this one, one of us wouldn't make it out alive."

"Thanks, Mac," Holden muttered then focused his attention on Lee. "This is Macbeth from the U.S. Marshals' office. She's your babysitter for the next few hours. I'll be back this afternoon. I'll grab some Chinese take-out for lunch."

Lee managed a smile and nodded. Holden left the warehouse apartment. The door made a distinctive humming as it locked behind him, reminding Lee that the attractive studio apartment was little more than a comfortable prison. Mac turned to Lee and smiled almost sweetly.

"I'm sure it seems like Agent Falcone and I don't get along," Mac announced reassuringly, "but believe me when I say, honestly, I can't stand the prick."

"He seems to have a chip on his shoulder."

Mac grinned as she passed Lee. "I'd be a little more graphic in the placement of that chip."

Lee hesitated a moment then laughed softly and followed Mac across the studio apartment. Mac looked around and marveled at the massive area.

"The feds certainly enjoy their toys," she remarked while grinning. "Pity they don't like to share them." Mac spun to face Lee with a slightly devious look on her face. "I'll bet this place comes equipped with panic rooms and one of those emergency escape hatches too." She again looked around. "Put this place in a cave, and I'd be in my glory." Mac eyed Lee. "I have a thing for superheroes. Do you like superheroes?"

"I used to read comic books when I was a little girl," Lee replied.

"Well, I'm starving," Mac announced. "Why don't I make us some breakfast while you tell me about your favorite comic book heroes?"

"You're on," Lee replied. "I'm starving. I haven't eaten since lunch yesterday."

"You're in luck. I make a mean omelet." Mac indicated the second floor. "Think bachelorette number two would like an omelet?"

"Maybe for lunch," Lee teased. "She'll sleep all day if you let her."

Mac appeared surprised. "Even after all the two of you have been through?"

"I know!" Lee shook her head. "I couldn't even convince my eyes to stay closed for more than a minute."

Mac casually leaned on the island counter and smiled sweetly. "I was like that when I first started out in this game," she announced. "You sort of get used to it. After a while, you can sleep through just about anything."

"You have an air of self-confidence about you unlike any woman I've ever met before," Lee remarked. "I thought I was confident and together, but the last twenty-four hours shattered any feelings of control." She shook her head and groaned softly. "You should see the size of this guy. He slung me around like a ragdoll. How do you fight someone like that and expect to survive?"

Mac grinned slyly and replied, "I heard you did, so you tell me."

"Blind luck," Lee remarked. "Literally. I nearly blinded him with a tube of lipstick."

Mac straightened while staring at Lee. She appeared pleased with the outcome. "Bravo. Just remember, it's what you do next that defines success."

"I gave him a shot to the groin," Lee replied timidly.

"Ah, the great equalizer," Mac announced cheerfully and appeared pleased. "They say size doesn't matter, and it's true. One good shot to the gonads and they *all fall down.*"

A metallic sound echoed throughout the apartment causing both to look at the ceiling.

"What's that?" Lee suddenly asked.

Mac slowly shook her head and crossed the living room, attempting to locate the source of the traveling sound. Lee followed a few steps behind her.

"Almost sounds like something rolling in the air ducts--" Mac began then suddenly gasped. She turned toward Lee with her mouth partially open. "In your room, now!"

Lee bolted for the stairs. A canister fell from the vent and onto the floor, expelling thick smoke. Mac grabbed Lee's arm and stopped her from running up the stairs.

"Never mind," she cried out. "The emergency exit!"

There was a loud bang at the main door. The smoke began filling the room.

"Go!" Mac yelled while removing her gun from a concealed shoulder holster.

"Tonya," Lee gasped then immediately choked on the smoke filling the room.

"She'll be safe! Go!"

Lee ran for the panel, flipped it open, and pressed the red button. The door slid open, causing an alarm to wail loudly. The bedroom doors could be heard electronically sealing. Lee leaped into the passageway. She turned around just in time to see Mac hitting the button to close the door behind her. Lee coughed several times and looked at the dimly lit stairs before her. Whatever triggered the alarm had apparently triggered the emergency lights on the steps as well. She knew help would be arriving soon. Mac and Tonya would be fine, she was positive. She had to find her way outside and keep watch for the responding officers. She paused at the bottom of the stairs and placed her hand to the doorknob before her. She looked out the concealed peek hole.

The area surrounding the warehouse was nearly empty, although she could barely hear the police sirens wailing in the near distance over the warehouse alarm. She saw a police cruiser enter through the warehouse gates. Lee opened the door to make her run for the officers. She stepped out of the one-way door and onto the warehouse grounds. The door shut loudly behind her, startling her. She spun around and saw Finn leaning against the door with a cheap grin on his moderately creepy face.

"Hello, darling," he announced in his best Southern drawl.

Lee cried out and attempted to bolt. Finn pounced on her with cat-like reflexes, catching her around her shoulders from behind, and placing her in a big bear hug.

"Where are you running off too so fast, missy?" he asked almost sweetly close to her ear. "I just want a moment of your time. No harm; no foul."

She was about to scream, even though it would never be heard over the wailing warehouse alarm. Finn swiftly spun her around and grabbed both her wrists with a vice-like grip. She fought against him as he pulled her toward the nearby black sedan. The back door opened from the inside, and he shoved her into the back of the car. Lee fell onto the seat and quickly straightened. Sal sat calmly on the backseat and stared at her. She attempted to flee the car, but the door wouldn't open.

"I'm sorry if Finn was a little rough with you," Sal announced calmly. "I'll speak to him about his manners."

Lee pressed her back against the door while staring at her boss. "What are you going to do with me?" she gasped.

"Nothing," he announced calmly. "I'd never hurt you, Lee, and I said I'd speak to Finn. No one here is going to hurt you, and that includes Finn."

Lee stared at him, but she was no longer convinced. She attempted to stop her body from trembling, but found it difficult. Although she had defended him to Agent Falcone, now, in his presence, she was a little less trusting.

"Jericho--?"

"I had nothing to do with Jericho's actions, Lee," he informed her in a calm tone, although she could hear the hidden anger behind the words. "He was acting on his own, I swear. I suspect he also killed Wiley, but the police seem to think he was acting on my orders."

"I don't understand," she gasped softly without taking her eyes off him. "Why are you telling me this?"

"Because, Lee, I trust you," Sal announced. "I have instincts about people. You're a good person, and I know you'd never knowingly set me up."

"You think Jericho set you up?" she asked as her body relaxed slightly.

"I don't know if he's smart enough to actually set me up himself," Sal replied. "But he definitely screwed me over. I have a dead accountant and a large hole in my data. He took something from my accounts, but with the entire server down, I have no idea what or why."

"Wiley said the bank accounts were short fifty million dollars," Lee announced then regretted giving him that information. Maybe she shouldn't have told him.

"Fifty million?" Sal cried out. He fell oddly silent as his mind reeled with the new information. "I have some clients who would be very unhappy if it turned out to be their money. With the system disabled, there's no way to tell what accounts have been compromised." He shook his head. "This is a very dark day for me and my company." Sal glanced at Lee and tilted his head in question. "Was Wiley in on it with him? Did they have a falling out?"

She slowly shook her head.

"I don't have any answers either," Sal informed her, "but I do know the feds are attempting to set me up to take the fall." He then stared at her. "Believe me, Lee; I had nothing to do with any of this."

"Why are you telling me this?" Lee again demanded.

"You're being held in protective custody," he announced then raised his brows, "supposedly from me. We can both agree that I have the upper hand here. If it were my intention to kill you, I easily could. Don't you agree?"

Lee uncertainly nodded.

Sal raised his hands with a look of innocence. "You're still alive. That should prove I'm not a threat to your life." His look softened. "I want you to trust me, Lee. Trust me as I trust you. I had nothing to do with Wiley's death or Jericho attacking you last night. Do you believe me?"

She stared at him a moment then nodded. "Yes," she replied softly. "I tried to tell Agent Falcone, but he's convinced you're into organized crime."

"Agent Falcone," he announced and smirked while casually nodding. "I haven't had the pleasure of meeting him yet, and I'm afraid I'm going to be late for that meeting. He's a smart guy--for a fed. I assure you, I won't be able to change his opinion of me. I need you to convince him of my innocence. Will you defend me to him?"

Lee drew in a deep breath and again nodded. "If they find Jericho," she informed him, "they may be able to prove you weren't involved."

"I'll personally hand him Jericho when I find him," Sal informed her. "Though I fear my circle of trustworthy people is shrinking dramatically."

"Are you going to let me go?" she asked timidly.

"You were never mine to start with," he replied in a gentle tone then revealed a tiny smile. "I'll have Finn escort you back inside, if you'd like."

"Thanks, but no thanks," she announced firmly. "I don't like him."

Sal smiled and chuckled softly. He leaned closer to her while raising his brows in suggestion.

"Neither do I," he whispered then laughed.

He reached past her, causing her to tense slightly, and tapped on the window. The door opened. Lee jumped away from the door and stared at Finn on the other side. He smiled deviously and extended his hand to her. Lee sneered at him and made a motion to get out of the car.

"Lee," Sal announced, catching her attention and forcing her to look back at him. His look was sincere. "I'd never hurt you, remember that. When this is all over, your job will be waiting for you. You have my word."

She stared at him with some surprise then smiled for the first time. "Thank you."

"Give my regards to Tonya," Sal announced then gave her a general nod and a slight wave.

Lee returned the nod and offered a tiny smile. She climbed out of the car and immediately locked eyes with Finn. His sleazy smirk was enough to stand her neck hairs on end, but she didn't allow him to see the fear she felt.

Chapter Nine

*A*gent Falcone hurried Lee and Tonya out of the warehouse, past several armed policemen, and into the awaiting black SUV. Mac climbed into the passenger seat only seconds before Holden hit the gas and sped away from the warehouse. An unmarked police car followed them. Lee leaned forward between the two in the front seat.

"Is this really necessary, Agent Falcone?" Lee asked. "He could have killed me, but he didn't. Can't you admit that it's possible Sal isn't part of this plot?"

"You're right," he announced gruffly. "He didn't kill you. Let's discuss what he did do. He found you at a highly classified safe house, penetrated the failsafe with a smoke bomb, and flushed you out onto the street where his thug tossed you into the backseat of his car."

Lee frowned.

"All so the lovable teddy bear could profess his innocence, and ask you to go to bat for him," Holden announced. His cruel smile mocked her as he shook his head. "Nah, no reason to worry about that. All innocent men risk being shot on sight to *talk* to their employees in protective custody."

Mac glanced back at Lee and offered a tiny, teasing smile. It was uncertain if Mac was on her side or not. Lee huffed and collapsed against the backseat.

"The safe house has been compromised," Holden announced firmly. "I don't know how he did it, but he's smarter and has a longer reach than I gave him credit."

"So where are you taking us?" Tonya asked.

"That's classified," Holden snapped.

"Even I'm not privy to that information," Mac gently informed the women in the backseat.

"All you need to know is I'm taking you someplace safe," he informed them. "I assure you, it's someplace no one will ever find you."

"You sound awfully confident, Agent Falcone," Tonya remarked with some disbelief in her tone.

"This guy flies so far beneath the radar, I don't even know where to find him most of the time," Holden remarked and seemed to grimace at the thought.

All three women gave him puzzled looks. It was Mac's turn to comment.

"If you don't know where to find him," Mac suddenly asked, "how are we getting there?"

✝

*A*gent Falcone's SUV pulled through the junkyard gate with the police cruiser trailing only a few feet behind. A man in dirty overalls sprang into action and pulled the metal gate shut behind them. Both vehicles approached a large clearing and stopped. All four got out of the SUV and looked around. Both women looked at Holden with shared surprise.

"You're leaving us in a junkyard?" Tonya gasped with horror in her voice.

Holden looked at his watch then to the sky. They heard the faint pulsating sound of a helicopter approaching. The three women looked to the sky in the same direction. A six-passenger helicopter approached and landed nearly dead center in the clearing before them. An attractive woman in her mid-twenties with long, dark mussed hair removed her sunglasses and climbed out of the helicopter as the rotors slowed. She glared at Holden with annoyance and took several aggressive steps toward him.

"You've got some nerve with that five minute notice bullshit," the young woman snarled at him. "I was briefing a room full of admirals when you called."

Holden smirked and cocked his head casually to the side, apparently doubting the young woman's story.

48

"Oh? So that's how we're spending our Saturday afternoons, Jackie?" he announced then raised his brows demandingly. "Playing poker with a bunch of retired Navy men?"

"No, of course not," she announced sternly. "Some afternoons we shoot a few hundred rounds at the shooting range." Jackie smiled slyly. "I like to mix things up."

Mac grinned and gave Jackie a quick once over then looked back at Holden. "I like her." Mac approached Jackie with her hand extended. "Deputy Macbeth, U.S. Marshal. You can call me Mac."

Jackie shook her hand. "Jackie Falcone."

All three women appeared surprised then looked back at Holden. He smirked and shrugged.

"What can I say? I don't get enough adventure in the field," he informed them.

"Okay, whoever's going, let's go," Jackie announced firmly. "AIS."

"AIS?" Tonya queried.

Mac snorted a laugh and grinned at Tonya. "Ass in seat." She gave Holden a quick once over as she passed him for the helicopter. "You've got a keeper there, Agent Falcone."

Tonya and Lee turned to follow Mac toward the awaiting helicopter. Lee looked back at Holden.

"You're not coming?" she suddenly asked.

"I think it's in my best interest to remain behind," Holden informed her. "You're in good hands."

Jackie grinned at Lee. "He's avoiding all contact with Monroe right now," she announced. "Holden rolled Monroe's Ferrari last month and the emotional wounds are still fresh."

The three women climbed into the awaiting helicopter and securely belted themselves in. Jackie approached Holden and smiled seductively.

"So, once I drop off the kids, do we have the rest of the weekend to ourselves?" she asked.

"Absolutely," he replied and hid his smile.

Jackie smoothed his tie and gave him an approving, quick once over. She winked at him an allowed her hand to slide down his chest.

"Bring your handcuffs, Agent Falcone."

He smiled his response and kissed her quickly but warmly on the lips.

"When you see Monroe," he began then immediately frowned, "tell him you haven't seen me."

Jackie laughed and returned to the awaiting helicopter. The helicopter no sooner started before lifting off. Holden watched it lift into the sky and fly away.

†

*T*he helicopter set down on a private stretch of beach not far from a luxurious, two-story beach house with a wall of windows facing the ocean. Within the detached two-car garage, one bay door was open to reveal an expensive, red Ferrari. Sand swirled into a mini sandstorm as the helicopter landed. Once it shut down, a neatly dressed man appeared on the lower deck. Monroe Dallas was a tall, lanky man in his mid to late thirties with a stylish flair to his expensive wardrobe. His light brown hair was neatly trimmed, although not nearly short enough to constitute a buzz cut. All four women climbed out of the helicopter. It had been a lengthy helicopter flight, taking the better part of six hours to reach the remote island off the coast of Florida. The three newcomers immediately looked around while marveling at the secluded beach and gorgeous beach house.

"Okay," Tonya announced while nodding her approval and barely containing her grin. "I can spend the next four to six months roughing it here."

Monroe jogged down the deck steps while eagerly smiling as he approached Jackie. They enjoyed a warm embrace and a quick, friendly kiss on the lips. Jackie pulled away and her pleasant smile turned into a stern glare.

"We need to talk about Atlantic City," she remarked firmly.

Monroe groaned and rolled his eyes as he stepped away from her. "I told you," he announced firmly and without concern. "That's your problem, and you need to deal with it. I'm not getting involved."

"Not getting involved?" Jackie cried out with hostility. "It's your fault I'm in this position!"

"So?" he remarked almost mocking her. "You're a big girl. You can get yourself out of it." Monroe gave her a stern look. "I'm already doing that crash test dummy husband of yours a favor by babysitting a few kittens for a week or two."

Mac folded her arms across her chest and cast a look at Lee standing alongside her. "Did that flamboyant mamma's boy just call me a kitten?"

"Well, us in general," Lee replied.

"Please, let's not upset our host," Tonya muttered to both women. "If I have to be incarcerated, I want to do it here and not some dirty, dingy warehouse."

Jackie threw her hands in the air with disgust at her friend. "Fine," she scoffed, clearly irritated at Monroe, and then pointed a warning finger at him. "Be that way, but this isn't over."

She stormed back through the sand to her helicopter and the three women standing nearby with their bags. Jackie eyed the three women then glared back at Monroe and smirked.

"He cheats at poker, his upper lip sweats when he's sexually aroused, and he screams like a little girl if he sees a spider," Jackie snarled.

"Jackie!" Monroe scolded with some surprise to the comment and immediately appeared embarrassed by her words.

Jackie grinned at the three women. "Enjoy, ladies."

All three women hurried away from the helicopter as it started, shielded their faces from the blowing sand, and watched through squinted eyes as the helicopter took off, racing into the horizon. The women glanced at Monroe, who could only shake his head while frowning with disgust.

"Let me guess," Mac announced while grinning slyly. "You two used to date."

"Thankfully, I didn't marry *that*," he muttered. Monroe managed a pleasant smile and nodded to the steps. "Come on, I'll show you to your rooms."

Chapter Ten

Monroe's beach house was just as amazing on the inside as it was on the outside. It was two stories of detailed wood, stone, and marble. The open floor plan gave it a roomy feel, and the sections of floor to ceiling windows stretched up to the second floor of the cathedral ceiling. The sun shining through the massive windows gave the home an island appeal. Monroe led the three women upstairs to the second floor while carrying Tonya and Lee's bags. Mac brought up the rear, carrying her own bag, and seemed to case the house for every possible entrance and exit.

"There are only three bedrooms," Monroe informed them while glancing back as he scaled the steps. "Despite Jackie's vulgar description of me, I'm the last of the true gentlemen. The three of you can take your pick of the bedrooms, and I'll sleep on the sofa in the living room."

Mac stopped by the first bedroom at the top of the stairs. "I'll take this room," she announced. "It gives me access to anyone attempting to sneak up the stairs."

Without awaiting a response, she entered the first room, leaving Monroe alone with Tonya and Lee in the open hallway overlooking the first floor.

"I can tell the U.S. Marshal and I are going to get along fantastically," Monroe announced while maintaining his smirk. "Who wants bedroom number two?" he asked while indicating the door closest to them.

Lee and Tonya exchanged looks and shrugged.

"I'll take this room," Tonya announced without care, collected her bag from Monroe, and entered the room.

Monroe smiled at Lee and indicated the last room. "Then you'll be stuck with my room. I just have to remove a few things before you get settled."

Lee entered the room with Monroe trailing after her. She looked around the large, well-appointed master bedroom with its own balcony. She looked back at Monroe as he hurriedly stuffed some personal belongings into a bag. He wasn't the most handsome man by any means, but he had a certain schoolboy appeal. That he was a snappy dresser possibly added to his appeal. Lee didn't doubt Tonya would be sizing him up for evening entertainment. Despite Monroe's relaxed disposition, Lee suddenly felt vulnerable in the room with double glass doors leading onto its own, private balcony. She glanced back at Monroe.

"Is it safe here?" she asked, unable to hide the concern in her tone.

He glanced at her and smiled more naturally. "Unless there's a hurricane, it's perfectly safe," Monroe replied. "I mean, not like that prison they probably stuffed you into originally. This place is safe because it's on a small island and located far enough from any populated areas."

"Agent Falcone seemed to think you're our safest option," she announced. "Your little tiff with his wife wasn't exactly encouraging."

"Ah, Jackie's always been like one of the boys," he informed her. "She was my commander's daughter. Trust me, putting up with the team while growing up made her the way she is today. She had to be tough to survive us."

"You were in the military?"

Monroe straightened and stared at her as if he'd been offended. "You say that like you find it hard to believe."

"Sorry," Lee replied and attempted to hide her embarrassed smile. "I didn't mean to offend you."

"No, it's okay," he announced and sighed. "I'm not offended. Frequently misjudged--but never offended. I guess I'm more of the brains of the operation than the brawn, you know."

Lee smiled and nodded. She wasn't about to say her thoughts aloud, but she had the feeling the fear of spiders might be true. Monroe finished placing things into his duffle bag, offered a timid smile, and then left the room. Lee groaned softly and shook her head.

"Oh, Agent Falcone," she remarked softly under her breath. "I hope you know what you're doing."

There was a soft tap on her door as it opened, revealing Tonya. She stepped into the room and looked around with amazement then nodded her approval.

"Well, you certainly did well with the room assignment," Tonya remarked then grinned at Lee. "I'm thinking cocktails on the beach in twenty minutes."

"I don't know that we should be on the beach," Lee announced and tossed her bag onto a nearby chair. "I feel so exposed here. What's to stop Jericho from walking through the front door and popping us off one-by-one?"

"Monroe, I suppose."

Lee snorted a soft laugh. "If bullets start flying, I'm hiding behind Mac. Monroe is all yours."

"I don't know," Tonya remarked and raised her brows seductively. "He's kind of cute."

Lee glared at her friend and shook her head. She couldn't believe she'd been right in her assumption.

"You've got to be kidding me," Lee huffed and folded her arms across her chest. "After what we've been through, you honestly think this is the time for a romantic interlude?"

"We're isolated, Lee," Tonya announced while looking around. "There's no way Jericho will ever find us here. It's a teeny tiny island. I'm guessing we're somewhere off the coast of Florida. We're a long way from Chicago." She collapsed onto the bed, reclined casually, and studied her friend. "Besides, there's an arrest warrant out for Jericho. It's not as if he's boarding a plane anytime soon. We'll ask Mac if it's okay to hang out on the beach."

Lee inhaled deeply and groaned while releasing her breath. "As long as Mac says it's okay."

✝

*T*wo days had passed without incident, allowing Lee and Tonya to relax for the first time since their nightmare began. Both women entered Monroe's beach house in their swim attire after a lengthy afternoon on the beach. They were already a lovely shade of bronze after just two days of sunning themselves. Monroe had been right; it was a secluded beach with no one else around. It was the first time Lee had felt safe since she found Wiley dead in his chair. Both women changed for dinner, which would be another evening of Monroe showing off his grilling expertise. His personal attachment to his grill was slightly unsettling, but Lee did have to admit, he was a grill master. Despite another relaxing dinner on the deck while watching the sunset, Lee was restless. Tonya easily seemed to forget they weren't on the island for a vacation getaway. Lee couldn't overlook the fact that someone wanted them dead, and there was a distinct possibility they'd eventually be found.

"Shouldn't we have heard from Agent Falcone by now?" she finally asked while shifting in her deck chair. "How hard is it to locate one man?"

"I guess that depends on the man," Monroe casually informed her. "I've known a few who are tough to find when they don't want to be found." He considered then grinned. "You're looking at one of them."

"Hopefully, he can stretch it out until Sunday," Tonya remarked. "I wouldn't mind a full week in paradise. I haven't had a real vacation in years."

"I just want this over with," Lee announced and frowned while watching the waves gently crash to shore. She was feeling almost defeated. "I want my life back."

"What life?" Tonya practically proclaimed. "You'd be at home cooking some sad little meal for one before going to bed to start yet another day at work. Let's face it, Lee; our lives suck at home. *This* is living." She looked at Monroe and smiled warmly, desperate to change the subject. "Are you self-employed, Monroe? I mean, what sort of work could you possibly conduct on a secluded island like this?"

"I'm an independent contractor," he replied casually. "I run imports and exports to and from Panama."

Mac suddenly glared at him and raised her brows in silent question. Monroe caught her look but didn't comment. She suddenly smirked, shook her head, and looked away.

"Oh," Mac muttered softly and held back her laugh. "This just keeps getting better and better."

"What?" Tonya suddenly asked and looked between Monroe and Mac.

Lee eyed both as well while equally curious. Her eyes suddenly widened as she stared at Monroe.

"Are you a drug runner?" Lee suddenly gasped.

Monroe sat up straight in his chair and appeared immediately offended by the question.

"No, I'm not a drug runner!"

Mac gave Lee and Tonya firm stares. "Let's drop the subject," she announced casually. "What Monroe does isn't any of our business, and as long as we're *guests* here, I'd like to keep it that way."

Lee knew that the normal response of an innocent man would be to announce exactly what his operation consisted. Instead, Monroe let the subject drop, seemingly unwilling to defend himself. Lee suddenly felt very uncomfortable. Who the hell was this guy?

Chapter Eleven

Romano's office building was eerily silent after the employees from all twenty floors had gone home for the evening. There was no one around and the lobby appeared empty. A strange snarling sound broke the silence. Jenner sat reclined in the leather chair behind the front desk with his feet propped up and his eyes closed. His snoring again sounded like a snarling beast. A loud thump alongside the desk woke the large man, nearly causing him to fall from his chair. He lurched forward and looked to the left of the desk. A neatly dressed man wearing a light leather jacket and baseball cap stood on the other side of the desk. His unusual briefcase set on the counter above the desk, which explained the loud thump. Jenner stared at the man with surprise or possibly disorientation from abruptly waking.

"I'm with ComServe," the repairman announced. "I'm here to fix your computer."

Jenner continued to stare at the man then finally stood, although his expression didn't change.

"How did you get in here?" Jenner demanded.

"Through the parking garage entrance," the repairman casually replied.

Jenner looked at the security monitors. Several were filled with static. He again looked back at the man.

"The door was locked and the alarm set," Jenner announced suspiciously.

"Sorry to disagree with you, but the door wasn't locked," the man informed him.

Jenner remained puzzled and continued to stare. He finally looked away from the man and removed his PDA tablet from the desk. He scanned the screen then looked back at the repairman alongside the desk.

"You're not due for another two hours," Jenner informed him.

"I had a cancellation," he replied and became impatient with the security guard. "Does your computer have a prior appointment that it can't see me early?"

Jenner sneered at the man, apparently irritated with his snide comment.

"Let's see your company identification," Jenner snapped as he locked eyes with the arrogant man.

The repairman rolled his eyes with annoyance and felt his pockets. He seemed unable to find his badge. He removed something from his pocket and flashed it at the guard. Jenner eyed the ComServe badge. Despite the terrible picture, it appeared genuine.

"I'll show you the broken computer," Jenner grumbled and snatched his baton style flashlight.

"That's not necessary," the repairman replied. "I think I can find it on my own."

"Company rules," Jenner snapped as he stepped out from behind the desk and led him to the elevators.

Both men rode the elevator in silence to the nineteenth floor. They departed the elevator and walked toward the computer closet at the far end of the hall. Jenner indicated the closet just a few doors down then looked in the opposite direction. He stared at a faint light coming from one of the offices. The repairman stared at the security guard, appeared disgusted, and then headed toward the computer closet. Jenner was now preoccupied with the light and headed in the direction of the dimly lit office. The security guard paused outside the partially opened door and noted the name on the office. It was Wiley's office. Jenner slowly pushed open the door with his baton flashlight. The metal flashlight scraped against the wooden door making a distinct rolling sound.

Jenner looked into the office. It was empty, but the small desk light was left on. Jenner sighed with relief and headed into the office toward the desk. He turned off the light, but noticed a faint glow partially lit the room. It was coming from the computer. Jenner appeared confused, since the computers were supposedly still down. He slowly rounded the desk and looked at the computer screen. The light from the hallway vanished as the door shut. Jenner gasped and turned on his flashlight, aiming it across the room. There was no one there. He reached for the desk light. From the glow of the computer, he saw the outline of someone standing next to him. Jenner spun with his flashlight clutched in his hand, prepared to strike, when he saw a gun aimed at him from only a foot away. He was about to scream when nearly silent shots were fired into his chest. He flew backward into the chair and fell to the floor. Blood rapidly seeped through the front of his blue uniform.

✝

*T*he ComServe repairman entered the computer closet and paused within the doorway. A man wearing a black leather waistcoat and black jeans kneeled before an open panel on the industrial computer.

"Who are you?" the repairman demanded.

The man kneeling on the floor glanced behind him, saw the repairman, and sat on his heels.

"I'm the tech guy," he casually replied.

"No, I'm the tech guy," the repairman launched back. "Who sent you? Let me see your badge."

The man in the leather waistcoat groaned and slowly stood. He removed something from beneath his jacket, revealed a semiautomatic with a silencer attached to it, and shot the repairman twice in the chest. The repairman flew back against the wall with a thump near the open door then slid down it, his eyes remaining open. Someone stepped into the open doorway. The man in the leather waistcoat aimed his gun then relaxed and lowered it. Jericho eyed the dead repairman on the floor and shook his head.

"We'll need to dispose of the bodies on our way out," Jericho announced. "The last thing this company needs is another police investigation."

"Bodies?"

"Yeah," Jericho replied and sighed softly. "The idiot security guard found me in the accountant's office."

"Huh, too bad for him," the man replied with little emotion as he replaced his weapon. "I thought the computer tech guy wasn't due for another two hours."

"Oh, well, shit happens," Jericho remarked.

"So did you get it?"

"The fucker emptied the dummy account," he snarled. "I'm sure he moved it to another account within the company account, but there has to be a thousand files in the system. He could have transferred the money just about anywhere and in multiple locations." Jericho leaned against the doorframe and casually folded his arms across his chest. "It'd take months to go through all those files. I don't have that kind of time. Without that money, I'm losing friends fast and hiding from the police is becoming more difficult."

"So what do we do now?"

"Shut the system back down," Jericho replied with little emotion. "The longer the system is out of service, the longer it'll take the feds to get ahead of us. Wiley must have left some clue as to where he transferred that money. He was smart enough to leave two dummy flash drives just to throw us off. Nothing on the one I found on him and bullshit on the lipstick USB he slipped in the girl's bag. That tells me he made alternate plans in case things went south."

"Think he told the girl anything?"

Jericho suddenly looked at the man in the leather waistcoat. "It's possible," he replied slowly and appeared deep in thought. "If he did, she isn't aware that she has the information, or she would have turned it over to the feds."

"It's a good thing you didn't kill her, huh?" the man remarked. "She could still be of value."

Jericho suddenly sneered and removed his cell phone from his pocket. "Yeah, it's a good thing I didn't kill her," he muttered as he left. "I'd better call off the dogs of war before that happens."

Chapter Twelve

*L*ee relaxed on Monroe's king-sized bed and stared at the full moon over the water beyond the part in the balcony curtains. It was nearly one o'clock in the morning, and she still couldn't sleep. Wondering who and what Monroe really was had plagued her mind most of the evening. Agent Falcone had to know what the man did for a living. Would he really trust their lives to someone dealing in criminal activity? Is that why he considered Monroe safe? Did Monroe have more mob connections than Holden claimed her boss had? She rolled onto her back and groaned while staring at the ceiling. She wished they had some way of contacting Agent Falcone. Lee wanted answers about this man she was supposed to trust with her life. Lee heard a faint voice outside possibly on the deck below her balcony. Had one or more of the others decided to stay up? Lee pulled her weary body up from the bed and approached the parted curtains to the partially opened balcony doors. She listened to the voice coming from the deck below.

"No, there's nothing happening here," she heard Mac saying softly.

Lee strained to see whom she was talking with. As Mac paced the deck, Lee realized she was on a cell phone. Ironically, Monroe seemed to indicate that it was impossible to receive a cell phone signal on his remote slice of heaven. Then it hit her. Mac had a cell phone! Lee was going to call Agent Falcone and express her concerns, and she didn't even care that it was the middle of the night. Lee slipped a button shirt over her tank top and hurried from her room. She had to catch Mac before she had a chance to hide the fact that she had a working cell phone. Lee hurried down the steps, making as little noise as possible, crossed the living room, and entered the kitchen. She then heard Monroe's voice on the deck as well, stopping her approach. Whatever had happened seemed to make Monroe angry with Mac. Lee moved closer to the glass doors in order to hear their heated conversation.

"You aren't supposed to have a cell phone," Monroe launched hotly. "You could jeopardize the entire safe house."

"Relax, Monroe," Mac lightly scolded him while offering a sweet smile. "It's just my mother. I promise you, she's not looking to assassinate anyone."

Monroe stared at her, his eyes wide, and shook his head with disbelief. "Who you called isn't the point," he lashed out. "If this Sal guy knows your frequent contacts, he's liable to have tapped their phones. Rich guys like that have all the good toys. A few minutes is all he needs to trace your phone call."

"He's not going to trace my phone call," she remarked hotly. "I'm smarter than that. Hell, I'm smarter than you." She then waved her cell phone at him. "This phone is government issued. It's untraceable."

Monroe snatched the phone from her hand, startling her. "You're not going to risk the lives of the women I'm protecting," he snapped. "I promised I'd keep them safe, which was the same promise you made."

"Damn it, Monroe," she demanded with annoyance. "Give back my phone."

Monroe sneered at her and popped the battery. "You want your phone?" He placed the battery in his pocket and tossed her the empty phone. "There's your phone."

She attempted to catch her phone, but it struck the deck and broke apart. A small transmitter fell from the phone. Both stared at the tiny, familiar object. Monroe met her gaze with his own astonished one.

"That's a tracker," he gasped.

"I swear, I didn't know that was there," Mac announced with a concerned look on her face.

Monroe stomped on the tiny device, shattering it beneath his shoe. He shook his head vigorously while glaring at her.

"I don't care if you're lying or not," he suddenly launched. "You're officially off this assignment." Monroe appeared to be considering his next move and suddenly turned anxious. "I have to get the women out of here."

As Monroe turned to head inside, Mac pulled a gun on him and maintained her innocent smile.

"I'm afraid not, darling," Mac informed him. "I'm in charge here, not you."

Lee stood within the kitchen by the partially open door just out of sight and stared with disbelief at Mac aiming her gun at Monroe. Lee looked around and attempted to figure out her next move.

"You're off this assignment," Mac snapped then tossed him a pair of handcuffs. "Cuff yourself to the grill, grill master."

Lee backed away from the partially open door, turned, and ran for the stairs. She had to alert Tonya. They had to run or hide. She wasn't sure which. Lee scaled the stairs quickly but quietly. Without hesitation or knocking, she slipped into Tonya's room. Lee nearly collided with Tonya, who had been hastily dressing. Apparently, she too had heard part of the conversation from outside as well.

"What's happening?" Tonya cried out in a state near panic while staring at her friend.

"We have to go--now," Lee whispered, attempting to hide her frightened tone for her friend's sake.

Tonya slipped into her shoes while keeping her eyes on Lee in the dim lighting.

"Mac attacked Monroe," Lee softly replied in rushed speech. "We have to get away from her."

"Mac?" Tonya gasped with horror.

Lee knew how her friend felt. She would have sworn they could trust Mac, but that wasn't the case. Maybe there wasn't anyone they could trust. Lee hurried to the bedroom door and peered out. She saw Mac crossing the living room for the stairs. Lee shut and locked the door then frantically motioned to Tonya.

"We have to go out the window," Lee gasped softly. "She's coming!"

Both women ran to the window, opened the screen, and slipped out onto the small ledge. Tonya looked down as Lee joined her on the ledge. It wasn't that far to the sand below, but neither was willing to jump.

"Toward my balcony," Lee ordered softly.

Tonya slid along the ledge toward the balcony only a few yards away. She easily climbed onto the balcony and helped Lee down from the railing. They hurried across the balcony and climbed over the railing on the opposite side. Tonya groaned with anxiety and watched as Lee shimmied down the support beam. She jumped the last few feet and landed softly in the sand. Tonya followed her, lost her footing, and cried out as she fell. Lee helped catch her, breaking her fall, and knocking both to the sand. As they scrambled to their feet, they saw Mac looking out Tonya's window at them. She saw the escaped women and quickly disappeared back inside.

"Run!" Lee cried out, no longer worried about keeping her voice down.

Both women ran through the sand and toward the back deck. Lee stopped Tonya and stared at the deck with surprise. Both Monroe and his expensive grill were gone. Tonya looked from the deck to Lee, her eyes wide with fear.

"What?"

"She handcuffed Monroe to the grill," Lee gasped.

"I'm sorry," Tonya gasped and grabbed Lee's hand. "Monroe is on his own." She tugged on Lee's hand, attempting to pull her along. "We need to get out of here!"

"And we will," Lee announced softly. "Wait for me by the garage."

"Where are you going?"

"For the car keys," Lee remarked. "Go!"

Tonya gave her a concerned look then ran around the back of the beach house and headed for the detached garage. Lee silently crept up the steps and approached the open deck doors. She peered in through the opening. The house was eerily silent, and the dim lighting lent a creepy feel. She thought for sure she'd see Mac on the stairs to cut off their exit. Had she gone out the front door, anticipating they'd head for the garage? Lee didn't have time to second-guess Mac. She hurried into the house and for the island counter where she last saw Monroe's car keys. She hesitated and stared at the empty spot on the counter where Monroe's Ferrari keys once set. Lee's heart pounded. She didn't have a backup plan.

"Looking for these?" Mac asked from nearby.

Lee gasped and turned to see Mac only a few feet away from her while dangling the Ferrari keys.

"Time for you, me, and Tonya to go for a little drive," Mac announced while maintaining her sweet smile.

There was a strange rumbling sound, startling both. As they turned toward the sound, they saw Monroe bodysurfing on the rolling grill straight for Mac. Mac screamed and attempted to leap from his path. The heavy, rolling grill clipped her and sent her flying into the nearby dining room table. Monroe leaped off the grill to which he remained handcuffed. He landed near the slightly dazed woman on the floor and patted down her pockets. He found the handcuff keys and attempted to unlock the cuffs. Mac slowly stood, sneered at Monroe, and punched him in the face, knocking him backward into the grill. Mac reached for her discarded gun, which sported a state-of-the-art silencer, and fired at him. Monroe leaped over the grill and raised the lid. The nearly silent shots struck the metal top, shielding him. Mac attempted to move around the grill for a better shot while Monroe frantically unlocked the handcuff attached to his wrist. He simultaneously turned the rolling grill to block her shot. He freed his wrist and looked up to see Mac aiming the gun at his face. A liquid suddenly sprayed into Mac's eyes, startling her as well as temporarily blinding her. Monroe looked alongside him and saw Lee tossing the can of non-stick spray over her shoulder. She snatched the discarded car keys and ran for the front door with Monroe on her heels. Mac recovered from the spray to her eyes and fired blindly at them.

Lee and Monroe ran for the garage where Tonya waited for them, practically hiding in the darkness. Lee tossed the keys to Monroe as all three piled into the two-seat sports car. Monroe backed the car out of the garage and sent it speeding away from the beach house. Mac ran out the front door but didn't bother aiming at them. It was too late. They heard a strange thumping sound coming from the sky in the near distance.

"Do you hear that?" Lee suddenly asked and attempted to look out several windows to locate the sound.

Monroe looked out the windshield and appeared alarmed. He turned off the headlights and skidded to the side of the road near some trees. He frantically motioned to both women.

"Get down!"

Lee and Tonya ducked in the limited space available and peered out the side window with Monroe partially lying on top of them to remain hidden. A helicopter whizzed overtop of them, flying lower than it normally should have been flying. All three lifted their heads and looked back toward the beach house through the back window. The front door stood open, but Mac was gone. The helicopter hovered before the house. The sound of rapid machine gun fire echoed through the silence as the shells tore through the house. The deafening gunfire seemed to continue non-stop. Monroe groaned and sank in his seat.

"No," he muttered softly.

There was a break in the gunfire as the helicopter continued to hover. All three stared back at the beach house with the same look of surprise.

"Seriously?" Tonya suddenly gasped with horror as her eyes widened. "They're reloading?"

A trail of smoke flew out the opposite side of the helicopter, startling Monroe.

"No, no, no!" Monroe suddenly cried out, ready to jump from the driver's seat.

A rocket launched from the helicopter and struck the house. Half the house exploded on impact with the remainder engulfed in flames. Monroe groaned, sank in his seat, and watched as his house was leveled.

"Not again," he muttered.

They watched the helicopter head in the opposite direction for the coast and eventually out of sight. Monroe cursed softly as he straightened, put the car into gear, and pulled back onto the road. They sped away from what was left of his burning house.

Chapter Thirteen

$\mathcal{F}$our hours had passed since the trio escaped the destroyed beach house. They spent nearly an hour on the dark, out-of-the-way back road to the abandoned airfield, where they had been waiting over three hours. Waiting for what, Lee had no clue. She was beginning to wonder if Monroe even knew what they were waiting for. Monroe hadn't spoken to either woman in almost three hours as he leaned against his Ferrari with his arms folded across his chest and a pouty look on his face. Lee and Tonya sat on the wing of what was left of an old plane. The airfield was creepy in the dim moonlight, casting shadows from the debris of destroyed planes and what remained of the hangars.

A couple of years ago, a hurricane had nearly wiped the island off the map, and the failing, private airfield was among the hardest hit. The airfield owner never bothered to deal with the repairs or clean up the destruction left behind. The nearby hangar looked as if it had seen some action, oddly resembling a military coup. Both women watched Monroe, despite their own desperate situation from the hostile takeover. They had nowhere to go, and neither was dressed appropriately. Lee still wore her shirt overtop her tank top and sleep shorts, while Tonya wore her nightgown over top of a pair of jeans. Lee again was barefooted, which was becoming an annoyingly common occurrence.

"Think we should ask if there's a plan?" Tonya softly asked her friend.

"I don't know," Lee muttered without taking her eyes off Monroe in the near distance. "He looked pretty pissed when he ended that call on his cell phone. Maybe we should wait until his mood improves."

"We've been here three hours without so much as a peep from him," Tonya remarked, their near death experience weighing heavily upon her now. "It's almost sun up. If there's a plan, I'd like to know what it is."

They heard the faint hum of an airplane in the distance. Monroe finally straightened although his mood hadn't improved any. Both women jumped to the sound and looked around.

"Did they find us?" Tonya gasped while attempting to keep from shivering at the sound.

"Doubtful," Lee muttered and hurried to join Monroe with Tonya on her heels.

They could see a plane coming into view. Monroe watched the plane without fear, indicating it was part of his new and improved plan.

"Please tell me that's someone friendly," Lee announced, now sharing Tonya's fears.

"On our side, yes," he announced then immediately frowned. "*Friendly* would be a stretch."

All three watched the plane hit the runway and come to a gradual stop several yards from the Ferrari. Lee and Tonya exchanged looks but didn't comment. They followed Monroe toward the twenty-passenger, private luxury plane. The door opened and the steps unfolded. A distinguished looking man in his early fifties casually walked down the steps, immediately locking eyes with Monroe. Monroe stopped halfway to the plane after having seen the man, cursed softly, and then put on a brave front as he continued his approach. Despite his age, the slightly graying man still maintained an impressive build. His steely gaze was enough to set both women on edge. Definitely intimidating, Ross Madrid didn't look the least bit friendly.

"For as often as I've had to bail your ass out," Ross demanded in a low snarl, "I have to ask myself why Holden would even consider you his best option in a crisis."

"He may have exaggerated how badly these guys want his witnesses," Monroe remarked in a tone that conveyed his respect or fear of the man before him.

Ross nodded without taking his eyes off Monroe. "Lucky for you, Jackie called in the big guns."

As the next man stepped out of the plane's doorway, Monroe's expression dropped even further.

"Ah, hell," Monroe muttered and looked away from the plane doorway.

Kirk Mandel stood an imposing 6'4" with broad shoulders and biceps the size of tree trunks. His buzz cut and thick facial stubble made him even more intimidating, if it were possible. He glared at

Monroe as he walked down the steps, stopped before him, and stared into his eyes with no emotion.

"I was in bed," Kirk snarled lowly. There was a tense pause. "With a hot redhead."

"I didn't ask them to call you, Kirk," Monroe protested. "Don't be mad at me."

He pointed a large finger in Monroe's face. "If she steals me blind, I'm taking it out of your ass."

"Hey," Monroe launched back. "This is all Jackie's fault. I just called for extraction, not your miserable ass. You want to take it up with someone? Go have it out with Jackie."

Kirk's expression suddenly dropped. "Are you kidding?" he nearly exploded. "That girl will rip off my testicles. The little bitch bites too."

Monroe smirked deviously while folding his arms across his chest. "She's standing right behind you."

Kirk appeared horrified and spun around to face another man with an equally grumpy look. The less intimidating man offered a slightly humored smirk.

"What's wrong, Kirk? Did you think I was the big mean witch?" Gil remarked.

Gil Rafferty, although a handsome man, shared the same serious expression as his counterparts. He was on the upper end of thirty if not in his early forties. His short dark hair, peppered with gray, gave him a slightly distinguished look. Lee and Tonya stared at the three strangers then exchanged concerned looks.

"Who the hell are these guys?" Lee muttered.

"I don't know, but they're hot," Tonya announced while giving each of the impressive men a lengthy once over.

Lee caught a glimpse of someone standing alongside her out of the corner of her eye. She looked alongside her and saw a shorter man in his early fifties standing only inches from her. He too studied the group of men by the airplane with great interest.

"I don't know," the man announced casually without looking at Lee. "I can't say I find any of them particularly attractive."

Lee cried out and jumped away from the strange man alongside her. All attention was suddenly on the women as they backed away from the man.

Monroe groaned and covered his eyes. "This isn't happening," he muttered then approached Lee and Tonya. "It's okay. That's just Zack. He's, uh, sort of like our mascot."

Zack suddenly grinned and chuckled, sending chills down Lee's back. She wasn't exactly sure what he found humorous about the comment, but he wasn't nearly as impressive as the other men were. Apart from being creepy, he didn't seem capable of tying his own shoes let alone being useful to them.

"Mascot," Zack scoffed and appeared almost pleased. "That's a good one."

"Weren't you supposed to be dead?" Monroe asked the strange man in a disinterested tone.

"Nah, that was just a misunderstanding," Zack replied then eyed both women. He smiled in a manner meant to be charming but seemed to miss the mark then politely extended his hand. "Zack Kinsley."

Both women suspiciously eyed him and his hand then glanced at Monroe for reassurance. Monroe frowned and shook his head at his friend.

"Go be annoying somewhere else," Monroe announced and shooed him away.

As Zack joined the other men by the plane, Lee glared at Monroe. "Who the hell are these guys?"

Monroe inhaled deeply and turned toward the plane with the men standing by the steps. All four stood with a wide stance and their arms folded across their chests while impatiently staring back at them. Monroe looked back at the women and offered a tiny smile.

"Meet Whiskey Tango Foxtrot," Monroe announced. "My former Navy SEAL team."

"Navy SEALs?" Tonya muttered and hid her lustful grin as she looked at Lee. "How hot is that?"

Lee refused to look at her friend, knowing what she was already thinking. Monroe guided both women toward the plane and the men. There was a brief introduction, and, despite their mood toward Monroe, the four men were pleasant enough toward the women. Jackie stood at the top of the steps with her arms folded across her chest and glared at them with an annoyed look.

"Are we having a tea party or are we blowing this joint?" she demanded.

Monroe smiled mockingly at the women. "And you've already met drill sergeant Jackie." He then looked at the guys and appeared curious. "Where's Beck? Too busy to come out here at five in the morning and bust my hump?"

"No, we're on our way to see him," Jackie announced then motioned to the doorway. "Let's go, girls!"

Lee and Tonya appeared surprised and exchanged looks. "Is she yelling at us?" Tonya asked.

"No," Ross replied as a casual smile crossed his face. "I believe she was talking to us." He turned to his men. "You heard the woman in charge. Move it out!"

Ross politely indicated for the women to take the steps into the plane. Both smiled and headed up the short set of steps for the plane door. The five men filed in behind them. Monroe entered the plane last and latched the door. As he turned, he nearly collided with Jackie, who glared at him.

"We need to talk about Atlantic City," she growled softly, catching Lee's attention.

"I think you have a plane to fly," Monroe informed her then offered a slightly mocking smile. "You don't want to keep Ross waiting."

"Fine," she snarled without taking her eyes off him, "but it's a little over four hours to Colorado. You're going to have to talk to me at some point."

"Actually, no, I don't," Monroe remarked while grinning slyly then pointed both front and back. "You'll be in the cockpit, and I'll be all the way back in third-class."

As he pointed toward the rear, Monroe saw a man in the last row of seats sleeping with a fedora covering his face. He glanced back at Jackie.

"I thought you said we were meeting Beck in Colorado," he remarked.

"We are," Jackie announced with a grin on her face. She patted him on the chest. "Enjoy third-class." She then headed for the cockpit.

Monroe walked past the two women and his team toward the available seats in the back near the sleeping man. He studied the man as he took a vacant seat alongside him. The plane engine started, rousing the man. He lifted his hat, straightened, and looked at Monroe. Monroe's expression dropped as he stared at the grinning man across from him.

"Bogart?" Monroe gasped with surprise that sounded more like alarm.

"Monroe!" he cried out enthusiastically.

The handsome, well-built man in his late twenties suddenly grinned and hugged Monroe against his will. Bogart was 'hunky actor' handsome with flowing golden-brown hair and sideburns a shade darker. The stubble on his youthful face only accented his dimples, adding to his charm and good looks. Bogart pulled back and was barely able to control his grin. His look then turned serious.

"I waited for you in Atlantic City, man, but you never showed," Bogart announced. He shook his head and appeared pleased as his grin returned. "It all worked out though. Did you hear? I ran into Jackie. What an amazing trip!"

Monroe stared at Bogart with his mouth hanging open and then attempted a smile.

"Uh, yeah, so I heard," he muttered.

"Yeah, it's been great," Bogart announced cheerfully. "I've been hanging with my girl and her federally for a few months at their place. Damned hospitable, you know, for a fed." He slapped Monroe on the shoulder while grinning excitedly. "I was almost reluctant to give up that comfortable gig to fly out here, but Jackie said you could really use my help with this one."

"Really?" Monroe muttered. "That was so *nice* of her."

Bogart straightened proudly in his seat and slapped his knee. "Man, we're going to be a great team, you and I. Just like that last job in Ecuador. That was one hell of an adventure." His eyes suddenly lit up as if another thought struck him. "How about after this job is finished, we hang out at your beach house like the good old days? I can't think of a better way to kill a few months than soaking up some sun on that private beach of yours."

Monroe weakly smiled. "Uh, well, the house was sort of blown up last night, but I'm sure Jackie--"

"Blown up?" he cried out with surprise then immediately turned noble. "Ah, hell, I'll help you rebuild. It'll be fun!"

Monroe attempted to hide his grimace.

Chapter Fourteen

*T*he luxury plane touched down on the private airstrip far from any major city. It was already late morning and the sun was shining. Gorgeous countryside and mountains stretched along the horizon. The view couldn't have been more spectacular, not that Lee could enjoy it. Apart from the hangar, a small mobile home, and a sports utility vehicle, there was nothing else around. The eight-passenger, four-wheel drive SUV was parked not far from where the plane slowed. A man in his mid to late thirties casually leaned against the front bumper of the SUV with his arms folded across his chest and watched the plane come to a stop. His sunglasses lent to the image that he was possibly a spy. He finally straightened as the door opened and the steps dropped. Beck Larue stood over six feet tall with an impressive athletic build. His light brown hair was moderately rumpled and the perfect length for running fingers through. His rugged good looks and sturdy gaze announced he was the final member of Whiskey Tango Foxtrot. He showed no emotion as the passengers disembarked the luxury plane with Jackie and Monroe bringing up the rear. Monroe was softly pleading with Jackie, who seemed contented to ignore him.

"We can't have him on this mission, Jackie," Monroe softly protested while casting a stray gaze at Bogart.

Bogart was cheerfully attempting to joke around with Gil and Kirk, although their expressions conveyed it was probably unwise of him.

"You want me to apologize for ditching you in Atlantic City?" Monroe asked while becoming slightly animated. "Fine, I'm sorry I ditched you to avoid Bogart, but I didn't know he'd invite himself to live with you guys for the last few months."

Jackie folded her arms across her chest while staring at Monroe and his desperate expression. He was obviously getting nowhere with the uncaring woman, and his mood toughened.

"He can't be here," Monroe insisted, now taking a stern approach. "And if you insist on playing your hand, I'll have to go above your head and talk to Ross. He's not going to want Bogart invading our protection operation. This is serious stuff. He's only going to get in the way."

Beck joined the other men, who seemed to be having a team meeting. Ross looked at Beck while maintaining his serious demeanor.

"Is everything ready?" Ross asked.

"The old lodge has never looked better," Beck informed him. "We'll be completely isolated and secure."

Bogart attempted to be a part of the meeting and made his way into the group. Kirk casually placed a hand to Bogart's chest without even looking back at him and pushed him back several steps, keeping him out of the conversation.

"And you got the necessary supplies?" Ross questioned.

"Everything we need," Beck replied then suspiciously eyed Bogart as he again moved closer to the conspiring men. Beck looked around the group and indicated Bogart with an accusing finger. "Who the hell is this guy?"

Bogart grinned charmingly and extended his hand. "I'm Bogart. I'm friends with Jackie and Monroe."

"One of Monroe's conniving conmen," Kirk snarled while glaring at the outsider.

"Hey, hombre, I'm a very *useful* conniving conman," Bogart announced in a defensive tone.

Beck poked his finger into Bogart's chest and forced him to take a step back. "It's men like you who get men like us killed in the field," Beck launched back. "Now back off!"

Bogart frowned but didn't argue with the hostile man. Looking like a dog with his tail between his legs, Bogart joined Lee and Tonya by the SUV. Unlike Bogart, Lee and Tonya were happy to stay out of the way and await orders. After a few more minutes of planning, Ross, Beck, and Gil approached Jackie and Monroe near the steps of the plane.

"Well, Monroe, it looks like you'll get your chance to plead your case to Ross," Jackie informed him and leaned against the railing to the steps.

Ross paused before Jackie and allowed a softer side to emerge. "We're going to be out of communication range on this one," he announced. "We have the satellite phone in case of emergency. Otherwise, one of us will contact Holden once a week from the nearest town with the clone phone."

"I understand," Jackie replied.

His look turned serious as he took a tougher stance. "I want you to tell Holden that we're even after this. If he wants any more favors, he'll have to contract our services. Some of us have other responsibilities."

"If I recall," Jackie announced, "you received a very lovely parting gift last time."

"That helicopter was reimbursement for the one we lost helping your husband on the last mission," Ross replied matter-of-factly.

"Whose brilliant idea was it to let Zack fly the helicopter in the first place?" she launched back.

There was an awkward silence as Jackie and Ross locked eyes. The other three men avoided looking at either and fidgeted. Somehow, Jackie had managed to keep the team wrapped around her dainty little finger, but it didn't seem as if Ross was about to be intimidated by the attractive, young woman.

"That's beside the point," Ross finally snapped, caving to her dominating personality.

Jackie hid her smile, knowing she won another round.

"We're getting off subject," Ross continued while waving his hands erratically. "I need you to fly Gil back to Chicago with you. Have Holden familiarize Gil with the head honcho who's after the young ladies."

"He's not going to be exactly keen on the idea, Ross," Jackie replied. "He wants the witnesses kept safe. I don't think he wants any of you going to war with the mob."

"Our way will get the ladies back to their lives sooner and in one piece," Ross announced. "Certainly, you can use your influence to convince Holden to let Gil poke around a little."

"Are you asking me to seduce a federal agent?" Jackie asked while cleverly raising her brows as she folded her arms across her chest.

"Considering he's your husband, yes, I'm asking you to seduce him," Ross replied firmly. "Will you do that?"

Jackie considered the question, straightened, and smiled. "I'll do that only if you agree to keep Bogart."

"Done," Ross replied without hesitation.

Monroe and Beck looked at Ross with surprise and simultaneously protested.

"You have got to be kidding," Beck exploded.

"You don't understand, Ross," Monroe attempted to explain. "Bogart is a fungus. Once he attaches himself to you, he's impossible to get rid of."

Ross eyed Monroe and appeared curious. "Isn't he supposed to be a friend of yours?"

"Friend is a bit strong," Monroe muttered. "I'm pretty sure the proper term is *leech*."

Ross looked at Jackie and smiled pleasantly. "Have a nice flight, Jackie."

Jackie grinned, pleased with herself. She and Ross exchanged quick kisses before she headed up the steps. Gil followed her up the steps and into the plane. Monroe secretly pouted while Ross's grin mocked him. Lacking enthusiasm, both men reluctantly followed Ross back to the others waiting by the SUV.

t

*C*ivilization was left behind almost two hours later. Lee and Tonya rode in the middle of the second and third rows of seats with the intimidating men on either side of them. Beck drove while Ross rode shotgun in the front passenger seat. Lee sat between the slightly psychotic Zack and the overly serious Kirk. She wasn't sure which was worse. Tonya remained stranded in the last row between the excessively talkative Bogart, and Monroe, who was already nearing insanity from the constant chatter. Kirk would cast glaring death threats at Bogart behind him, leaving Lee feeling uneasy every time she saw the evil in his dark eyes. Beck's constant glares through the rearview mirror weren't helping ease Lee's tension either. If Lee didn't maintain faith in Agent Falcone's judgment of the men, she'd be taking bets on which man would kill Bogart first.

Apart from the lengthy, tense ride inside the SUV, Lee couldn't help stare out the window at the beautiful landscaped countryside on the long stretch of road. They only passed a few vehicles in the last hour, and she couldn't recall how long it had been since they'd seen sign of a house. She wondered how much further it would be, but she didn't feel comfortable talking to either of her seatmates. Tonya gently rubbed her temples and appeared ready to explode any moment.

"How much longer?" Tonya finally blurted out the question Lee had been desperate to ask.

"It's about another hour--" Beck announced from the driver's seat.

Lee held back her groan, but Tonya wasn't nearly as concerned with hiding her feelings.

"--until we reach town," Beck continued. "The lodge is another two hours from there."

Despite not being able to see one another's expression, Lee and Tonya shared the same shocked look.

"Three more hours?" Lee gasped, beating Tonya to the outburst. "Are you serious?"

Zack casually leaned forward toward the front seat and over Beck's shoulder. "I think we need a potty break," he casually announced.

Lee felt her cheeks immediately redden. She didn't need a bathroom break, and if she did, she certainly didn't need Zack announcing it to the entire transport vehicle. She secretly seethed then shifted in her seat. Now that he had said the magic words, she suddenly had the urge to urinate.

"Great," Tonya scoffed while throwing her hands in the air. "Now I have to go."

Zack smirked proudly as he sank back in his seat. It was almost as if he knew the comment would set the mood. Kirk squirmed in his seat as well.

"Yeah, me too," Kirk muttered.

"Well, you're in luck," Beck announced cheerfully and nodded out the front windshield. "There's a restroom just up ahead."

Both women looked out the side window and strained to see where Beck had indicated. The timing was uncanny. The SUV pulled alongside the road not far from a large boulder, which was the restroom in question. Lee held her breath and refrained from commenting. Zack removed a semiautomatic from his hidden shoulder holster and cocked it, causing both women to jump. He grinned deviously.

"I'll check for snakes!"

Lee and Tonya stared after him as he sprang from the SUV and stalked the large boulder with his gun prepared for a shock and awe on any slithering wildlife. Tonya leaned forward and touched Lee's shoulder.

"We're gonna die out here," Tonya whispered near Lee's ear from behind.

Lee would have laughed if she actually thought it was a joke, but she was starting to get the same uneasy feeling regarding the men Agent Falcone assigned to protect them.

†

*T*he SUV pulled up to what remained of an old lodge that had seen better days. Once an impressive resort, the fifty bedroom hotel showed years of neglect. There were several boarded windows, the paint was peeling, and the wraparound porch appeared to be eroding. The men got out of the SUV and showed no reaction to the condition of the lodge. Lee and Tonya stared at the dilapidated building with their mouths slightly open. There were no polite words to describe how they were both feeling.

"What a hell hole!" Bogart proclaimed, causing all eyes to fall upon him.

Lee was certain Bogart wouldn't be alive by morning. Kirk tossed a duffel bag at Bogart, which he barely caught and almost knocked him to the ground. Bogart was about to protest when Kirk threw another bag at him, as if playing some sick game to knock him down.

"Make yourself useful," Kirk demanded of the pretty boy.

Monroe grabbed two bags and approached Lee and Tonya. He observed their expressions then offered a reassuring smile.

"Don't worry," he informed them. "It's not nearly as bad as it looks."

Tonya and Lee weren't convinced but they followed Monroe and Beck onto the porch. All three entered behind Beck. The magnificent, rustic lobby appeared painstakingly refinished to its original condition. Both women remained equally shocked by the beauty of the place. The old-fashioned front desk was possibly antique and added class to the lobby. A large, walk-in stone fireplace took up the entire back wall. An open, wooden staircase led to the second floor rooms, which overlooked the lobby.

"What is this place?" Tonya asked to no one in particular.

"Back in the sixties, it was a luxury hotel where the rich and pampered went to escape the bustle of the city," Ross informed her while looking around. "When it outlived its usefulness, it was auctioned off in the eighties and bought by a group of fifty hunters. They restored most of the main building."

"My grandfather was one of the last surviving members of the hunting club," Beck continued while proudly looking around. "I was willed a large portion of the estate, leaving the guys to buy out the remaining heirs."

"Few people know about the lodge," Monroe announced. "We use it as a safe haven from the rest of the world."

"Since I sold my used car lot," Beck casually informed them, "I spend most of my time here. It's pretty much my home." He headed toward the front desk, removed some old-fashioned keys, and then indicated the elevators. "The elevators function, but I recommend you don't use them. They're unreliable. We'll all stay on the second floor close to the stairs. I have a two-bedroom suite for our guests, which offers a connecting door to a possible third bedroom. Ross will take the connecting bedroom." Beck handed Ross both sets of keys. "Even though no one should be able to find us this far out, one of us will remain on guard duty in the lobby at night."

"So geographic isolation is your only security?" Tonya asked and appeared concerned.

Beck shrugged slightly and offered a tiny smirk. "Understand; I'm not exactly paranoid--"

He then approached the steps, moved the large ball at the end of the railing, and revealed a button. Beck slammed his palm on the button. Steel panels fell down across the windows, in front of the main entrance, and metal doors slammed shut toward the back of the main lodge. The sound of crashing metal was almost deafening, causing both women and Bogart to look around with surprise. Kirk grinned for the first time, apparently pleased with the lodge's defense system. Lee and Tonya looked from the sealed windows and door to Beck, who smirked in response.

"But I like being prepared," he announced casually.

Zack walked past both women and muttered to them, "Don't believe what he says. He's paranoid."

Chapter Fifteen

*A*gent Falcone sat in the driver's seat of his SUV and kept watch of Romano's office building from across the moderately busy street. He clearly had a lot on his mind judging by the transfixed look in his eyes. The passenger side door opened without warning, startling him. He had his weapon in his hand surprisingly fast and aimed it at the door. Gil showed no emotion to the gun aimed at him as he climbed inside Holden's SUV, but instead raised his brow in response.

"Jumpy, Holden?"

Holden frowned and replaced his gun to his shoulder holster. "Gil," he muttered his greeting then returned his attention back to the building across the street. "What brings you to my stakeout?"

"Fifty million dollars, two hot witnesses, and one pain in the ass federal agent," Gil replied.

"Always a pleasure, Gil," Holden remarked with disinterest. "What can I do for you now?"

"Just wondering about your endgame."

"My endgame?" he questioned while looking at Gil. "What's that supposed to mean?"

"Just that you have nothing on this guy, Romano," Gil announced. "You have my team watching those women, but you're not any closer to pinning anything on this guy than you were the day his accountant was carried out feet first."

"I'm aware of that," Holden remarked then looked back toward the building. "The fifty million is our motive. Once we find the flash drive, we'll have our proof. We just need to figure out what Romano did with the money, and then we have him."

"Congratulations," Gil announced without cracking a smile. "You have a man embezzling money from his own company. If you're lucky, you may be able to pin money laundering on him. You still won't have anything to prove that he murdered the accountant or that he ordered a hit on those women. He's already denounced his right-hand man, Jericho, who we know broke into Lee's apartment. You know--the guy on the lamb."

Holden avoided looking at Gil, a self-proclaimed know-it-all; although he couldn't hide his annoyance at what he undoubtedly already knew.

"Once you arrest Jericho, the women will be out of danger, and Romano will have handed you your scapegoat for the accountant's murder," Gil continued while casually playing with several buttons on the center dashboard.

Holden slapped Gil's hand to prevent him from flipping any switches. Gil cast a glare at him.

"I assume you're attempting to make some point," Holden grumbled.

"Yeah, case closed," Gil replied while studying him. "At best you have Jericho for breaking and entering. A good lawyer will get him off on the death threat charge with the 'he said; she said' defense. It's his word against hers and with Sal's money backing him..." Gil shook his head as if shaming Holden. "You don't even have a case against him for the dead accountant or the attack on Monroe's beach house."

Holden finally looked at Gil while maintaining his irritation. "I'm buying some time until I can get something on Romano. I know it doesn't look good, but it's the best I can do at the moment."

"Yeah, it's the best *you* can do," Gil remarked. "You give me twenty-four hours, and I can give you all the dirt you need on this guy to put him away for good."

"You're suggesting I let you go rogue to get that information?" Holden demanded.

"I'm not suggesting you *let* me do anything," Gil announced sternly. "I'm asking you to stay out of my way, so I can end this for you."

"I'd love to let you loose on my town, Gil," Holden informed him. "But there's nothing you can do illegally that my team can't do within the boundaries of the law."

"You're spending the afternoon watching a building like a teenager watching for a thong sighting," Gil retorted in his usual monotone voice. "You must realize that any information of value is at his country mansion."

"I'm not helping you break into his mansion," Holden announced with irritation.

"One strategically placed bug in Romano's office; a transmitter of Beck's design on his home computer, and we have access to phone calls and emails coming to and from his office. I'm not asking you to help me break into his mansion," Gil responded firmly. "I'm just asking you not to arrest me if I get caught.

"I won't have to arrest you if you get caught," Holden snapped. "You'll be dead."

Gil suddenly grinned. "I knew I could count on you," he announced and left the car.

Holden stared after him with a look of shock. "What? Gil, wait!" He groaned softly and shook his head. "Every relationship comes with baggage," he scoffed. "Why did mine have to come with a six-pack of SEALs?"

✝

*R*omano's country mansion was nestled on a large parcel of land beyond tall, stone walls. The professionally landscaped estate didn't have a hedge out of place. Weeping willow trees and faux split rail fencing lined the long driveway. The driveway split off to circle a large fountain outside the front door, while the remaining driveway branched off to the left. The driveway led to the kitchen, staff wing, and eventually to the massive, detached, eight-car garage. Gil remained partially hidden behind a large tree and watched the mansion through a pair of small binoculars. Despite the grandeur of the mansion, it lacked extensive security one would expect from a mafia kingpin. Apart from the security guard at the front gate, there wasn't a guard to be found. A few strategically placed cameras seemed to be the only security measures.

Gil lowered his binoculars and watched the mansion a while longer being not completely convinced that the place was so unprotected. A delivery truck pulled up to the security gate and stopped. The security guard approached the truck from outside the gate. A large silver sable German shepherd ran across the lawn and jumped at the gate while barking at the truck. A man yelled from the house. The dog ran back to the house. Gil stared a moment longer and frowned.

"I hate dog alarms," he muttered.

Gil made his way along the outer area beyond the gate and headed toward the backside of the mansion. There was a second, unmanned gate, but it appeared to be on lockdown. He again studied the surrounding area. He spotted a large hangar between the back gate and the large garage. A four-passenger helicopter sat on a landing pad near the hangar. Beyond the eight-car garage, several men were working on landscaping in the backyard. They appeared to be pitching a concert tent for some large gathering. Gil removed his cell phone and pressed a single button. He waited a moment for the person on the other end to answer.

"It looks like they're having a party, Holden," Gil announced into the phone. "Something going on?" He awaited a response then smirked. "Birthday party this Saturday afternoon, huh? Yeah, I think I can use that to my advantage. Can you get me a copy of the secretary's plan book for this week?" There was a brief pause as Gil rolled his eyes. "It's a simple request, Holden. Call me back in an hour." Gil disconnected the call and frowned. "With all Jackie's military options, why'd she have to marry a fed?" he muttered with annoyance.

†

*L*ater that afternoon, Gil waited near the main gate while keeping out of sight in the tree line. He looked at his watch and frowned. A landscaping truck approached the gate. Gil grinned and waited for the vehicle to stop. The guard greeted the truck and spoke to the driver. As the guard headed back into the guardhouse, Gil silently darted for the back of the vehicle and easily scaled the tailgate, dropping into the back with the equipment. As the truck drove through the gate and up to the back of the mansion, Gil dropped out just prior to the vehicle stopping. He mingled with the other workers, carried a plant behind them, and then slipped off to the side, disappearing out of sight.

Gil casually walked through the staff wing of the house, ducking into doorways each time he heard voices. He eventually found his way to the kitchen. He slipped silently across the massive kitchen while an older man and woman talked at the opposite end. Gil entered the attached dining room, which contained a massive, carved table with seating for twenty. The dining room looked more like a ballroom than a dining room. He approached the main dining room door, was about to leave, and then suddenly hesitated to the sound of women's voices. Two young, attractive maids passed the doorway and headed into the kitchen. Once they were gone, Gil slipped out of the dining room and entered the grand hallway, which seemed to extend forever. He observed the many rooms as he passed, mentally noting which rooms were where. He paused before a closed door, assessed his situation, and then entered the room.

Expensive, antique furniture filled the elegant study, tastefully decorated with a distinguished man in mind. Obviously, Romano was rich enough to hire people with excellent taste to decorate for him. Gil passed a wall lined with bookcases, approached the desk, and planted a device under the front edge. He then rounded the desk and attached a second device to the back of the computer tower. Once he'd secured the devices, he wasted little time slipping out of the study. He casually shut the door behind him and headed toward the kitchen area. He heard the same female voices conversing just up ahead. Without slowing, he changed direction and headed back along the grand hallway and toward the front door. He opened the front door and saw a red light on the security panel alongside the door flash. Gil groaned with disgust, realizing he'd set off an alarm.

"Who sets a door alarm in the middle of the day," he muttered as he casually removed his cell phone. He waited for someone to pick up on the other end. "Yes, I'd like to report an intruder at 954 Sona Lane," Gil announced into his cell phone. "Can you send someone out right away?" He hesitated and awaited a response. "Thank you, I appreciate your assistance."

Gil immediately returned the cell phone to his pocket as the guard with the German shepherd ran onto the porch. Gil placed his hands in the air and remained motionless as the dog snarled at him. The guard aimed a gun at the intruder. Police sirens wailed in the distance. Being arrested for illegal entry wasn't exactly the smartest move, but for a man with a 'get out of jail free' fed card, it had its advantages.

"Don't move," the guard shouted as the dog growled and barked his disapproval.

"I'm not moving," Gil replied with little emotion.

"It's okay, Lenny," a male voice announced from the foyer behind Gil.

Gil slowly glanced over his shoulder to the man standing behind him. It was Jericho! Gil recognized him from photos Holden had in his file. The fact that he was inside Romano's mansion was almost enough to incriminate Lee's boss.

"I've got this," Jericho announced and smiled deviously. "I'm sure he just made a wrong turn from the backyard. Tell the police there's been a misunderstanding."

The man with the dog nodded and commanded the dog from the porch with him. Once they were out of sight, Gil turned toward the wanted man behind him. Jericho zapped him on the side with a stun gun. Gil immediately dropped to his knees while twitching slightly, although handling the sudden surge of electrical current better than most men would. It obviously wasn't his first time being tased. He attempted to gather his strength for retaliation, but it was too late. Jericho punched him in the face, driving him the rest of the way to the floor, allowing him no chance to fight back.

Chapter Sixteen

Lee leaned on the second floor railing, carved from an actual tree trunk, and overlooked the rustic lobby below. The five men from Whiskey Tango Foxtrot were standing near the check-in desk while having a serious discussion. Lee was unable to hear their conversation, which didn't actually bother her. Bogart was conveniently left out of their meeting, which obviously bothered him, judging by the way that he paced the opposite end of the lobby. Tonya appeared from the second floor corridor, joined Lee by the sturdy railing, and leaned on it alongside her. Both women had finally changed out of their hastily thrown together outfits from their night of hell and into some clothes Jackie had donated to their cause. Tonya watched the men with moderate fascination then smiled her approval.

"So," Tonya announced while slyly raising her brows. "Which one do you want?"

Lee glanced at her friend and shamed her with a disapproving look. "I'm not interested, Tonya," she announced. "We were nearly killed last night."

"I know that," Tonya huffed. "But we weren't. We're safe here."

"I remember those famous last words at Monroe's house too," Lee muttered.

"That was different," her friend remarked. "Mac sold us out. Now she's out of the picture. No one's going to find us here. Hell, I'm not even sure where *here* is. This seems like a pretty good place to relax and forget about our problems for a while." Tonya indicated the men in the lobby below. "There are some pretty fine specimens of manliness down there. I assume we're going to be here a while, so we may as well make the best of it and enjoy ourselves."

"You're seriously thinking about hooking up with those guys?" Lee demanded.

"Well, one of them," Tonya replied and stared at her friend with astonishment at her tone. "Are you seriously telling me you're not?"

"I'd think you know me by now," Lee replied and looked away with disinterest.

"Yeah, I don't suppose any of them qualify as a cowboy," Tonya teased then turned to face Lee. "Come on; make the best of a bad, dull situation. What else is there to do around here? Have you noticed? No television. No computer. No internet. No phones. I'm shocked we have electric and indoor plumbing." Tonya flopped on the railing and groaned while holding her chin in her hand. "Did you see the books and magazines in the lobby? Unless you're into fishing, birdwatching, and improvised booby traps, there isn't even anything decent to read around here."

Lee shook her head but didn't have the energy to engage in another sexual debate with her love-starved friend.

"I'll pass, thank you."

"I know our situation sucks," Tonya announced while looking at her friend. "I'm just trying to find a way to make the best of it. What's the big deal?"

Lee sighed and hung heavily on the railing. "I'm sorry," she announced with a soft groan. "You're right; we're going to be here a while. You should entertain yourself, if it's what makes you happy. I suspect the guys won't mind."

"I know what we can do," Tonya suddenly chirped and straightened with enthusiasm. "Let's pretend we're at the nightclub. I'll pick out overnight company, and you tell me what's wrong with each of them. Help me choose the right one. It'll be just like a typical Friday night."

"Except it's not night and it's not Friday," Lee casually informed her.

"Just play along."

"Okay," Lee reluctantly announced and straightened. "Who's up first?"

Tonya gave a nod to Bogart across the room. "What about that one? Bogart. He's sort of dashing. A little talkative for my taste, but he looks like he'd be energetic in bed."

"He's almost certainly a womanizer," Lee replied. "I don't know that you'll find enough condoms around here to want to play with that one."

87

"Hmm, good point," Tonya replied. "We'll add him to the 'cuddle list'." She looked across the room to the five members of Whiskey Tango Foxtrot and indicated Kirk while smiling lustfully. "What about that one? Mr. Big and Brawny."

"Kirk?" Lee practically gasped. "Can you imagine a guy with no emotions in the sack? What would that be like?"

Tonya sank into thought, grimaced, and shook her head. "Oh, you're right. It'd be like wild kingdom. Three seconds of heaven for him and then he'd roll over and fall asleep." Tonya studied the men and indicated Zack. "Can we both agree we need to avoid that one in all situations?"

"That's a safe assumption," Lee replied in a low tone. "There's something not right with that guy. Probably sniffed too much napalm back in the day."

Tonya held back her laugh then indicated Beck. "Okay, now that one has some potential."

"Has a bit of an attitude; possibly slightly unstable, but he seemed nice enough toward us," Lee replied. "I'd put him in the 'potential' column."

"Ross has that whole 'man in charge' thing going," Tonya announced. "He's a little too serious for my taste."

"Yeah, he's pretty serious," Lee replied. "He's also a little old for you. Even if he's not too old for you, you're too young for him. I don't think he'd warm up that fast."

"He'd probably turn all gentlemanly," Tonya remarked then suddenly frowned. "Or fatherly. Oh, that kills that fantasy. That just leaves Monroe."

"Monroe is decent enough," Lee informed her and studied him by the desk. "I mean, he's cute and dresses nice."

"Definitely not gay," Tonya added then considered her own comment. "Although, he's oddly attached to his personal possessions. Kind of spoiled that way."

"So which one will it be? Monroe or Beck?"

"I don't know," Tonya announced. "I think it'll be fun letting fate decide. Shall we get to know our captors?"

"Sure, why not," Lee announced with a bored sigh.

They headed down the open stairs and into the lobby. As they approached, the five men immediately broke up their meeting. Ross was the first to engage them. He offered a pleasant smile and made them feel comfortable among the intimidating men.

"I trust your quarters are suitable," Ross announced to both women.

"They're fine," Lee replied and returned the smile.

"We were hoping someone would show us around our prison away from home," Tonya announced teasingly, although only Zack seemed humored. She then looked at Beck and smiled sweetly. "Since this is your home, we thought maybe you'd want to give us the tour personally."

Beck seemed unusually tense by Tonya's seductive grin but managed a weak smile. "Uh, yeah, sure."

†

*G*il slowly woke and attempted to focus on the bland, dimly lit room. The German shepherd dog stared into his face and snarled softly while exposing sharp teeth. Gil slowly lifted his head and looked around what was clearly a room within the basement, although its resemblance to an interrogation room was uncanny. He immediately pulled on the handcuffs wrapped around the arm of the heavy chair. Jericho stood from where he sat on an old desk toward the opposite side of the room. He casually approached Gil and grinned.

"I see you're awake," Jericho announced. "I was worried I'd killed you for a minute there."

"I appreciate your concern," Gil replied dryly.

"Let's skip the pleasantries," Jericho snapped. "Who are you and what are you doing here?"

"I'm with the landscapers," Gil announced.

"I prefer if you don't lie to me," he said sternly. "There are five landscapers. Five signed in, and five signed out. Are you with the police?"

"Did you find a badge or a gun?"

"No."

"Then I'm not with the police."

Jericho grinned and nodded. "Oh, so you want to play that way," he replied. "Well, I'd love to stay and chat with you all evening, but I have other plans. We can continue this conversation in the morning. Until then, feel free to scream your head off. No one will hear you, and even if they did, they wouldn't care. Have a nice night." Jericho looked at the dog. "Darth," he announced and then spoke in German.

The dog stared at Gil and snarled.

"Don't worry; Darth will keep you company," Jericho announced then grinned. "I, uh, wouldn't make any sudden movements...or any movements for that matter. He's hungry, and it wouldn't take much for him to tear your leg off."

Jericho left the room, locking the door behind him. The dog stared at Gil and continued to snarl. Gil studied the dog.

"Darth, huh?"

The dog snarled viciously.

"Is that mean man starving you, so you'll obey him?" he asked in a coddling tone.

Gil tilted his head, stared back at the dog with soulful eyes, and whimpered softly. Darth tilted his head and listened to the sound Gil made.

"I'll bet you'd love something to eat," Gil baby-talked the dog. "Puppy want something to eat?"

Darth again tilted his head while staring at Gil. Gil said something in German. The dog suddenly leaped to his feet and licked his muzzle. He said something else in German and stuck out his booted foot. The dog grabbed his boot by the heel and tugged on it. Gil continued to repeat the word. The dog tugged harder until the boot came off. He pulled the boot closer to him with his foot and repeated the command to the dog. Darth grabbed Gil's foot, causing him to cry out.

"Easy!"

The dog pulled his sock off.

"Good boy."

Gil used his toe to pull a thin piece of metal from his boot liner, although it took a little effort. He held it up between his toes, and raised it to his awaiting, cuffed hand. He began working on the handcuff lock and looked at the curious dog. He said something in German. The dog barked excitedly. Gil laughed softly.

"Such a good boy!"

Chapter Seventeen

*D*espite only being a little before ten o'clock that evening, Lee was still exhausted from last night and their long morning. Eluding Mac, witnessing Monroe's house blowing up, and several hours of flying and lengthy car rides up treacherous canyon passes had taken its toll on her. Several of the guys had called it a day, being most were up before dawn themselves, leaving Lee and Tonya comfortably seated in the lobby with Beck, Zack, and Bogart. Tonya was attempting to flirt with Beck, but Bogart seemed to be an interested party and continually thwarted her plans by asserting himself into the conversation. Beck was clearly annoyed with the interloper; although Lee didn't think it was over the battle for Tonya's affections. On the contrary, Lee was fairly certain Beck had little interest in her friend. Although outwardly friendly, he seemed to be keeping his emotions in check around them. Was he just maintaining a certain level of professionalism? Or was he hiding a dark, mysterious past? Perhaps some woman had broken his heart many years ago.

Lee knew Tonya would never forgive her if she didn't stay up and create a buffer between her and Bogart. Eventually, Tonya would have to give up her sexual quest for Beck. Zack, on the other hand, was a mystery all to himself. He sat comfortably in an overstuffed chair while sipping tea from a delicate china cup. He held the teacup daintily in one hand and the saucer in the other. He seemed interested in the current conversation. Zack projected a regal, gentlemanly appearance, yet Lee somehow doubted he was much of a gentleman. His earlier actions and an uncomfortable five-hour drive to the lodge seated alongside him told her there was something creepy about the mousy looking man. He certainly wasn't much to look at. Physically, he was much shorter than the other guys were and certainly built less muscular. She wondered what he offered to their group. Was he some sort of computer genius?

The fact that Zack hadn't spoken much since dinner successfully freaked Lee. He reminded her of a serial killer rather than a Navy SEAL, not that she'd met any Navy SEALs prior to meeting Monroe. She actually found it difficult to believe Monroe had been a Navy SEAL as well, let alone someone non-impressive like Zack. Zack finally leaned forward and set down his delicate teacup and saucer on the coffee table.

"You know," Zack finally announced, startling everyone by finally speaking, and looked at Tonya. "It would probably speed things along if you just conveyed your interest in fornication so Beck can turn you down and be done with it."

All eyes were on Zack. Lee and Tonya stared at him with their mouths hanging open, while Beck and Bogart appeared mildly embarrassed by the unfiltered comment. Beck placed his hand over his eyes and groaned softly.

"Or, if you'd like to make it more entertaining for those of us watching this train wreck, you could simply throw yourself at him, so that the rest of us will have something interesting to think about in the shower."

"Enough, Zack," Beck finally growled while glaring at him with disapproval.

"What's wrong with you?" Tonya suddenly lashed out at Zack with horror and embarrassment clearly on her reddened face as she bolted up from her seat near Lee.

He stared back at her with an innocent look and appeared almost offended. "Not a damned thing, my dear. I've just never seen a ship take so long to sink before. Had you been paying attention, you'd realize Beck hasn't shown any interest in your flirtatious exploits, but Bogart has been writhing in his seat prepared to pounce since you sat down and batted your lashes."

"You're disgusting!" Tonya practically shouted.

"Can we not wake Ross," Beck muttered softly and gently rubbed his temple while casting stray looks between the irate Tonya and Zack.

"I'm not disgusting," Zack announced calmly and with little reaction to her outburst. "I'm merely stating the obvious. Beck, although not entirely opposed to meaningless sex, has grown out of that phase of his life, unlike Bogart, who seems eager to take you on his magic carpet ride."

Lee stared at Zack, almost wondering if he was for real. If it hadn't been so degrading to her friend, she would have found his comment slightly humorous.

"I'm sorry," Beck announced to Lee and Tonya as he fidgeted and shook his head. "I'm afraid Zack has seen a lot of action over the years. The filter between his brain and mouth stopped working a long time ago."

Zack glared at Beck and appeared irritated. "Did I say something that wasn't true?"

"That's not the point, Zack," Beck nearly shouted them smiled meekly and attempted to remain calm. "That's not how you talk in front of mixed company."

"So you're saying I should just be quiet and die a slow, painful death waiting for one of you to put an end to her pointless flirting?" Zack demanded.

"I don't need to take this," Tonya bellowed out. "I'm going to bed!"

Tonya stormed for the stairs. Bogart turned on the loveseat and watched her walk away, clearly disappointed at the loss.

"I don't share any of Zack's crude comments," Bogart called after her. He now resembled a mutt in heat. "Can't we at least discuss this?"

She stopped near the stairs, glared at Bogart with a look of annoyance, and then groaned.

"Fine," Tonya scoffed then headed up the steps.

Bogart appeared surprised by her response. He dove over the back of the loveseat and hurried after her. Beck shook his head, sank into his seat, and attempted a weak smile at Lee.

"I'm really sorry," Beck announced and gave a slight nod to Zack. "Zack operates out of his own world."

"There's nothing wrong with my world," Zack responded hotly to his friend.

"No, you're just scaring the straights," Beck snapped. He groaned and stood. "I'm going to bed. Don't destroy the place, okay?" He then turned to Lee. "Would you like me to walk you to your room?"

Lee gave a slight nod, indicating Zack in the nearby chair. "Is he dangerous?"

Beck eyed Zack and appeared to hesitate, taking a little too long to consider the comment before responding. Zack stared at Beck and grinned in response. It was hard to tell what devious thoughts were circulating in his demented mind. Beck looked back at Lee and slowly shook his head.

"Nah, not to you," Beck replied. "He's just demented in a mad genius sort of way."

"In that case, I think I'd like to give Tonya and Bogart a head start before I go to my room," Lee announced then cringed at the thought. "I don't know if the walls are soundproof, and I certainly don't need to hear them going at it."

"Yeah, I understand," Beck replied while holding back his chuckle. "Shout if you need anything." He then hesitated and gave her a stern, serious look. "Just remember, the louder you scream, the more guns you'll see."

She hid her smile, nodded, and watched Beck head for the steps. Lee suddenly felt uncomfortable as if she were being watched. She uncertainly turned her head and realized Zack was staring at her from where he sat casually reclined in his chair.

"I'm not demented," he scoffed.

"Maybe not," she replied simply, "but you're a long way from normal."

There was an awkward silence, and she immediately cursed herself for making the comment aloud. It probably wasn't wise to offend the man, especially while alone with him.

"I'll give you that," he replied simply, surprising her. "But in my defense, I did nearly die six times."

Stunned by his admission, Lee suddenly proclaimed, "That's terrible!"

"Add that to the four times I actually did die--" He grinned and chuckled softly. "Let's just say there's a lot of wiggle room for fuck-ups."

Lee stared at him with her mouth hanging open to the comment. "Died? You mean died as in--?"

"As in, 'oh, fuck, I'm dead," he casually replied then raised his brows. "Would you like some tea?"

She stared at him, uncertain know how to respond to his Jekyll and Hyde personality. She actually liked him better when he was silent and creepy.

✝

*R*omano's secluded estate was peaceful for the late night hour. Several outside lights remained on, keeping the property and gardens well lit. Apart from the fountain, there were no other sounds. Within Sal's office, Gil sat behind the desk in the mostly dark study and typed into the computer. He ate a sandwich as he transferred data to a remote server. He glanced at the dog sitting alongside the chair intently watching the sandwich in his hand.

"You already had two of your own," Gil sternly informed the dog. "Your boss will be upset if he thinks you have a full tummy in the morning."

Darth licked his muzzle and watched the sandwich. Gil smiled at the dog and gave him the rest of his sandwich. He watched the dog devour it.

"Want some milk with that?"

The sandwich was gone in seconds. Gil shook his head with disbelief.

"My God, you eat like Kirk," he remarked. "I used the good mustard too. Did you even taste it?"

The dog let out a soft 'woof'. Gil held his finger to his lips to silence the dog. He returned to the computer and came to a password-protected program. Gil casually looked around the desk a moment, saw a framed picture of an attractive, young woman, and picked it up. He turned the framed photo over and noted the password written on the back. He again looked at the dog.

"Romano isn't exactly the criminal mastermind Holden seems to think he is," Gil informed the dog. "I think Holden needs to go back to fed school."

The dog tilted his head while watching Gil. Gil typed in the password and gained access to the program. He saw the dog's look and shook his head.

"Don't even get me started on Special Agent Holden Falcone," he announced to the dog then returned his attention back to the computer. He opened several files and then hesitated with a look of surprise. "Well, well. What do we have here? I'd better send this to Beck for analysis."

Chapter Eighteen

$\mathcal{I}$t was early the following morning. The secluded woodlands surrounding the lodge were peaceful, although it was like that most of the day. Lee wearily shuffled out of her shared suite with Tonya and headed down the open staircase to the lobby. She wished she could sleep late like her promiscuous friend, although, by the sounds coming from Tonya's room at all hours, she didn't get much sleep. Lee sometimes wondered if Tonya didn't have the right idea about men and relationships. Her friend seemed happy enough, particularly after marathon sex with men she barely knew. Lee wasn't sure she could ever live that lifestyle, although she sometimes envied her friend for having male companionship. Lee never considered herself a beautiful woman, but she also never lacked men at clubs wanting to take her home either. She wanted more than a casual fling, but it didn't seem as if the cowboy of her dreams would ever come along and rescue her.

Since they'd be stranded at the lodge for weeks, possibly months, maybe a long-term fling wasn't completely out of the question. She almost shamed herself for thinking such things. Besides, there wasn't even a spark of attraction despite the high levels of testosterone and the charismatic good looks of the SEAL team. She was beginning to wonder if her flame hadn't burned out from years of avoiding relationships. Perhaps this cowboy fantasy was just a way of looking toward the impossible, so she wouldn't have to worry about falling in love. Lee entered the kitchen and found Ross pacing the terrace beyond the large wall of windows. He had a larger phone-like gismo to his ear, and his expression was hard to read. She watched him pace while listening, but he didn't talk to the person on the other end. Lee decided it was none of her business and turned toward the stove. She nearly collided with Zack, who stared past her at Ross and his continuous pacing. Lee cried out with surprise and jumped away from him.

"Damn it," she cried out and held her chest, feeling her heart pounding. "You scared the crap out of me!"

Zack didn't react or acknowledge that he'd frightened her. He nodded toward the man pacing on the terrace outside.

"What's with Ross?"

"I don't know," Lee replied while attempting to control her breathing. "I just got here myself. I guess he's talking to someone on the phone."

"That's the satellite phone," Zack informed her. "Emergency use only. That means it must be Agent Falcone or Gil. No one else has the number."

"Do you think it's good news?" Lee quickly asked and looked back to the pacing man on the terrace.

"He's not saying anything," Zack informed her while observing Ross. "He'd never let someone do that much talking without getting his two-cents in." He considered his own comment. "It has to be Jackie. You don't interrupt her when she's talking."

Lee glanced at him and appeared curious. "Why's that?"

"She's scary," he replied in a matter-of-fact tone. "Given half a chance, she'd rip a man's testicles off." He suddenly grinned. "God, I love that girl."

Lee gave him a strange look, but he didn't comment further. Ross disconnected the call and entered the kitchen. He practically ignored Lee and approached Zack.

"Gather Monroe and Beck," Ross ordered. "I want the three of you to head into town and see if you can get that satellite dish of Beck's to work."

"I thought we weren't using that," Zack replied and appeared curious. "You said it was risky."

"It just became worth the risk," Ross informed them. "Some guy just contacted Holden. He claims he caught one of his men poking around and is holding him hostage."

"Gil?"

"Holden thinks so," Ross replied. "He wants to trade Gil for Lee."

Zack glanced at Lee then looked back at Ross as if she wasn't even there. "Just her?" He suddenly snorted a laugh. "Huh, I'm guessing he doesn't know the value of his prisoner. I'd ask for both girls."

Lee stared at Zack's profile with her mouth hanging open and a look of surprise.

"So, are we going to trade her?" Zack casually asked, appearing serious.

"Hey," Lee cried out feeling offended. "I'm standing right here!"

Ross looked at Lee and offered a tiny smile. "Zack's only half serious. Ignore him." He looked back at Zack and turned serious. "What's more interesting is the message I received after the ransom demand. It's encrypted, but it appears to be from Gil. He must be using an unsecured computer somewhere. I don't think he's as much a prisoner as his captors seem to believe. I need you to attach a computer to the dish and find out what he was trying to tell us...or possibly, what he's sent to our secured server. It could be important."

"I'll wake the guys," Zack announced and hurried from the kitchen.

"I'd like to go along," Lee informed Ross without hesitation even if she knew he'd say no.

Ross stared at her with surprise. A twisted smile crossed his face, almost mocking her.

"As if that's going to happen," he remarked and crossed the kitchen toward the counter and a fresh pot of coffee.

"That town is in the middle of nowhere," Lee protested while watching him. "It's not as if Jericho or Sal will be looking for me there. I can be of some use. If Gil found something on Sal's computer, I'll know what to look for. I'm very good with computers."

"So is Beck." He picked up the coffee pot and glared at her. "You have no idea how foolish it would be to allow you to go into town," Ross remarked sternly then fell silent as he stared at her. "Find a baseball cap and sunglasses." He set the coffee pot down and pointed a warning finger at her. "You stay close to Zack and do whatever he tells you."

"Zack?" she replied with surprise. "I have to admit, I don't understand the faith you put in that one. At best, he's a delusional nutcase."

"Don't let his nutcase act fool you," Ross informed her. "Zack is cunning and devious. If anything happens, you'll want to be standing behind him. I trust him with my life, so I should think you'd do the same."

She uncertainly nodded, studied Ross a moment, and then smiled timidly while rocking on the balls of her feet.

"Can I have a gun?"

Ross suddenly snorted a laugh, picked up his cup of coffee, and walked away. Lee frowned at the response. If she hadn't marveled at his commanding presence just moments ago, she'd be deeply offended by his attitude.

✝

*T*he interrogation room door within Romano's mansion was unlocked and opened. Jericho entered without bothering to look at the chair where he'd left his prisoner handcuffed. Jericho grinned deviously then finally looked toward the chair across the room.

"How was your night?"

Gil raised his head and glared at Jericho without comment from where he remained handcuffed to the chair. The dog excitedly ran from the room for his morning bathroom break. Jericho laughed softly and followed the dog, shutting the door behind him. Once he was gone, Gil smirked.

"Productive, thanks for asking."

✝

*I*t took nearly two hours to drive to the small out-of-the-way town. Lee sat in the middle row of seats with the highly overrated Zack. Beck again drove and was currently in a heated debate with Monroe about the limited number of radio stations available. They were having a difficult time agreeing on what sort of music they should play. Lee was growing tired of the conversation, but she refrained from commenting. Zack casually removed his seatbelt, leaned between the two front seats, and pressed the 'off' button on the radio. Both men looked at him with surprise.

"I prefer the silent station," Zack snapped, glared at both men, and then returned to his seat.

Lee was actually surprised they took that from the meek looking man. There had to be something more to Zack than what she was seeing. Perhaps it was his demented attitude that kept them fearful of the small man.

Although Lee made it a point to stress that the town was small, it was larger than it had seemed on their way through yesterday. The little town had a population of nearly five thousand. It had its own

99

nightclub, which was probably something more country and less modern, several restaurants, a movie theater, bowling alley, and at least four bars. They passed a small motel on the way into town, although Lee wondered who'd need a motel room in the middle of nowhere. Beck found a secluded area to park behind the lounge toward the back of the small lot. While Beck and Monroe assembled the elaborate satellite dish on top of the vehicle roof, Zack walked across the parking lot toward the main thoroughfare. Lee looked from the busily working men to Zack as he walked away. She made her decision and hurried after Zack. Beck and Monroe immediately began yelling at her.

"Whoa, whoa, whoa!" Monroe bellowed. "Where do you think you're going?"

Lee stopped, looked back, and innocently pointed after Zack, who now stopped and stared at them as well.

"With him."

"I don't think so," Beck announced with a soft, humored laugh. "He's just looking to get into some trouble, and he certainly doesn't need you tagging along."

"We're in the middle of deliverance," she boldly announced. "What can possibly happen?"

"With Zack? Anything and everything," Monroe casually informed her.

The mystery of Zack was starting to bug Lee. What was so special about this man? He looked like a nerdy science teacher. Apart from boring her to death, she didn't understand the big deal. Monroe motioned Zack to continue without Lee. He left without a care. Lee frowned as she returned to the SUV and watched the two men on top of the roof while connecting the dish. She leaned against the fender and folded her arms across her chest in a mild temper tantrum. Both men noted her look.

"This town isn't as small as you seem to think," Beck informed her in an attempt to explain their decision. He focused his attention on the dish. "They get a lot of rowdies from neighboring towns. Miners and farmers with too much time on their hands and not nearly enough female entertainment."

"It's in the middle of the day," she informed him. "I assume they'd all be working the fields or mining their mines."

Beck eyed Monroe. "She's a sassy one."

"Yeah, she's a regular ray of sunshine," Monroe muttered. "Like Jackie lite."

Both men chuckled. Ignoring their taunting, Lee casually glanced around the quiet town.

"So what's the big draw for all these famers and miners?" she asked. "Is the bar scene that good?"

"Actually," Beck announced while tightening the bolts on the dish, "there are a few acts at the lounge that draw in some pretty big crowds."

"Strippers?"

Beck suddenly stared at her as if she spoke a foreign language. "This is a family town," he shamed her. "There aren't any strippers around here. You're not in the city anymore."

Lee straightened and leaned across the hood while watching them work. "So these women just sing? And the famers and miners are happy with that?"

"Think of this town as Camelot," Beck announced cheerfully. "Back in the medieval times, knights would sacrifice their lives for the women they loved, even if they'd never even kissed." He grinned his approval. "It's romantic."

"You're so full of shit," Monroe remarked and attempted to keep from laughing. He looked at Lee while leaning on the dish. "There's this really hot lounge singer with world-class--" Monroe made a motion of huge breasts but stopped himself. "--voice. They all come to see her."

"And does this goddess have a name?" Lee asked, not daring to admit she felt slightly jealous of the woman already. She doubted any man would ever describe her with such fondness.

"Pinto," Monroe announced cheerfully while grinning. "She's got this whole hot, European thing going."

Lee slowly straightened while staring at Monroe. Her mouth fell open with surprise. "Pinto?" she suddenly gasped.

"Yeah," Beck replied and appeared humored. "Not like the horse. There's a small town in Madrid--" He stared at her and fell silent. "Something wrong?"

"Sal's daughter changed her name to Pinto when she ran away from home and moved to Colorado," Lee informed them and then raised her brows. "Tonya said she became a lounge singer."

Monroe and Beck exchanged looks.

Chapter Nineteen

$\mathcal{I}$t was a little over two hours later when the SUV pulled up to the lodge, having raced up the driveway. Beck jumped from the vehicle and hurried toward the main entrance as Ross stepped outside. Ross looked around with concern then glared at Beck.

"Where's Lee?"

"I couldn't get her to return," Beck announced with a sense of urgency. "She insisted she wanted to stay. Monroe took her with him to the public library to access our server through the computers there." He appeared anxious. "I know it may be nothing, but if his daughter found something incriminating on his computer--?"

"Since they don't get along, you're thinking she may roll over on her father, huh?" Ross inquired then groaned softly. "That's one hell of a long shot."

"It's not as if we have anything better to do with our time," Beck informed him. "I don't mind wasting my time checking her out." He hesitated then gently cleared his throat. "What do you want to do with this information?"

"I want you to take me to town," Ross announced firmly. "I think it's worth taking a closer look at Sal's daughter. Kirk will stay with Tonya. Where's Zack?"

"Who the hell knows," Beck muttered. "Running with the bulls, tipping cows--the possibilities are endless."

"We'll need to find him," Ross announced and walked with Beck toward the vehicle. "I want him to stay with Lee while we investigate Sal's daughter."

"Can I come along?" Bogart asked from the doorway.

Both men looked at Bogart standing at the lodge entrance, not realizing he'd been eavesdropping. Beck groaned, rolled his eyes, and cursed softly under his breath. Ross frowned and nodded Bogart to the SUV.

$$t$$

*T*he public library was almost as old as the town itself, once being a historic home converted into a library. The original walls of the old home could still be seen beyond the bookcases. Monroe stood over Lee's shoulder while she worked on one of the computers toward the back of the library. There were a few school-aged children wandering the nearby aisles of bookshelves but almost no adults. Lee rapidly typed on the keyboard.

"Are you sure that thing you installed will keep anyone from locating us?" Lee asked while frantically typing.

"Yes, I'm sure. It's scrambling our location," he replied while watching the screen. "If anyone on the other end realizes it's you, they won't be able to locate your position. Unfortunately, you only have ten minutes before it can be unscrambled."

"I'm working as fast as I can," Lee informed him. "You breathing over my shoulder isn't exactly helping."

Monroe became excited and pointed at the computer screen. "That's it," he announced. "That's our secured server. If Gil left something for us, it'll be there."

"It's a big file," Lee informed him.

He handed her a flash drive. "Download it," Monroe instructed. "We can view it off-line back at the lodge. It's safer to do that anyway."

Lee snatched the flash drive, hastily inserted it, and transferred the files to the drive. They watched the information download a little slower than acceptable. Monroe frowned and glanced at his watch several times. He looked around the library then suddenly froze and his expression dropped.

"What the hell--?"

Lee looked up to see what caught his attention. Mac stood in the main room just beyond the archway while talking to the librarian at the counter. Monroe crouched alongside Lee's chair, so he wouldn't be seen. Lee sank in her chair and stared at Monroe.

"How did she find us?" Lee gasped.

"How is she still alive?" he launched back.

"What do we do?"

"Nothing," Monroe replied softly. "We can't let her see us. How's the download coming?"

"Complete," Lee replied and removed the flash drive.

Monroe extended his hand, but Lee was already stuffing it down the cleavage of her shirt.

"How do we get out of here?" Lee demanded while looking around then saw the back door and became enthusiastic. "There's a back door."

"No, that's an emergency exit," he informed her. "You open that door, and the alarm will sound." Monroe removed his cell phone and stared at it. "I have a weak signal. I can try calling Zack, but there's no telling where he is and if he'll have a signal. Keep an eye on her at the desk."

Lee peeked around the side of the monitor to have a look at the mysterious woman. Mac was now leaning on the desk while the librarian checked something on her computer. Monroe crawled around the floor behind the monitors until he found a stronger signal. He sent a text that simply read, '911 library; front desk'. As Mac turned in their direction, Lee dove to the floor near Monroe. A few kids walked past and stared at them huddled on the floor together. Lee and Monroe remained still and silent. Monroe looked around the side of the desk from their position on the floor. Mac kept her attention on the librarian. Zack entered the library and paused near the desk. He casually looked around.

Monroe texted him, 'Distract woman at desk!' Zack looked at his cell phone then replaced it to his pocket. He glanced at Mac then casually walked past her. He pressed a stun gun into her hip as he passed. She twitched and collapsed to the floor, alarming the librarian. Zack jumped to her fallen side.

"Help, I think she's had a seizure!" Zack cried out.

Monroe rolled his eyes and hurried Lee from the back room, past the front desk, and out the door. As the librarian joined Zack alongside the woman, he straightened.

"I'll go for help," he announced and hurried from the library only a few seconds after Lee and Monroe.

The librarian patted Mac's hand. She slowly came to and looked around with surprise.

"What happened?" Mac demanded.

"You collapsed," the librarian replied. "You should remain still until help arrives."

Mac sneered her annoyance and slowly sat up. "I'll be fine," she hissed while gingerly rubbing her hip.

Just outside the library, Zack walked around the corner of the nearby building and almost collided with an enraged Monroe.

"What's wrong with you?" Monroe demanded. "That's the woman who was posing as a U.S. Marshal. She's going to know someone tased her."

"What did you want me to do?" Zack demanded. "My options were limited. I didn't know how serious the danger was."

"Can we just go?" Lee demanded. "She could come this way any minute."

All three hurried toward the back of the buildings and into the parking lot. The black SUV pulled up to them, startling Lee. The side door opened. Monroe pushed Lee into the vehicle and climbed in behind her. Zack jumped in after them and shut the door. The SUV drove around the building and parked somewhere less obvious. Beck and Ross turned around in the front seat to look at them while Bogart leaned forward from the last row.

"Beck says Sal's daughter has a musical set in a few hours," Ross announced.

"We have bigger problems right now," Monroe informed him. "That woman posing as a U.S. Marshal is here. She somehow found us."

"That's impossible," Ross bellowed.

"I assure you, it was her," Monroe announced.

"If this chick works for Romano," Bogart chimed in, "how do you know she's not here to see his daughter?"

All eyes were suddenly on Bogart.

"He does have a point," Lee remarked and received several glares.

Ross straightened in the passenger seat. "I'll find our girl and keep an eye on her. Monroe and Zack will stay in the SUV with Lee." He glanced at Beck in the driver's seat. "You'll make contact with Romano's daughter."

Beck nodded and was about to get out of the SUV when Lee protested.

"So we're just going to sit here for a couple of hours?" she demanded.

"Think of it as a stake-out," Ross informed her. "I can't have you and Monroe running around town and chance this woman seeing either of you, especially if she's not looking for you."

"What about me?" Bogart asked. "I can do something. Give me an assignment."

"What can *you* do?" Beck snarled with irritation.

"I'm pretty damned useful," Bogart retorted, taking offense to the comment. "I know how to handle myself." He then looked at Ross. "I also know how to tail people without being caught."

"And if you're caught?" Ross demanded.

Bogart grinned charmingly. "I'll improvise," he announced proudly. "I'm a master at improvising."

There was an odd silence as Ross stared at Bogart. Beck glared at Ross with annoyance.

"You're not seriously considering letting him--?"

"He may be some use," Ross announced to Beck then looked at Bogart and grinned. "Fine, you're in. Zack will go with you, since he's seen her. I'll stay with Monroe and Lee for now."

Bogart grinned boyishly. "I won't let you down."

"So I'm still stuck in the car?" Lee demanded.

"You wanted to come along," Ross remarked without care then motioned for the men to leave.

The three men left the vehicle, leaving Lee with Ross and Monroe. Lee sank back on the seat, folded her arms across her chest, and pouted.

"Was that really wise?" Monroe asked Ross.

Ross shrugged without concern. "Worst case scenario, Zack kills Bogart."

Lee suddenly looked at him with surprise. Ross grinned and chuckled softly. She sneered at him.

"You guys definitely have a warped sense of humor," she muttered.

"It helps keep us alive," Ross replied.

Chapter Twenty

$\mathcal{K}$irk sat on the bottom step of the lodge stairs with the sports section of the newspaper in his hand. The sound of the upstairs bedroom door opening caught his attention. He earmarked the page on the book carefully hidden beneath the newspaper and closed the paperback. Judging by the hot woman with a gun on the cover, it was undoubtedly a romantic thriller. He concealed the book within the pages of the sports section and pretended to read the paper. When there was no sound on the stairs, he looked up them to the second floor. Tonya wasn't there. Kirk appeared curious, set his paper on the steps, stood, and headed for the second floor. He walked a few yards down the corridor and knocked on the suite door. There was no response. He removed his gun from his shoulder holster and opened the door. After a moment of looking around, it was obvious Tonya wasn't in her room. Kirk returned to the hallway, appeared curious, and looked around.

"Tonya?"

There was no response. Kirk headed along the hallway in the opposite direction. He approached the rarely used backstairs. Without hesitation, he headed down the stairs, which brought him in the corridor not far from the kitchen. He entered the kitchen and looked around.

"Tonya?"

There was still no response. It was hard to tell if Kirk was concerned or irritated as he left the kitchen. He walked along the main corridor, looking into each room as he passed. He suddenly hesitated, backed up, and entered the lounge. The lounge appeared to be empty.

"Tonya?" he gruffly announced.

Tonya popped up from behind the bar with a container of orange juice in her hand. She smiled and managed a soft, tense laugh while placing her hand to her chest.

"God, you scared me," she gasped then attempted to relax. "Where is everyone?"

"Town," he replied without altering his stern expression as he studied her.

"Without me?" she playfully pouted then removed a glass and filled it with orange juice.

"What are you doing?" he inquired.

"Having some orange juice," she replied and shook the carton. "I didn't see any in the kitchen, but I remembered Bogart making a screwdriver last night." She studied him and appeared curious. "Did Lee go too?"

"Yes, she went with them," he replied and finally returned his gun to his holster.

She fidgeted from his lack of emotion and the way he intently watched her.

"I can't believe she didn't wake me. The bitch," Tonya muttered and sipped her orange juice from the scotch glass. "I would have gone."

"I doubt you would have been invited," he replied firmly. "Ross was reluctant to let her go either."

"Huh?" Tonya teased while grinning slyly. "I wonder how she rates?"

Kirk maintained his stare and didn't comment. She fidgeted slightly while studying him.

"You're a ray of sunshine in the morning," Tonya muttered under her breath.

"It's almost late afternoon," he curtly replied. "While it's just us alone in the lodge, you need to remain in my sight. Don't make me chase you again."

Tonya appeared surprised by his gruffness but attempted to hide her concerns.

"Fine," she scoffed and walked out from behind the bar. "I'm going to the kitchen for something to eat."

She walked past him and out the lounge door. Kirk watched her then looked back at the bar, hearing a faint humming sound. He approached the bar, leaned over the top, and looked behind it. Kirk straightened with the satellite phone in his hand. It hummed softly. He turned off the power. The humming ceased. He headed for the lounge doorway with the phone in his hand. He walked down the hall and entered the kitchen. Tonya removed a container of yogurt from the refrigerator and turned as Kirk approached the massive island counter. She saw the strange phone in his hand, appeared curious, and immediately indicated it.

"What's that?" she asked.

"This?" he questioned while raising his brows, showing some emotion for the first time. "This is a satellite phone. It's our only communication with the rest of the world." He indicated a switch on the side. "This switch turns it on and off." He flicked the phone into the 'on' position. The humming returned. He then pointed to a button beneath the numbers. "This little button automatically redials the last number called." Kirk pressed the button and placed the phone to his ear.

Tonya's expression suddenly dropped as she watched him. "What are you doing?"

"Seeing who you called," he replied casually.

She frowned and leaned on the counter with less enthusiasm. "I'll save you the trouble," Tonya replied while looking guilty. "I called my mother."

A female voice answered on the other end.

"Is Tonya there?" Kirk asked in his usual, gruff tone. He was silent a moment. "I see. Do you know where she is?" There was another pause. "No, I'll try again later." Kirk disconnected the phone and pointed it at Tonya while glaring at her. "No phone calls without our permission. You realize your mother's phone is probably tapped."

"I know," Tonya protested, "but I only talked to her for a minute. I just wanted her to know I was okay. I told her I was in Florida, in case someone was listening."

"Don't let it happen again," Kirk warned her with a chilling look for added emphasis. "Agent Falcone has been known to put his witnesses in the nuthouse for their own protection. You wouldn't want to spend the next three to six months there."

Tonya appeared horrified and quickly straightened. "I won't use the phone again without permission, I promise."

t

*B*ogart chattered endlessly to Zack as they walked along the sidewalk in the small town. Mac remained several yards ahead of them and just within sight. She seemed unaware of the two men tailing her.

"The whole secret to tailing someone," Bogart continued, "is to keep your distance and act disinterested. Typically, I like to have my nose in my cell phone while wearing sunglasses. Damn, I wish I'd remembered to bring my sunglasses." He grinned more to himself while keeping his eyes on Mac in the distance ahead of him. "Always being aware of your surroundings is essential. Nothing gets past me. I think I'd make a great member of your team. I'm observant, you know?"

Bogart looked alongside him. Zack was gone. He stopped and looked around, but Zack was nowhere to be found. Bogart frowned and shook his head.

"That little prick ditched me."

Mac entered the country bar and lounge. Bogart waited a moment and then entered after her. Despite still being daylight outside, the lounge remained dimly lit with mood lighting on small, round tables. Larger tables and booths were off to the sides. A massive bar lined the back wall of the large room. The lounge was nearly empty, since the live entertainment wouldn't start for another hour. The few patrons were seated at the bar grabbing drinks and an early dinner. Mac stood before the bar and talked to the bartender, who seemed charmed by the attractive woman. Bogart approached the bar and took a vacant seat far enough away to avoid being noticed. He snacked on some free peanuts and eavesdropped on Mac's conversation with the bartender.

"I'm sorry," the bartender informed her. "Pinto doesn't like being disturbed before her set. She's a private lady."

"I'm aware of that," Mac announced while attempting to remain cheerful and slightly flirtatious. "I represent her father's estate. If I could just have a moment of her time--"

The bartender suddenly straightened and turned stern. Any romantic interest he had in Mac faded. "She won't see you," he announced gruffly. "I'll have to ask you to leave."

"But--"

"Pinto wants nothing to do with her father," he informed her sternly. "If you don't leave, I'll have you removed."

He nodded across the lounge to a tough looking man, who suddenly stood from his stool near the front door. Mac looked toward the large man then glanced back at the bartender and smiled gently.

"Thank you for your time."

Mac left the lounge in more of a hurry now. Bogart slid off his chair and casually trailed behind. As he stepped outside the lounge, he saw Mac get into her rental car and drive away. He watched a moment in silence while frowning.

"Guess that solves that little problem," Zack remarked.

Bogart jumped with surprise and looked at Zack, who now stood alongside him.

"Where the hell did you come from?" he demanded.

"Me?" Zack asked innocently. "I was following you. If you were half as observant as you prided yourself to be, I'd think you would have noticed."

Bogart cursed Zack under his breath.

Chapter Twenty-one

*I*t was nearly six o'clock that evening and the lounge was starting to fill with patrons from nearby towns and farms. Beck sat alone at one of the tables near the wall with an untouched glass of beer before him. His eyes shifted around the lounge in a slightly uncomfortable manner. He was unusually tense. Bogart and Monroe joined him at the table. He saw them, sank back in his chair, and groaned.

"What are you two doing here?" Beck demanded.

"Ross sent us," Monroe informed him. "He's keeping an eye on our other girl, so we decided to help you keep an eye on *your* girl." Monroe's grin mocked his friend.

"She's not my girl," Beck growled softly. "Just because I'm considered local, that doesn't--"

"Okay, don't get your panties in a bunch," Monroe announced sternly.

"Someone's got a crush," Bogart teased.

Beck straightened in his chair, leaned across the table closer to Bogart, and pointed a warning finger at him.

"Would you like to sit on that seat or have it shoved down your throat?" Beck snarled.

Bogart raised his hands in the air defensively, acted surprised, and leaned back.

"Chill, brother."

"I'm not your brother," Beck launched back softly then glared at Monroe. "Seriously, get him out of here."

"Relax, Beck," Monroe announced while staring at his comrade. "What's gotten into you lately?"

Beck sank back in his seat and avoided looking at Monroe. "Nothing."

Monroe and Bogart exchanged looks and silent conversation. The small crowd of mostly men applauded, indicating the show was about to start. All eyes were on the stage. Beck suddenly sat up straight and gave his full attention to the stage area. Monroe and Bogart glanced at him and noticed his focused gaze.

"I called it," Bogart muttered then returned his attention to the stage.

The lounge owner, a man in his sixties, stood center stage with a microphone in his hand.

"Thank you for coming tonight," the lounge owner announced. "Please give a warm round of applause for Pinto!"

The crowd roared and applauded. A gorgeous woman in a slinky, sequin dress walked onto stage. Her long, copper-colored hair was pulled up to one side and held in place with a sequined clip. She smiled beyond bright red lips to the applause. Monroe and Bogart glanced at Beck and his starry-eyed gaze. A tiny smile crossed his once hardened face.

"My God," Monroe muttered to Bogart, although loud enough for Beck to hear. "I think he's blushing."

Beck's look immediately hardened. Despite not looking at Monroe, he kicked him under the table. Monroe yelped. Once the attractive, young woman started singing, the room fell silent to her vibrant, strong voice. The men within the room appeared to fall helpless to her singing. Or was it the dress revealing plenty of leg and cleavage that caught their attention? Once she finished the song, there was a roar of applause. She took her bow and immediately started a second song. Monroe leaned across the table toward Beck, breaking his trance-like stare on the attractive woman.

"So how do we approach her?" Monroe asked. "Security is tight backstage."

"And they're seriously protective of her," Bogart added. "The moment Romano's hired henchgirl mentioned her father, the bartender nearly had her thrown out."

"I may have a 'get out of jail free' card," Beck informed them then removed a delicate, antique diamond tennis bracelet from his pocket.

"Where'd you get that?" Monroe asked with surprise while staring at the bracelet.

"He lifted it," Bogart announced while grinning. "He wanted it as an icebreaker, literally."

"Wipe that smile off your face, before I wipe if off for you," Beck snarled at Bogart then looked at Monroe. "The clasp is broken.

It must have fallen off during one of her performances a few weeks ago. I hadn't gotten around to returning it."

Bogart raised his brows and attempted to contain his knowing smile. Beck pointed a warning finger at Bogart, threatening him without even looking in his direction. Bogart shifted uncomfortably. Beck kept his attention focused on Monroe.

"I'll inform the waitress that I found Pinto's bracelet, and she'll invite me for a drink," Beck informed him.

"No offense," Monroe announced boldly, "but with a woman like that, this is going to require someone with a little more experience. You know; someone who's a little more worldly with women."

"Fine," Bogart announced with a reluctant sigh. "I'll do it. Give me the bracelet."

Beck glared at Bogart while placing the bracelet into his jacket pocket.

"You're going to stay away from that girl, got it?" Beck snapped at Bogart with annoyance. "We're trying to get intel on her father, not get her into bed. I think I can handle this." He looked toward the passing cocktail waitress, easily caught her attention, and motioned her toward their table. He placed a ten-dollar bill onto her serving tray. "Would you tell Pinto I think I found a bracelet that belongs to her?"

"You could give it to me--" the waitress began.

Beck smiled politely but remained persistent. "I'd like to return it myself, thank you."

The waitress attempted a smile as if understanding his meaning, nodded, and left their table. Once Pinto's song ended, the waitress approached her as she headed backstage. She looked toward their table across the lounge. Beck immediately fidgeted and looked anywhere but at her. Bogart and Monroe eyed him then exchanged looks and strange grins.

"It's working," Monroe announced enthusiastically. "She's coming over."

Beck straightened while running his fingers through his hair, collected himself, and looked up as Pinto approached their table. He immediately fidgeted and appeared to lose his nerve.

"I'm told you found my bracelet," Pinto announced while staring at Beck.

"I, uh, think so," he stammered then fumbled in his pocket and revealed the bracelet.

Pinto groaned softly then smiled excitedly. "I didn't think I'd ever see that again."

He handed her the bracelet, seemingly grazing her hand on purpose. She accepted it, appeared curious, and then eyed him suspiciously.

"I lost this three weeks ago," she announced. "When did you find it?"

"Uh, two weeks ago," he easily lied. "I, uh, found it in the parking lot. I thought it might be yours, but I hadn't been back to town to return it."

"You could have left it with the manager," she announced while studying him.

"Like I said," he began, "I wasn't sure it was yours, so I thought I'd better return it in person."

Pinto studied him a moment then smiled almost knowingly. "Guys do find interesting ways to ask a woman to have a drink with them," she remarked.

Monroe and Bogart leaped up from their seats and pulled their chairs out for her. Pinto smiled at both and took Monroe's chair. He smiled mockingly at Bogart then took the vacant seat on the other side of her. Bogart sneered at Monroe and returned to his seat.

"I'm Beck and these are my, uh, friends," he remarked and indicated the men. "Monroe and Bogart."

She smiled politely at each man. The waitress brought another round of drinks for the guys and mint iced tea for Pinto.

"You don't drink?" Bogart asked while indicating the tall glass of iced tea.

"Not while I'm working," she replied. "The mint helps sooth my throat. The smoke gets bad toward the end of the night." She eyed the three men and grinned. "You're not my typical stalkers. There's no dirt under your fingernails." She then glanced at Beck and appeared curious. "I've seen you around a few times, but you can't be local."

"Local enough," he replied. "I have a place a couple of hours from here. I only come to town for supplies."

"Ah, a recluse," she announced cheerfully. "We get plenty of those."

"We know you're busy," Beck gently announced while shifting in his chair. "So it's probably best if we get to the reason for this visit."

Monroe and Bogart displayed their displeasure with Beck's 'getting to the point' approach.

"I have this friend with the FBI," Beck announced while fidgeting without taking his eyes off her. "We'd like to ask you some questions about your father--"

Pinto's expression suddenly dropped into something resembling a sneer, and she abruptly stood.

"We're finished here," she announced gruffly.

Monroe and Bogart stood just as quickly, alerting the large bouncer at the door. He began his slow and intimidating approach toward their table.

"We know you and your father had a falling-out," Monroe announced in a verbal attempt to stop her.

"Yes, we had a falling-out," she proclaimed. "And I don't want to discuss him with you or anyone else."

She spun on her heels to leave. Beck bolted up from his chair. The bouncer picked up his pace toward their table.

"Two women from his office were nearly killed by one of his goons," Beck firmly announced.

Pinto stopped with her back to the men. The bouncer approached her and glared at the three men. All three stared back at the intimidating man. He was even bigger close up.

"Is there a problem, Pinto?" the bouncer asked in a gruff tone.

She eyed the bouncer with an oddly solemn look then glanced back at Beck.

"No, everything's fine," she replied and returned to her seat facing the men.

All three took their seats.

Beck stared at her with a soulful look. "Thank you," he announced softly.

"Which two women?" she asked gently.

"Tonya, the receptionist, and Lee from payroll," Beck replied.

"Tonya," Pinto gasped softly then allowed her head to fall into her hand. She looked back at Beck. "Is she okay?"

"Yeah," he replied. "She's in protective custody, but there have been a few attempts on her life."

"I'm glad she's okay, but I don't know what you think I can do," Pinto announced and lifted her head. "I haven't talked to my father in almost two years. Most of what he has to say, he says through Tonya."

"The feds are searching for a flash drive left by the accountant before he was killed," Beck informed her.

Her eyes suddenly widened. "Wiley?" she gasped with alarm. "Wiley's dead?"

"Yeah," Beck replied. "He was murdered a few days ago. It would seem he found something while going through the files. He even went as far as to alert the FBI, but someone killed him before he could talk to the agent on the case. He crashed the server and left a flash drive that no one can seem to find. It's possible your father thinks Lee has evidence against him."

"I still don't know how this involves me," she replied while appearing uncomfortable. "I always suspected my father was into something less than ethical, but I never would have guessed he'd go so far as to kill someone."

"Fifty million dollars is a big motivator," Monroe bluntly informed her.

"Fifty million?" she suddenly questioned then relaxed. "I can't imagine him killing someone for fifty million dollars. You realize he's worth more than that, right?" She inhaled deeply and studied Beck. "What do you expect me to do?"

"We'd like you to have a look at some files on his computer," Beck gently informed her.

"You don't seriously expect me to show up at my father's house and hack into his computer, do you?" she suddenly erupted and appeared ready to bolt from her seat.

"No, of course not," Beck announced in a calm tone meant to relax her.

"We already have someone available for that task," Monroe informed her.

"I have working knowledge of his system and files," she replied. "But you can't access that information remotely." She hesitated. "I would have to be at his computer, but I'm not willing to integrate myself back into my father's life. Not even for Tonya. It wasn't easy escaping his tight grip the first time around. If I go back, he'll never let me go."

"We have access to some information," Beck insisted. "You wouldn't have to go anywhere near his house, I promise. We'd bring the information to you."

She eyed them suspiciously then groaned softly. "If you want to waste your time, fine," she scoffed. "You'll be looking for a file named 'Rhonda'. It was my mother's name. That's where he has all his important files. If he's doing anything illegal, it'll be hidden in there, but I don't think you'll get past his firewall and password protection. That computer is like a vault. I've done it once or twice, but it wasn't easy." Pinto glanced at the stage and the singer entertaining the crowd. She looked back at Beck. "I'm up in two more songs," she announced. "Good luck. You're going to need it."

"We'll be in touch in a day or two," Beck announced and extended a business card. "In the meantime, if you think of anything, no matter how unimportant it seems, please give me a call."

Pinto accepted the card, glanced at it briefly, and then stuck it down the front of her dress, catching each man's attention. She stared at Beck a moment longer with a strange look that conveyed moderate concern.

"If you're poking around in my father's business," she announced, "I suggest you tread very lightly. He's extremely private, and at times, he has one hell of a temper."

Pinto stood and left the table. All three men watched her walk away. Bogart groaned softly and grinned. Monroe looked back at Beck.

"You heard her," Monroe announced. "She's not going to return to her father's mansion, and the computer can't be accessed remotely. We don't even know what Gil sent us. It could be nothing. We're wasting our time on the daughter angle."

"And you never even asked her what she found on his computer that time she supposedly hacked it," Bogart remarked.

"Are you kidding?" Beck announced while straightening in his chair. "She would have bolted at the mere mention of that, and we'd be bounced out on our asses. A woman like that can't be conned or intimidated. We have to gain her trust before she'll open up to us." He then relaxed in his seat. "I'll take a look at what Gil sent us then bring it here for her to examine. I can get more information out of her then."

"We should probably get back to Ross and head home," Monroe announced with a defeated sigh.

Beck leaned back in his chair. "We have time to listen to her next set," he announced firmly and returned his attention to the stage.

Chapter Twenty-two

*B*eck's SUV remained near the back of the lounge parking lot, conveniently parked further away from the new collection of trucks. Lee squirmed impatiently in the passenger seat of the SUV while Ross sat casually reclined in the driver's seat across from her. Lee wore a baseball cap and sunglasses to conceal her identity, despite that it was nearing sunset. Zack had spread out on the third row of seats with his fingers laced behind his neck and his eyes closed. It was quite possible he was asleep. It was half-past seven. Ross fidgeted for the first time. Even he was growing impatient with the amount of time that had passed. Ross looked at his watch, groaned with annoyance, and then glanced at Zack in the far backseat through the rearview mirror.

"See what's taking them so long," Ross announced.

Without a word, Zack sprang to his feet and jumped out of the vehicle. Judging by his cat-like reflexes, he hadn't been asleep after all. Lee glanced through the side mirror to watch him, but Zack was already gone.

"He's like part Ninja or something," Lee commented aloud, although she hadn't intended to.

"Zack's a special breed," Ross replied. "He's already used most of his nine lives."

"So I've heard," Lee remarked.

She felt compelled to study the older man. He had a quiet sophistication she'd never really seen before. Lee found herself oddly intrigued by him.

"Do you get roped into helping old friends a lot?"

"More than you'd think," he replied with a deep sigh. "Holden, Agent Falcone, has bailed us out on numerous occasions since he got together with Jackie. She's the daughter of our late commander." Ross drifted out a moment then looked at her and smiled. "For the situations we've gotten ourselves into, it's helpful having a federal agent on our side. We return the favor when he needs us. It's a workable relationship."

"Would I be safe in assuming none of you are married?" Lee asked while hiding her smile. "I can't imagine too many women dealing well with what you do."

"You'd assume correctly," Ross replied then laughed softly. "A few of us have tried to live a semi-normal life, but it never really works out in the end."

"You were married?" Lee asked then immediately regretted asking such a personal question, at least aloud. "Sorry. I don't mean to pry."

"No, it's okay," Ross remarked and shrugged with little concern. "I foolishly thought I'd be married once I left the military." He snorted a soft laugh. "I became a SEAL, because I wanted to save the world. Your team is your family, and that's all you need. At least, for a while. I was involved with a spirited Naval Officer. She was around enough that she was practically one of us. Probably the longest relationship I'd ever had." He sank into thought and held his breath. "Our last mission out nearly got the entire team killed. It was time to re-evaluate our priorities. After our CO died, none of us wanted to break in a new commander, so we took our leave." Ross stared out the windshield, inhaled deeply, and sighed softly. "I was ready to settle down and play house with my spirited Naval Officer." He then glanced at Lee and smirked. "It never occurred to me that she wanted to be a career officer. I suppose I mistook our time together as something more. I don't hold it against her, but I often wonder what our life together would have been like."

Lee studied him then smiled gently. "You're just a hopeless romantic at heart."

"In our own special way, I suppose all of us are," Ross informed her. "Even Kirk, who'd like everyone to believe he's such a bad ass, has his moments. After Zack blew one of the buildings we'd raided, we found a momma cat and her three kittens in his backpack. It was tough getting him to give up those kittens." A humored smile crossed his face. "Gil's been married twice to the same woman, and Beck falls hopelessly in love with women he never intends to approach."

"What about Zack and Monroe?" Lee asked while maintaining her humor with stories about the other men.

"Monroe can be a womanizer at times," Ross replied with reluctant honesty. "I'm guessing he's still hung up on Jackie. I can't be sure, but I think they got together once, because he seemed convinced they were going to get married despite her disinterest. The commander, her father, got into it with him, and that ended that. After that, he stepped up his game with one attractive woman after another." He hesitated then considered his next comment. "Zack is a lover by nature, if you can believe that."

"I find that hard to believe."

"It's true, although he tends to make bad choices in women," Ross informed her. "When he does in fact die, and stays dead, it'll be at the hands of a lover. He has a weak spot for Russian spies. Despite one particular woman trying to kill him on several occasions, he keeps meeting up with her for romantic interludes. Last time they got together, he came back with ten stitches where she tried to stab him."

Lee gasped with surprise and stared with disbelief. "And he keeps going back for more?"

"Hell, yeah," Ross replied and chuckled softly. "He turns all dreamy if you even mention her name. He's like a mongoose playing with a cobra."

"I never would have imagined the six of you being so interesting in that respect," Lee replied.

"Well, we're not all shooting bad guys and blowing up shit," Ross replied with a humored smile.

Lee laughed softly at the look on his face. She glanced out the windshield and saw Mac getting out of her rental car parked not far from them. Lee's expression dropped.

"Ah, shit! She's back!"

Ross looked across the parking lot and saw Mac. He pulled Lee down in the seat and across his lap, holding her down by her head. Lee struggled slightly against his grip that nearly smothered her face into his crotch.

"What's she doing?" Lee muttered into Ross's crotch, well aware where her lips were pressed.

"Ah, hell," he groaned softly. "She's going back to the lounge. If she sees Monroe, we're screwed."

Lee continued to stare at Ross's crotch from her close-up position. The thought of speaking with her mouth pressed where it was slightly disturbed her, although she wasn't completely turned off either.

"Is she gone yet?"

Ross released her head. "Yeah, she went around the corner. Probably into the lounge. Damn it."

Lee slowly sat up, feeling slightly dazed from being thrown down on his lap and the moderately compromising position. She attempted to compose herself, although she could feel her cheeks burning with embarrassment. As she glanced at Ross, lustful images flooded her mind, and she subconsciously glanced at his crotch. Ross removed his cell phone and sent a quick text to Beck and Zack. When they acknowledged the text, he groaned softly.

"Hopefully they're in a position to get Monroe out of there unseen," Ross announced. "If she sees him, she'll know you're somewhere close by. You'd better climb into the back, in case she returns before the guys do."

Lee nodded and climbed over the console and into the back. She couldn't help but stare at Ross's profile from the seat behind him. At that moment, something stirred inside her.

†

Mac entered the lounge with her attention focused on Pinto, who was performing on stage. Mac paused by one of the smaller standing tables near the back, possibly to avoid the bartender seeing her. She'd taken the time to change into a different outfit, so she wouldn't be spotted and again thrown out by the bouncer. Across the lounge, Monroe remained hidden behind Beck, having switched chairs with Bogart.

"We need a diversion," Monroe muttered to Beck.

All three men saw Zack approaching Mac's table. Beck and Monroe showed their concerns.

"No, no, no," Beck gasped softly as his eyes widened. "Not that kind of diversion!"

"I've got this," Bogart announced and jumped up from his seat before anyone could protest.

Beck groaned softly and covered his eyes. "Oh, God. This is going from bad to worse."

Bogart nudged Zack as he passed him, silently indicating he was taking care of the situation. Zack stopped and glared at Bogart as he passed him. He was possibly offended that Bogart was invading his territory. Bogart circled Mac's table and approached from the direction of the bar, so that she'd turn her back to Monroe's table and the door. Bogart paused by her table and smiled charmingly, catching her attention, but not necessarily in a good way. She glared at him and smirked almost deviously.

"Sorry to bother you," Bogart announced, maintaining his cheerful disposition, "but my friends--" He casually indicated the bar behind him to no one in particular. "--and I have a little wager."

122

Mac smiled sweetly at him. "Take a hike."

Bogart didn't give up despite her disinterest or her tone of hostility. "I know you get this sort of thing all the time," he continued, annoying her further.

Beck and Zack hurried Monroe from the lounge. Zack stopped by the door and decided to watch the train wreck.

"You're that newscaster, right?" Bogart announced cheerfully. "The investigative reporter. The guys didn't believe that it was you, but I told them it was most definitely you. That breaking story you did on E.coli was amazing."

She stared at him a moment with a strange look. He slipped her a napkin.

"I'd love to get your autograph," he announced while grinning boyishly then waved his cell phone. "And maybe a picture of us together for bragging rights."

Mac appeared humored by the question and laughed softly. "I'm sorry; you have me mixed up with someone else," she replied more naturally.

Bogart grinned and put on his best country boy act. "I know, but you probably get tired of the same pick-up lines, and a woman as classy as yourself deserves all-new pick-up lines."

She laughed softly and appeared to fall helpless to his charm. "I'll give you an 'A' for originality."

He raised his brows while grinning and indicated the napkin. "Is that enough to earn me your telephone number?" He again waved the cell phone. "And a selfie?"

"I don't make it out this way too often," she informed him. "Why don't you give me your number, and I'll call you the next time I'm in town."

"Deal," he chirped and wrote his number on the napkin. He slid it toward her and maintained his grin. "And the selfie?"

She reluctantly nodded. Bogart joined her, grinned charmingly, and took their picture together. He stepped away from her and remained cheerful.

"I look forward to your call the next time you're in town," he announced then headed toward the door.

Zack ducked out just before him. Bogart stepped outside the lounge and didn't even flinch when Zack filed in alongside him. He walked with Zack toward the lounge parking lot then glanced at the picture he'd taken. Zack stood in the background, his neck stretched to get into the picture, and his middle finger in the air. Bogart glared at Zack and frowned.

"Classy."

"I hope you didn't give her your real phone number," Zack remarked.

"I gave her my answering service number," he replied.

"You have an answering service?"

"Several, actually," Bogart informed him while grinning. "In my business, it pays to have several phone numbers attached to a multitude of phony businesses. It's easier to disappear that way. You understand."

"I suppose that would be easier than faking your own death half a dozen times," Zack remarked then eyed Bogart and smirked. "But I like getting flowers."

Bogart stared at him then slowly shook his head. "You are an odd man."

Chapter Twenty-three

*O*nce the six had returned to the lodge, Kirk was waiting on the porch to greet them. His mood was typical for the brawny, emotionless man. He glared at Beck as he approached them from the porch. The two men locked eyes as if having a secret discussion before they exchanged any words.

"We have a serious *rat* situation," Kirk informed him lowly. "It needs to be taken care of immediately."

Beck stared with a look of disbelief at Kirk, who continued past him with an obvious mission in mind. Beck groaned softly, placed his hands on his hips, and looked at Ross.

"I hate rats," Beck muttered.

"Yeah, me too," Ross remarked.

Kirk continued on his mission, passing everyone, and headed straight for a concerned looking Bogart. Kirk grabbed him by his jacket and slammed him backward into the side of the SUV. The sudden assault stunned Bogart.

"You and I need to have a little talk," Kirk snarled then grabbed Bogart by the back of the neck and said something into the alarmed man's ear.

The others watched with surprise, but no one commented or attempted to intervene. Kirk gave Bogart's neck a firm squeeze as he glared into his eyes.

"Are we clear?" Kirk demanded.

Bogart stared at him with a fixed expression and uncertainly nodded. "Yeah, I hear you, bro," he replied while straightening his shirt. "I'll take care of it."

Kirk shoved Bogart away from the SUV. Bogart hurried for the lodge and away from the large, intimidating man. Tonya was now standing on the porch watching the scene unfold. She had a strange look on her face then glanced from Kirk to Bogart as he approached her.

"What was that all about?" she gasped.

Bogart frowned and glanced back at Kirk while gingerly rubbing his sore neck. "Just too much testosterone." He placed his arm around her shoulder, managed a tiny grin, and guided her back toward the main door. "Wait until you hear what happened in town."

She eagerly entered the lodge with him.

Ross approached Lee and casually extended his hand. "I believe you have Monroe's flash drive."

Lee nodded and removed the flash drive from its resting place down the front of her shirt. Ross's eyes followed her hand into her cleavage. His brows raised as she handed him the warm flash drive. He laughed softly and turned away to avoid looking her in the eyes. His lighthearted expression toughened as he looked at his men and handed Beck the flash drive. Becks' eyes subconsciously strayed from the flash drive he held to Lee's cleavage as well.

"Kirk and Beck are with me," Ross announced. "We'll get Kirk up to speed on what happened in town."

Ross looked back at Lee, where she stood for some odd reason as if awaiting further orders. She couldn't help the sudden pang she felt as he stared at her.

"You're with Monroe," Ross announced then turned toward Zack. "Zack, take care of the rat situation."

Zack gave a firm nod as he removed his semiautomatic from his shoulder holster. He cocked his weapon and headed for the lodge.

†

Monroe entertained his friends with his grilling skills while they hung out on the back patio a little after ten o'clock that evening. It had been a long day, leaving most hungry enough to eat their steak rare if necessary. After they had returned from town, Ross had spent nearly half an hour with Beck and Kirk in the lounge. Lee could now see Ross in the kitchen leaning against the island counter while talking with Zack. Lee cast several glances at the two men through the glass doors. She couldn't stop staring at Ross, and she wasn't sure why. He was rather distinguished, but he wasn't her type. Lee knew it had to be the incident earlier in the car that had her helplessly staring at the man. It seemed ridiculous that one little sexual gaffe would put all sorts of questionable thoughts into her head. Consumed with everything that happened in town, she was completely unaware of the others on the patio.

Tonya sat on the edge of the inground pool and soaked her feet while Bogart remained glued to her side. He was laying on the charm, possibly attempting to secure another night of sex games with the attractive woman. Tonya's mood that evening was hard to read. She almost appeared disinterested despite the good time she'd had with the handsome conman the night before. Lee finally returned to reality and noted Tonya's odd behavior regarding Bogart. She hoped Tonya wasn't planning to chase Beck again. Her friend had to have more morals than attempting to seduce a second man in their group. It would seem any hopes Tonya had of getting one of the other men into bed ended the moment she slept with Bogart. Lee wasn't sure how men felt about such things, but she personally found it creepy and in bad taste.

Ross and Zack finally joined them on the patio. Zack immediately approached Monroe at the grill, obviously wanting to check the status of their already late dinner. As Ross approached, Lee felt her heartbeat quicken. She couldn't understand her body reacting as if she were attracted to the older man. Now wasn't the time or place to take an interest in anyone, and she had to keep reminding herself that he wasn't her type. She was almost positive he wasn't. Could Tonya be right? Had she deprived herself of physical intimacy too long? Was this her body's way of telling her she needed to 'scratch an itch'? It wasn't like her, and she refused to give in to some primal, sexual need like her promiscuous friend. Lee found herself staring at Ross. He had an odd look on his face that was almost concerning.

"Everything okay?" Lee asked.

"Yeah," Ross replied while casually looking around. He met her gaze and seemed slightly uncomfortable. "Actually, no, everything isn't okay."

Ross nodded her toward the opposite end of the patio. She walked alongside him while feeling her heart pounding in her chest. The suspense was killing her. What had happened? What was with the secret meetings? They paused away from the others. Ross stood unusually close, allowing Lee to feel the heat coming from his body. She resisted the urge to throw her arms around his neck and kiss him. Her thoughts were all over the place, and she didn't like the way it felt. As he stared at her a moment in silence, she gazed almost helplessly into his blue eyes.

"What's wrong?" she asked gently, hoping to get on with the conversation, casting her back into reality.

"After our near encounter with Romano's hired, uh, henchwoman, I've been having some concerns about our security measures here at the lodge," he announced then hesitated and drew a deep breath. "I'm issuing a room change, and I don't think you're going to be very happy about it."

"A room change?" she suddenly asked with surprise. It wasn't exactly what she was expecting to hear from him. "What sort of room change?"

"More like a roommate change," he replied while seeming slightly uncomfortable with his announcement. "It's not an easy call, so I'll let you decide, but you'll be partnered with either Zack or Kirk tonight."

Lee felt her heart nearly pound out of her chest at the words. She was almost too stunned to respond.

"You're kidding," she suddenly burst out and then attempted to collect herself. She lowered her voice and glared at Ross. Lee was no longer in the mood to be civil. "You're giving me a choice between the psychopath and 'Kirk the barbarian'?"

"This isn't up for debate," he informed her. "We don't want to alarm Tonya, so you won't let her know the real reason why you're staying with one of my men."

"What?" she suddenly asked then waved her hand. "Whoa, wait. Are you saying that you want me to share a room with one of those two guys and make Tonya think it's a hookup?" She resisted exploding. "Are you insane?"

"Don't make me argue the point with you, Lee," he announced sternly. "I realize it sounds morally compromising by allowing your friend to think you're 'hooking up' with one of my men, but I wouldn't insist if it wasn't important. We don't know what brought that woman to town. We don't know that she bought into any of Romeo's stalker act." He straightened proudly. "Tonya doesn't need to know of my concerns for now. There's no reason to upset her about something that may not be an issue. She'll be fine in Bogart's protection. That leaves you. You're not staying in a room alone tonight. Swallow your pride and make a decision, or I'll be forced to make it for you."

"Why not Beck or Monroe?" she demanded then reconsidered. "Forget that, I know why not Monroe." Her look hardened. "Why not Beck?" She hesitated then slyly raised her brow. "Or you, for that matter?"

"Beck has a sleep disorder," Ross informed her. "He'd be up half the night talking your ear off."

"Okay, fine," she announced firmly and folded her arms across her chest. "I choose you."

"It doesn't work that way," he replied.

"Why? Do you have some sleep disorder I should know about?" she suddenly demanded, throwing it back at him. "Or is it *your* image you're worried about? Because, you know, I have an image too. Maybe you need to lead by example and swallow *your* pride instead."

He seemed surprised by her comment and tone. For a moment, he was reluctant to respond.

"Fine," he finally announced with little emotion. "Kirk snores and Zack would just end up in your bed spooning against you all night."

"I wouldn't doubt that," she muttered. "He's like an annoying little dog."

"More like a pit bull," Ross muttered then sighed deeply. "After dinner, we'll just slip away from the others. Let Tonya come to her own conclusions. It'll be easier. Hopefully, if all goes well, I'll be less paranoid in the morning."

"And tomorrow morning, if Tonya asks what happened, what do I tell her?" Lee almost demanded.

"If everything checks out in the morning, you can tell her I was just being cautious and nothing happened," he replied. "If I get reports of perimeter breaches or if anything seems suspicious, we'll have an entirely different problem to worry about."

Lee groaned softly. "I'm sorry for being such a bitch," she remarked gently. "I know you're only doing your job. It's just...the whole situation is very uncomfortable."

"I get that," Ross replied. "But if it makes you feel any better, the guys are going to torment the hell out of me, so you've played your hand well."

She held back her grin. "So we're both going to be embarrassed by this, huh? Good to know."

"Yeah, well, don't get too cocky," Ross suddenly announced. "I suffer from PTS nightmares. You could be in for one hell of a night."

She considered Ross's response and wondered what that actually meant.

†

129

*T*he lodge was peaceful in the remote woods. The only sounds were those of woodland wildlife. Within the lobby, Kirk sat on the stairs, again reading his romantic thriller without the need of a newspaper to cover it from prying eyes. It was so quiet; the grandfather clock's minute hand echoed throughout the entire lobby. Upstairs, Beck's bed was rumpled and it appeared as if he had attempted to sleep but was unsuccessful. Beck sat up on his bed in only a pair of shorts with his laptop comfortably over his bare thighs. The flash drive Monroe and Lee had created at the library stuck out of the port on the laptop. Beck's eyes narrowed and his nose wrinkled at the contents within the file on the flash drive. The file contained several pictures clearly taken by a police photographer. They revealed several shots of a mangled car and a dead woman with horrific injuries. Apparently, she had been thrown from the car upon impact. There were also pictures of several objects with numbered markers, indicating they were possibly evidence for a criminal investigation of the accident.

"What the hell--?" Beck stared at the pictures a moment longer and scratched his moderately mussed hair. "Why would Sal have crime scene photos?" He rubbed his weary eyes then glanced at the pictures again. "Someone blackmailing you, Romano?" He then considered the question and raised his brows. "Or is it the other way around?"

†

*B*ack at Romano's estate, Gil remained sitting in the sturdy chair still handcuffed to it and looked extremely bored. He glanced at his watch, groaned, and shook his head.

"Not gracing me with your presence this evening?" Gil muttered. He removed the lock pick from his sleeve and unlocked the handcuff. "Haven't you people heard of bathroom breaks?"

He casually stood and headed for the door. Within a few minutes, Gil was slipping into the dimly lit kitchen. He glanced around, but it was late and everyone had gone to bed. The snarling of a dog caught his attention. He glanced across the kitchen while attempting not to make any sudden moves. Darth saw him, whimpered excitedly, and ran to greet him. Gil breathed a sigh of relief and scratched the dog affectionately.

"Such a good watchdog," he announced in a coddling tone meant to excite the dog.

Darth let out a quick bark, startling Gil. He placed his finger to his mouth and shushed the dog. He approached the refrigerator and routed around. He removed a plate and grinned while looking at the excited dog.

"Hmm, looks like pot roast," he announced. "I hope the cook made those little potatoes."

He helped himself to some pot roast then tossed a chunk of meat to Darth. The dog practically swallowed it whole.

"That's not good for digestion," Gil informed the dog. "You should learn to savor your food." He then considered the comment and shrugged. "But we are pressed for time." He tossed the dog a few more pieces of beef and shoved some into his own mouth. Gil held up a small potato and grinned between chewing. "I was right," he said to the dog. "Little potatoes."

He tossed one to the dog. Darth jumped up and caught it in his mouth, again swallowing it without chewing. Gil stuffed two into his mouth and returned the plate to the refrigerator.

"Come on, Darth," he announced with his mouth full. "Time to check our social network page. See if the guys found anything useful."

Chapter Twenty-four

It was a little after three o'clock in the morning. Lee had been sound asleep within Ross's room when she awoke to the sound of someone shouting. A loud bang followed. Lee jumped up in bed and looked around the dimly lit room. Within the bed next to hers, Ross thrashed beneath the covers, clearly having a violent nightmare. Although she was relieved they weren't under attack, she watched him reliving some traumatic moment and wondered if she should attempt to wake him. She was certain she didn't want to touch him in his current state, knowing it might startle him and possibly injure her. Lee slowly turned on her bed and listened to him blurt out something beyond her comprehension. Whatever his nightmare, it was severe.

"Ross," she announced in a gentle but firm tone, hoping to wake him. When he didn't wake and his thrashing continued, she spoke a little louder. "Ross!"

Ross suddenly flew up in bed with his semiautomatic in his hand and aimed it at the dresser. He then scanned the room with the gun leading the way. Lee dove from the bed and onto the floor furthest from his bed to avoid being shot. Ross realized there was nothing there and slowly lowered the gun. He strained to recognize Lee on the other side of the bed.

"What's wrong with you?" he suddenly demanded while attempting to control his breathing. Ross turned on the bedside light between the two beds. "That's a good way to get shot. What the hell were you yelling about?"

Lee slowly peeked over the edge of the bed at him where he sat partially beneath his covers with the large semiautomatic resting on his lap.

"What's wrong with me?" she suddenly blurted out and straightened on her knees. "You're the one who aimed a loaded gun at me. What the hell are you doing sleeping with a loaded gun? With the way you were thrashing around, you're liable to shoot someone...possibly yourself!"

There was an urgent pounding on the door, alarming Lee. She sprang up from the floor, darted across her bed, and practically dove into Ross's bed, hiding behind him. She clung to his arm and stared at the door. Her heart was pounding, and she could barely control her heavy breathing.

"Go away, Kirk!" Ross shouted at the door.

"Everything okay?" Kirk announced through the closed door. "I thought I heard the girl screaming."

"Yeah, they tend to do that when you accidentally aim a gun at them," Ross replied without moving from his bed.

Lee released Ross's bare arm and sneered at him, although he couldn't see it.

"Duct tape and zip ties," Kirk announced through the door. "I keep telling you."

Ross glanced at Lee and the horrified look on her face. He smirked and chuckled softly.

"He's joking," Ross informed her.

"Yeah, I'm sure he is," she muttered.

"Three seconds for the code phrase, or I'm busting the door down," Kirk announced firmly.

"Bust down the door and I'll shoot you in the head," Ross growled back.

"Pleasant dreams," Kirk announced and was heard walking away from the door.

"That's the code phrase?" she remarked while staring back at him.

Ross shrugged while smirking. "Basically, it's anything involving bodily harm to the other. Just don't ever ask Zack for the code phrase. You may get an education."

Lee watched Ross switch the gun's safety to the 'on' position. She then realized she was still in his bed only inches from him wearing her oversized man's button shirt and a pair of floppy shorts. Leaping from the bed as fast as possible crossed her mind, but she didn't want to give him the impression that she was anxious about being in the bed alongside him. A more casual retreat would serve her better. She didn't want him to think she was just another frightened woman. Although dignity went out the door the moment she superman leaped into his bed in the first place. He looked at her and appeared almost sympathetic.

"I'm sorry if I startled you with my, uh," he fumbled then indicated the gun, "quick reflexes."

"With the way you were jumping in your sleep, you're eventually going to shoot yourself," she lectured then stared with concern. "Do you always sleep with that thing under your pillow?"

"Oh, no," he replied defiantly.

She was glad to hear that.

"I usually sleep with a revolver," he announced casually. "Less chance of it discharging accidentally."

She looked at him with surprise. Ross grinned slyly. Lee rolled her eyes and attempted to hide her smile. She wasn't sure if he was serious or not. She looked at the bedside clock, groaned, and ran her fingers through her long, mussed hair.

"With the number of guns in this place, I'm surprised none of you have shot one another by now," she announced then realized Ross was staring at her. She stared back at him with a curious look. "What?"

He was silent a moment then forced a smile. "Not a fan of firearms?"

"I don't have a problem with guns," she remarked, feeling slightly offended as she stared at him. "It's the sheer number of guns you and the other guys are carrying on your bodies at any given time that I find staggering. I mean, if I randomly searched any of you, how many weapons would I find?"

Ross looked beneath the covers at himself then met her gaze with a sly grin. "I'm a little light on weapons at the moment." He extended the semiautomatic to her handle first. "Your ass is on the line," he announced simply. "You should have a working familiarity with firearms."

She uncertainly accepted the gun and marveled at the weight. "I used to spend many summers on my grandfather's farm in the country," she informed him. "He taught me how to shoot a rifle and a shotgun."

"Same concept," he announced. "I'll give you a crash course in handguns."

Ross took the gun from her, skillfully ejected the clip, and popped the bullet from the chamber. Lee had to admit that the sounds and his fast actions were enough to set her on edge. He squeezed the trigger, allowing the slide to snap back into place while creating a terrifying sound. She jumped slightly. He handed her the empty gun. Once she held the gun, he showed her how to hold it properly and steady her aim. She already understood how to line up a shot, although it was slightly different with a handgun versus a rifle. She had to admit, she enjoyed the closeness of his body and his hands touching her arms and wrist. He then showed her how to cock the gun, which required some practice on her behalf. He had her aim the gun at the dresser and then squeeze the trigger. She listened to the click of the empty gun, although the sound wasn't nearly as terrifying with the gun in her hand. He then showed her how to load the clip and again cock the gun, this time allowing a bullet to enter the chamber. He flipped on the safety switch and removed the gun from her while grinning.

"Nothing to it," he announced cheerfully and leaned back to replace it under his pillow.

She watched him stretch out on the bed to replace the gun and marveled at his toned body despite his age. He was probably in better shape than men half his age. As he straightened, he met her gaze. She hadn't been able to look away fast enough; although she wasn't sure she wanted to.

"Maybe we'll do some target shooting tomorrow," he announced while maintaining his pleasant smile.

"I think I'd enjoy that," she replied, although it was his company she was actually referring. Lee felt her cheeks redden and attempted to cover with some small talk. "I guess this assignment is pretty boring for you, huh? I can understand wanting to make the best of it."

"Actually, I just enjoy seeing a woman with a gun in her hand," he replied then allowed a throaty chuckle to escape. "There's nothing sexier than a woman shredding a target with an AK-47 assault rifle."

"Your idea of foreplay, huh?" she teased then immediately regretted having said it aloud.

The comment was completely inappropriate. Lee hid her embarrassed look and shifted on the bed.

"I don't know why I said that," she remarked softly and fidgeted.

Ross shrugged casually. "I'd like to believe it's because you find me attractive, but I guess that would be wishful thinking on my behalf."

She stared into his blue eyes a moment as her heart pounded from the thoughts racing through her mind. There were several ways to respond to the comment.

"I do find you attractive," she replied softly then immediately wondered why she had to go with 'blunt honesty'.

There was a long silence as they stared at each other, almost uncertain what to say. Ross took her hand in his and gently caressed it while smiling boyishly.

"Honestly," he announced then chuckled nervously, "I don't know what to do with that information. I've been out of the dating scene a long time."

"How long is a long time?" she asked delicately while hiding her smile.

She found it almost difficult to believe that she was sitting on a bed with a man, both half dressed, and zero worries that he would jump on her.

Ross looked up and appeared deep in thought. He glanced back at her and smiled timidly. "I'm not sure," he replied. "Two maybe three--" There was a moment of hesitation and possible consideration. "--years."

She stared at him with surprise. "Wow, you've got me beat by a year or two."

"Give or take twenty-five years," he teased while caressing her hand.

She enjoyed the way his hands caressed her hand with great warmth and affection. Despite that she didn't normally move very fast, she was secretly yearning to make love to this man. It'd been a long time, and he was what she needed and wanted in a fling. He lifted her hand to his lips and kissed it warmly, sending a flood of pleasure throughout her entire body. She'd never had a man kiss her hand like that before. How was it possible that it was so erotic? He smiled almost as if reading her thoughts and resumed caressing her hand.

"I'm thinking romantic picnic lunch for two just a short walk from here," he announced cheerfully. "There's a freshwater pond. It's breathtaking."

"Now?" she asked with surprise.

He laughed softly. "No, of course not now," Ross replied. "Tomorrow afternoon. A moonlit stroll to a pond only leads to skinny-dipping and bad behavior."

"No," she teased and held back her giggle. "We wouldn't want that."

He reached for the bedside lamp between their beds and turned out the lights. She tensed slightly as he leaned back toward her. He pulled the covers down for her. She met his gaze through the dim lighting.

"Just to be safe, though, we should probably stay close," he informed her and hid his tiny smile. "I promise to be a perfect gentleman."

Lee studied him a moment through the dim lighting, hid her smile, and slipped under the covers on his bed. He joined her beneath the covers, nuzzled against her, and held her in a warm embrace. She couldn't deny how wonderful it felt being nestled in his strong, protective arms. She peacefully slipped off to sleep.

Chapter Twenty-five

Around four o'clock in the morning, Lee woke from her light sleep and noticed the strong, male arms encircled around her from behind. She could feel Ross's body firmly pressed against hers. Although nothing had happened between them, she felt alive and rejuvenated. He stirred slightly and nuzzled the back of her neck, sending shockwaves of lust throughout her body. It was something she hadn't felt in a long time. She couldn't deny how badly she wanted to roll over and seduce this man, but the thought of that romantic picnic he'd suggested made her want to wait and see what he had planned. She had to concede that he wasn't exactly a cowboy, but it didn't make him any less attractive. Besides, being former military was sort of like being a cowboy.

As much as she hated leaving his secure arms, she needed to use the bathroom with some urgency, and she couldn't hold out much longer. Monroe's overly marinated steaks had also created a terrible thirst. She would need something to drink if she intended to sleep anymore tonight. Since it didn't seem as if Ross was going to part ways with her backside, she'd need to slip out of his arms. It was sad but necessary. Lee pulled away from him and got out of the bed without waking him, or so it would appear. She used the bathroom then approached the hotel room door and unbolted it. Although not loud, the sound abruptly woke Ross, who flipped over while simultaneously reaching under the pillow for his gun. He saw her by the door and relaxed slightly. He ran his fingers through his slightly graying, mussed hair.

"Where are you going?"

"Just getting a drink," she informed him. "Did you want something?"

"Yeah," he replied firmly. "I want you to refrain from leaving this room without an escort."

His response puzzled her. When did she become a prisoner within the lodge? She'd gone down to the kitchen in the middle of the night for a drink before and no one cared. His tone was almost startling.

"Since when is that a big deal?" she asked with a little more bite to the question than she had intended.

"Since the woman sent to kill you was seen in town not two hours from here," he replied then got out of the bed, allowing her to see him in his form fitting boxer briefs.

Lee had to admit, it was a sight worth witnessing. She considered looking away but took in a sweeping eyeful, since he wasn't checking her for a reaction. She waited while he slipped into a pair of pants, hastily threw on a shirt, and grabbed his gun from under his pillow. He carelessly placed the gun down the back of his pants then buttoned his shirt as he approached without regard for shoes. If she substituted that glass of iced tea for a glass of wine, she'd be ready to seduce the man when they returned to the room. He must have noted the tiny smile on her face and attempted to keep from grinning.

"Care to share that last thought?" he asked teasingly and paused before her.

Lee felt her cheeks redden and avoided looking at him; instead, she turned toward the door.

"It'd only make you blush," she replied casually as she opened the door.

His hand pushed the door closed, surprising her. As she turned, he pulled her against him and kissed her quickly but passionately. Ross released her before she had a chance to react. His kiss left her surprisingly dizzy, and she felt a dull ache shoot through her body. Everything within her screamed she should seize the moment. He met her gaze and smiled slyly.

"I can play the role of a gentleman 95% of the time," he informed her. "But if encouraged, that 5% is just waiting to reveal itself."

She felt her heart pound as her body ached simultaneously to the comment. A thousand dirty images flashed through her mind, which didn't help. As she scrambled for any reason not to throw her arms around him and tackle him to the bed, he casually opened the door and politely extended his hand, allowing her to go first. She pushed the erotic images from her mind, smiled at him, and exited the room. His self-control was astounding. Somehow, it just made her want him more. They headed down the back corridor toward the backstairs, avoiding the man on guard duty in the lobby. It was, after all, a shorter route to the kitchen.

†

*M*onroe sat on the steps in the lobby leading to the second floor. He casually flipped through a magazine on sports cars then opened the centerfold. He studied the red muscle car and groaned softly.

"Now *that's* gorgeous."

His eyes became heavy as he suppressed a yawn. Monroe picked up his travel mug, took a large swallow of lukewarm coffee, and immediately made a face.

"Piss warm," he muttered aloud but obviously to himself. "Too much work to make a fresh pot of coffee, Kirk?"

Monroe set his magazine aside and attempted to stand, but he appeared uncoordinated and sat back down. He held his head a moment and seemed slightly puzzled. He picked up his travel mug and looked at it.

"What the--?"

His eyes rolled back as the travel mug slipped from his hand, and he collapsed onto the steps behind him.

†

*B*eck slept peacefully beneath the covers on his bed within his room. A light suddenly flashed, waking him. He stirred, saw the light flashing from his laptop computer, and leaped up from the bed. He turned the laptop toward him and stared at the screen, which revealed a blueprint style map of the lodge and surrounding property. There were several moving blips, which were heat signatures representing people. A red light blinked at what was obviously the front door, indicating a breach in their secured perimeter.

"No," Beck gasped with surprise. "That's impossible."

He hurriedly pulled on his pants, slipped into his shirt and shoes, and grabbed his semiautomatic from the nightstand. As he stuffed the handgun down the back of his pants, he grabbed an assault rifle from its hidden location behind the headboard, cocked it, and hurried for the door. Beck slipped into the corridor and immediately headed toward the front stairs. He tapped on two doors as he passed them. Once he approached the area of the stairs, an intruder slipped out of the linen closet and headed for the two-bedroom suite. The intruder jimmied a credit card alongside the lock and easily unlocked the door. He silently opened the door and slipped into the suite.

As the intruder entered the two-bedroom suite, Tonya appeared from the first bedroom. She stopped when she saw the man dressed in black standing within the living room and nearly cried out. He aimed a gun with a silencer at her. She held back her scream and stared with horror at the gun.

†

*B*eck hurried down the main stairs and checked on Monroe, who remained unconscious on the steps. Beck looked around and appeared to consider his next move.

"What's happening?" Kirk asked in a loud whisper from the top of the stairs.

Beck looked up the steps to the hastily dressed Kirk, who only wore a pair of pants. He held an assault rifle against his muscular, bare chest and his semiautomatic was partially exposed down the front of his pants. Beck motioned him back the way he'd come. Kirk nodded and hurried back down the hall. Kirk approached Ross's bedroom door and tapped twice. When there was no response, he kicked in the door with a thunderous crack. He stepped into the room with his assault rifle leading the way. Within two seconds, he was back in the hall. A fully dressed, heavily armed Zack was standing directly behind him. He gave a curious nod to Kirk. Without words, Kirk signaled to Zack. Zack nodded and ran down the corridor toward the backstairs. Kirk approached the suite door, tapped on it twice, and awaited a response. When there wasn't one, he kicked in the door with the same vigor as the last. He slipped into the room with his assault rifle aimed and ready to fire at a moment's notice. The women's suite was alarmingly silent. The living room was empty and both bedroom doors were open.

"Bogart?"

There was no response. Kirk immediately headed for Tonya's bedroom. He threw his back against the doorframe and aimed the assault rifle into the dimly lit room. Kirk flicked the light switch, brightening the room, which revealed Bogart lying on the floor alongside the bed in only his manly pink briefs. Kirk hurried to the fallen man and assessed him for injuries while hastily checking for a pulse. Apart from some blood in his hairline, Bogart wasn't badly injured. He possibly suffered a concussion from a blow to his head. Kirk gave him a slight, reassuring pat on the shoulder.

"Hang in there, buddy."

Kirk straightened and hurried from the room.

Chapter Twenty-six

*R*oss and Lee sat at the island counter with glasses of iced tea before them. They talked and laughed softly. Lee realized she had been wrong about Ross when she'd first met him. He wasn't nearly as serious as he portrayed himself to be in front of his team. Perhaps she'd been wrong about all of them. Maybe none of them were as serious and tough as they wanted others to believe. Were they really even Navy SEALs? Or was that all just an act to garner business? Their good time was interrupted by the sound of a faint clunk from the floor above them. Ross eyed the ceiling, appeared concerned, and sprang to his feet while removing his gun from his pants. His quick reflexes with his gun enforced his skilled training. She was about to comment when the back door was kicked open with a thunderous crack. Lee screamed in response as she turned then froze at the sight of the intruder dressed in black aiming a gun at her.

"Down!" Ross cried out.

Even though she was frozen with fear, Lee heard his words and instinctively ducked on command. Ross shot the intruder twice in the chest. Despite being thrown back by both shots, the man didn't go down. The intruder fired back at Ross, who was already returning fire. The bullet made contact with the man's forehead, snapping his head back. Lee watched as part of the man's skull exploded out the back, spattering blood and brain tissue against the door behind him. Lee cried out with surprise then looked back at Ross, who clutched his bleeding right arm. She sprang to her feet with a look of alarm on her face while staring at his bleeding arm.

"Stay down," he ordered despite the pain.

Lee couldn't take her eyes off Ross's bleeding arm, and his order didn't register. Before she could comprehend what was happening, another intruder entered through the doorway. Unaware of the second attacker, Lee stood in Ross's line of fire, obstructing his shot. Ross lunged past her with his gun aimed and a wildly unpredictable look on his face. Lee turned toward the doorway, saw the second man with the gun aimed at her, and cried out. The second intruder's body suddenly jolted in unison to loud, rapid gunfire, which sent him to the floor. Body armor aside, the force of the powerful shots was enough to knock him down. Lee turned toward the side kitchen door where Zack stood with his assault rifle. Much to Zack's surprise, the intruder sat up with his weapon raised. Zack casually shot the man in the head with a single shot. The massive assault rifle shell took out a large portion of his skull. Lee cried out and dove behind Ross. She couldn't tear her eyes away from the gruesome sight as the man's blood poured across the floor. Possibly disturbing her more was Zack's expression never changed. There was no fear and no emotion on his face.

"Go with Zack!" Ross ordered while shoving Lee toward Zack and the side doorway. "Upstairs!"

As if sensing some unseen monster, Zack suddenly spun in the doorway behind him and fired at some unknown attacker. Ross whirled Lee around him by her arm and pulled her toward the main kitchen door.

"What about Tonya?" Lee cried out.

"You let me worry about Tonya," Ross informed her as he hurried her from the kitchen.

As they ran along the corridor, more gunfire sounded throughout the lodge. Lee clung to Ross's hand, although she wasn't sure if he was squeezing her hand tighter than she clutched his. The pain in her hand was the least of her worries. Her heart was pounding with each faint gunshot. Despite Ross's skillful look into each doorway they passed, Lee could feel panic sweeping through her body. It sounded like a war zone within the lodge, and she could only imagine Whiskey Tango Foxtrot meeting their demise along with poor Tonya. There was gunfire from behind. Lee screamed as a bullet whizzed past her head and hit the nearby wall, exploding plaster only a few feet from her.

Ross whirled her behind him and returned gunfire, although the gunman dove into the safety of a nearby room. Lee ducked while covering her head. The fear that she would die tonight scared her beyond rational thought. Ross hurried her along the hallway and toward the lobby. He suddenly stopped and tackled her behind the front desk, reacting to an intruder she barely even saw. The tackle was amazingly hard, although impact with the floor was far worse, being Ross landed on top of her. Gunfire seemed to be coming from every direction, which was louder now that they were in the lobby. Ross moved off Lee, poked his head around the side of the front desk, and returned fire. He was careful to make each shot count, being he only had one clip in his semiautomatic. Lee saw the blood on her shirt then looked at Ross, who concentrated on shooting at several intruders. There was a large amount of blood soaking through his shirtsleeve where he'd been hit. She could do little more than stare helplessly at the blood. She couldn't believe he'd been shot and acted as if nothing had happened. She didn't know whether to scream or cry.

Beck and Kirk, positioned at opposite ends of the lobby, exchanged fire with two of the intruders. The intruder appeared from the corridor where Lee and Ross had just come. To their surprise, another intruder suddenly tumbled down the main stairs. Lee looked up from her position behind the front desk and saw Zack on the second floor. He signaled something to Ross. Ross turned to Lee and held her face in his bloodied left hand, forcing her to stare into his eyes. It was the only way he could be sure she wasn't in shock and would listen to him.

"Do exactly what I say when I say it," he announced firmly. "Don't hesitate and don't think. Just do it."

Lee slowly nodded. Ross half pulled her to her knees near the edge of the desk and indicated Zack at the top of the stairs. He then met her gaze.

"When I tell you to run, you're going to run straight up those stairs to Zack."

"But the man--" She attempted to indicate the man in the back corridor not far from them.

Ross poked his head out from behind the desk and shot the man in the head, dropping him to the floor. As the man collapsed, Ross looked back into her eyes.

"I need you to trust me, Lee," he announced firmly. "Run to Zack. Don't stop and don't look back."

She slowly nodded while feeling her body tremble. Ross stared into her eyes and kissed her quickly on the lips. He offered a tiny smile.

"It's going to be okay, I promise."

Despite his kiss bringing her out of her moderately shocked state, it filled her with a different fear. She had a terrible feeling that it was a kiss goodbye and that she'd never see him again. She was suddenly more concerned for Ross than herself. Ross turned toward the desk and motioned to Beck and Kirk. Both men partially stood and opened fire with their automatic weapons. The sound of assault rifle fire filled the lobby to near deafening levels. Objects exploded, plaster splintered, and glass shattered. For a brief moment, theirs were the only weapons firing as the intruders took cover from the barrage of bullets.

"Go! Now!"

Lee held her breath and ran across the lobby, as gunfire seemed to come from every direction. The bullets were nowhere near her, but she swore she could feel them whizzing past her through the air. She ran for the stairs and scaled them to reach Zack, who joined his comrades in rapid fire at the two intruders, keeping them from shooting at Lee. She was nearly to the top of the stairs when she saw another intruder appear in the hallway behind Zack. She suddenly stopped on the stairs and cried out in horror. Her expression was all Zack needed. He spun into a high, roundhouse kick and knocked the man several feet away and to the floor. Lee now stood frozen on the steps, silently screaming for her body to react, but she couldn't seem to move. She no longer heard the gunfire, only the pounding of her heart. She imagined the sting of a bullet shredding through her flesh, and the brave men of Whiskey Tango Foxtrot dying because of her. She was too terrified to move from the third to last step to the second floor.

He should have yelled at her, but instead, Zack leaped down the last couple of steps to her, grabbed her arm, and catapulted her over him to the landing just behind him. She rolled across the floor just near the corridor then flipped onto her backside. The fallen intruder near her recovered and raised his gun to shoot Zack. Zack caught a glimpse of the intruder aiming his gun. Zack flipped through the air, wrapping around the man like a python. Without slowing his momentum, Zack caught the man around the neck with his legs and tossed him through the air. As they struck the floor together, Zack flipped over with the man's head locked between his legs and effortlessly snapped his neck. Lee heard her own voice cry out at the hideous cracking sound. She hadn't even realized she screamed. Zack shoved the man's lifeless body to the floor, sprang to his feet, and reclaimed his assault rifle on the way to her. She stared with horror at the dead man.

Before she even realized what had happened, Zack had her by the wrist and yanked her to her feet. He fired a few shots to the lobby below then pulled her down the corridor behind him. More men appeared in the back corridor from the rear stairs, blocking their escape route. Without hesitation, Zack changed direction and pulled Lee into a nearby room. She finally came back to life as Zack bolted the door. She wanted to scream but held it back.

"They're going to get through," she gasped softly while staring at Zack.

"Probably," he casually replied and hurried her toward the window. "But we won't be here when they do."

Zack aimed his assault rifle at the large window and shot out the thick glass. Lee screamed and ducked as the glass shattered. She slowly straightened and approached him and the broken window. Lee looked out the window then to the pool below. She looked back at Zack, who just stared at her without comment.

"Oh, no!" Lee backed away from him. "There's no way I'm jumping from a second story window into a pool."

Zack offered a slightly humored smile as he flung his assault rifle over his shoulder by the strap.

"Don't be ridiculous," he announced and offered an unsettling chuckle. "I would never expect you to jump from a second story window into that pool."

Lee exhaled softly and attempted to control her rapidly beating heart. "That's a relief."

Zack suddenly swept her off her feet and into his arms then turned toward the window. She clung to his neck while screaming in horror.

"No, no! Don't you dare throw me!"

"I wouldn't dream of doing that," Zack casually replied.

Without a second thought, Zack ran for the window with her in his arms, leaped onto the ledge, and jumped out the shattered window. Lee clung to his neck and screamed the entire way down. They landed in the pool with a loud splash, parting the water in a large tidal wave. Lee felt the water rush past her. She wanted to scream but feared drowning. Before she could panic, Zack pulled her to the surface and released her.

"Swim," he ordered.

Lee gasped and attempted to scream but nothing came out. She started swimming toward the steps with Zack lazily swimming behind her. As they stepped out of the pool, Lee doubled over and attempted to catch her breath. Zack casually grabbed her by the wrist as he walked past and pulled her behind him. She wanted to protest but lacked the strength. He half dragged her beyond the pool area and into the woods. He stopped several yards from the lodge and pointed up a tree. She continued to breathe heavily while looking up the tree to the sturdy tree stand several feet above her.

"You're going to wait there. I have to go back and help my team," he informed her then appeared stern. "I don't want you to make a sound until one of us comes for you. Got it?"

She slowly nodded. Zack grabbed her by the waist and hoisted her up to the first rung, which was eight feet up the tree. She climbed the rungs the rest of the way to the tree stand, which was twelve feet above the ground. As she sat on the platform and looked down at him, Zack pointed a warning finger at her, indicating for her to heed his words.

$$\dagger$$

*K*irk, Beck, and Ross continued to fire upon the two remaining men near the main entrance. The exchange was fierce as assault rifle bullets tore through the furniture, walls, and windows. Zack slipped unnoticed into the lobby through the front door. By the time the first intruder saw him, Zack pulled the trigger and shot him in the head. As the second intruder turned to shoot Zack, Kirk took his shot and fired two rounds from the assault rifle into the man's head, exploding most of his skull. The firing ceased and all was quiet. All four men slowly straightened and looked around.

"We need to sweep the lodge for any stragglers," Ross ordered gruffly.

"My laptop has the heat sensors," Beck informed him. "I can do a live body count."

Ross motioned him up the stairs then looked at Zack. "Is Lee safe?"

"Safely tucked away," Zack informed him.

"Good," he replied. "I want you and Kirk to find Tonya and Bogart. Keep alert for stragglers."

Kirk ran up the stairs after Beck while Zack headed down the main corridor. Ross found an emergency first aid kit beneath the front desk, opened it, and removed some gauze pads and wraps. He quickly and skillfully patched his injured arm to stop the bleeding then headed across the lobby. He snatched an assault rifle from one of the dead men and approached the still unconscious Monroe. He crouched alongside Monroe and attempted to wake him by tapping his face a little harder than necessary. Monroe groaned softly and looked around while holding his head.

"What the hell--?"

"Yeah, exactly," Ross replied. "Someone must've knocked you out."

"More like drugged me," Monroe replied as he sat up then casually looked around. "Looks like I missed one hell of a party." He then eyed Ross. "Is Lee okay?"

"Yeah, she's safe," Ross replied. "I'm going to retrieve her now. You just take it easy and keep an eye on things down here. We don't know if there are any hostiles left alive."

"Yeah, sure," Monroe announced and removed his gun from his shoulder holster, although it required some effort.

Ross hurried for the main door and left the lounge.

Chapter Twenty-seven

*B*eck hurried across his dimly lit bedroom, set his assault rifle on the bed, and picked up his discarded laptop. He scanned the screen for viable blips, particularly those moving. His expression dropped at the number of added blips since the alarm first alerted him to intruders. Despite having eliminated several unwanted visitors, there were several more on the property.

"Oh, we've got company," he muttered.

Beck turned as Kirk entered his room. Kirk scanned the area, met Beck's gaze, and indicated the laptop.

"What's that thing showing?"

Beck shut the laptop then tossed it onto the bed. "We're looking at possibly four hostiles. It's picking up four warm bodies outside. One should be Lee."

"Ross probably went to retrieve her," Kirk announced as he routed through one of the dresser drawers and removed a full magazine for his assault rifle.

Beck held up his hand. Kirk tossed him a spare magazine as well. He easily caught it and exchanged it for the nearly spent one in his own assault rifle.

"Zack is heading into the kitchen area, and Bogart is unconscious in Tonya's room," Kirk announced while exchanging his own rifle magazine.

"With Monroe downstairs, that means there's someone else upstairs with us. I'm guessing that's Tonya. Her location is at the other end of the hall. She's probably hiding. I doubt she went downstairs with all that gunfire. That means there are probably two bad guys downstairs and two outside," Beck announced. Both men locked and loaded their weapons. "You take the kitchen then circle around out back and make sure Ross has Lee. I'll head for the lobby, put Monroe on alert, and search the front half of the lodge."

They heard a floorboard creak just outside the partially opened bedroom door. Both men spun toward the door with their guns aimed. The door slowly opened to reveal a slightly unsteady Monroe with his own gun aimed at them. Both men relaxed.

"Are you up to some recon?" Kirk asked Monroe.

"Yeah, just point me in the right direction," Monroe announced and steadied himself.

"You're with me," Kirk announced. "You can search the back of the lodge, and I'll head out back to find Lee and Ross."

Monroe nodded and followed Kirk from the room with Beck on their heels. They then went their separate ways with different missions.

†

*L*ee sat on the tree stand platform while hugging her bare legs to her wet shirt. She shivered slightly from the chill in the air. Even during the summer, nights in the wooded mountains were cool, and being soaked from her dip in the pool wasn't helping. She heard someone moving within the woods. Lee held her breath while remaining silent and still. She saw Tonya darting through the woods, but she was too far away for Lee to call out without attracting attention to her location. She had to reach her friend and bring her to the safety of the tree stand. Lee climbed down until she reached the last rung eight feet from the ground. She dangled from the rung and allowed herself to drop to the ground. She landed softly, although it was uncomfortable in her bare feet, and hurried through the woods in the direction Tonya headed.

"Tonya," she called in a hushed whisper, attempting to catch her friend's attention while minding where she stepped in her bare feet. "Tonya!"

Tonya suddenly stopped and turned from nearly twenty yards away. She saw Lee and appeared relieved. Tonya took a few steps toward her then stopped as horror swept over her face. Lee's expression dropped. She quickly turned and came face-to-face with Jericho. Before she could scream, he struck her on the head. Lee dropped to the ground. Tonya stared at her fallen friend then met Jericho's evil gaze from nearly twenty yards away. His devious smile mocked her.

t

*O*nly moments later, Ross approached the large tree and looked up to see the empty stand. As concern swept over him, he scanned the surrounding woods, but there was no sign of Lee. His expression hardened to something resembling hostility. Ross hurried through the woods and back toward the lodge. There was the faint sound of movement, causing him to spin with his assault rifle aimed. Kirk aimed his weapon at Ross as well. Both men relaxed. Kirk looked around then met Ross's gaze as his brows knitted in silent concern.

"Where's Lee?" Kirk demanded.

"She's not in her perch," Ross announced sternly. "Get Beck on that damned laptop. I want her position, and I want it yesterday. I'm going to sweep the grounds. If you find anyone who doesn't belong, take them alive."

Kirk nodded and ran back for the lodge and entered through the kitchen, casually stepping over the pool of blood collecting around the two dead men. As he headed into the back corridor, he nearly collided with Beck, who was on his way down the backstairs. Beck looked thoroughly confused.

"You didn't find anyone either?" Beck asked.

"Ross said Lee is missing," Kirk informed him. "He wants you to pull up heat sensors on your toy. I'm going to continue my search down here. Maybe she ran back inside."

Beck nodded and hurried back up the rear stairs. He ran along the second floor hallway and entered his room. Tonya sat on his bed with his laptop open in front of her. She looked at him, jumped up from the bed, and gasped slightly as he aimed his weapon at her. He slowly relaxed and lowered his assault rifle.

"We've been looking for you," Beck remarked and approached her where she stood near the bed. He indicated the laptop. "What do you think you're doing?"

"I was just--"

Beck removed his handgun from his pants. "You know what," he announced curtly and aimed the gun at her while shaking his head, "I don't even care."

She gasped when she saw the semiautomatic aimed at her. "What are you--?"

"Save it, sweetheart," Beck snarled. "Lee is missing, and if I find anything has been tampered with on my laptop, I'm putting a bullet in your head."

Tonya's stunned look suddenly turned hateful. "Well, that's just rude."

A shadow loomed over Beck. As he started to turn, someone struck him on the side of the head. Beck dropped to the floor, both his weapons clattering as they struck the hardwood floor alongside him. Tonya raised a skeptical brow and looked at the man standing near Beck's unconscious body. Jericho grinned and aimed his semiautomatic at Beck's head.

Tonya suddenly leaped forward and gasped, "No!"

Jericho looked at her and appeared surprised then irritated. He anxiously tightened his finger on the trigger.

"What possible reason is there to keep him alive?" he demanded in a gruff tone.

"There's something very important on his laptop. He was interested in something Monroe brought back on a flash drive, but I can't open the file," Tonya informed him. "I don't know what information was passed along to him or who it came from, but it could be important to us. We need to know what he was sent, and if it's stored somewhere else in case we need to delete it. We need him alive."

Jericho frowned with disapproval and lowered his weapon. "I certainly hope that's the only reason you want him alive," he snapped. "Because if I find out--"

Tonya carried the laptop beneath her arm and approached Jericho. She smiled seductively.

"You don't need to worry about that," she informed him and touched his face. "You're the only one I love."

Jericho grinned, pulled her roughly against him, and kissed her aggressively. He broke off the kiss as quickly as he had initiated it then looked at Beck on the floor.

"Let's get him out of here before the others find us," Jericho announced. He swiftly zip tied Beck's wrists behind his back and duct taped his mouth.

Tonya opened the laptop and studied the screen that revealed the body heat of those still alive within the lodge. She cast a quick glance at Jericho.

"Did they get Lee away from here?" she asked then resumed studying the computer screen, checking the location of the rest of the team.

"Yeah, she's halfway to the rendezvous by now," he announced while straightening.

Tonya looked up from the computer screen. "You have a clear path to the front door," she informed him. "The guys are all toward the back of the lodge and the rear grounds. I'll be ten minutes behind you," Tonya informed him then stuffed the laptop into his backpack. "I just have one loose end to tie up, and then we won't have to worry about Whiskey Tango Foxtrot ever again."

"Ten minutes," he threatened while slinging the backpack over his shoulder. "If you're not at the meeting place, you'll have to keep up this charade for another few days."

"I understand," she replied. "I'll be fine. Go."

Jericho nodded and swiftly picked up Beck, tossing him over his shoulder, and approached the bedroom door. As Jericho headed toward the main stairs, Tonya snatched Beck's discarded semiautomatic and headed in the opposite direction toward her suite. She hurried across the suite and into her bedroom. Bogart clutched his bleeding head but seemed barely conscious where he sat on the floor alongside the bed. He wasn't even aware she had entered the room. Tonya approached him, paused only a few feet away, and aimed the gun at his head. Bogart sank against the bed with a groan and never even opened his eyes. He was out more than he was awake. Tonya's finger tightened on the trigger. Someone grabbed Tonya around the neck from behind, causing her to gasp, as a cloth covered her nose and mouth. She struggled only a moment before her eyes rolled back and her body fell limp into her captor's arms. Mac lowered Tonya to the floor, grinned, and casually tossed the cloth aside.

"This just isn't your lucky day," Mac informed the unconscious woman as she opened a large duffel bag.

Chapter Twenty-eight

Mac casually crossed the quiet lobby strewn with blood and dead bodies. She carried the duffel bag over her shoulder and stepped over several bodies on her way to the main entrance. She heard the sound of a gun cocking behind her. Mac suddenly stopped, hesitated a moment, and then slowly turned to see Kirk standing behind her with his semiautomatic aimed at her.

"Put down the sack," he ordered gruffly, "and put your hands in the air...or I put a bullet between your eyes."

Mac stared at Kirk a moment, smiled sweetly, and hoisted the duffel bag from her shoulder.

"Just relax, handsome," she announced. "I'm not looking for trouble."

Mac suddenly swung the duffel bag at Kirk. He couldn't shoot in fear of killing the person in the bag. The heavy bag struck him, taking him to the floor. Kirk flung the bag from him and sprang to his feet, but his gun was left pinned beneath the bag. He faced Mac and sneered his annoyance.

"That was a mistake," Kirk informed her.

He threw a fast, hard punch for her face. Mac blocked his punch and struck him in the face with her own fist, startling him. Before he even had a chance to defend himself, she kicked him twice in the side and punched him in the face. Mac then spun into a roundhouse kick and struck him in the chest, knocking the large man down to his knees. She seemed pleased with herself and straightened while grinning at the fallen man. A high-flying foot suddenly struck her in the chest, sending her rolling several feet across the floor. She came to a stop in a crouched position and glared across the lobby. Zack straightened while staring at her, his face void of emotion. Mac glared at Zack and appeared annoyed.

155

"Oh, you wanna play?" she snarled then smiled sweetly. "I'll play with you."

Zack removed a baton from his back pocket and gave it a flick, extending it to two feet.

"So that's how you want this to go down?" she demanded.

Zack remained in attack position with his eyes locked on her. His silence was chilling. Mac suddenly ran for him. Zack swung with his baton. Mac slid between his legs and struck the bottom step with her booted feet. Zack spun, prepared to strike. Mac leaped to her feet, kicked out one of the wooden railing rungs, and leaped over the railing as Zack swung at her. He struck the railing instead of her. She grabbed the discarded rung where it now lie on the steps. As Zack went for a return strike, she deflected his baton with the wooden rung. Zack ran up the outer side of the stairs, leaped over the railing from above, and kicked Mac with both feet on his way down. She toppled down the last three steps and struck the floor. As Zack approached her, she sneered while standing and straightened her leather jacket.

"Now you're just pissing me off," she snarled.

She lunged for him. Zack and Mac punched and kicked each other with amazing martial arts skills. Batons, fists, and feet were flying in every direction, although each was blocked by the other. Kirk gathered his strength after his surprise attack and stumbled toward the discarded duffel bag. While matching Zack blow for blow, Mac spun in time to kick Kirk in the chest, knocking him back to the floor. She turned in time to block Zack's flying kick. Kirk writhed in agony on the floor not far from the duffle bag. After another minute or two of kicks and punches, Zack deflected Mac's right fist only to have her left fist connect with his crotch. He doubled over in agony. Mac straightened near him while grinning proudly and cocked her head to the side.

"The great equalizer," she informed him.

Zack punched her in the crotch. Mac cried out with pain and surprise, clutched her crotch, and nearly fell to the floor. Zack straightened, showing some discomfort from the groin shot he'd received.

"Oh, I'm sorry," he snarled softly. "Did that hurt?"

She sneered at him while slowly straightening and removed a small bottle from her jacket pocket. She hurled the bottle at him. He easily deflected the bottle flying for his face. The small bottle shattered against his palm. He flicked the liquid from his hand, took a step toward her, and then suddenly stopped. His eyes rolled back, and he collapsed to the floor. Mac smiled slyly at him and then collected her duffel bag.

"We'll play again some other time," she announced sweetly. "Nighty night."

She hoisted the bag over her shoulder and left through the main door. Kirk crawled across the floor and attempted to reach his discarded gun, but by the time his fingers touched the handle, she was gone.

"Son-of-a-bitch," Kirk snarled then collapsed to the floor with a groan.

✝

*B*ogart slowly woke to Ross crouching over him and lightly slapping his face. He groaned while clutching his head and nearly fell back to the floor alongside the bed.

"It was that bitch, Tonya," he muttered to Ross.

Ross stood over him while Monroe stood just inside the doorway holding an assault rifle.

"And you were supposed to keep an eye on her," Ross snarled his annoyance for the newcomer. "How the hell did she get the slip on you?"

Bogart frowned and shrugged. "Just one of those things," he replied lowly.

"You rolled over and fell asleep," Monroe launched back with disgust.

"No, I didn't roll over and fall asleep," Bogart snapped while glaring at Monroe. He then fell silent and groaned. "That girl has the stamina of a mechanical bull."

"I knew it was a mistake depending on you," Ross remarked and pointed a demanding finger at him. "You had one assignment. Keep an eye on Tonya, and you blew it!"

"We'll find her," Bogart announced and attempted to stand, although he was having a difficult time maintaining his balance from his head injury. He made it to his knees and stopped, clutching the bed to keep from falling.

"She's gone," Ross launched back with a look of rage in his eyes. "She's gone and they took Lee!"

Bogart stared at Ross and the look of hostility on his face. He frowned, unable to hide the shame of his incompetence. Ross turned to Monroe.

"Find the others," he demanded. "I want to know why Beck hasn't reported the location of those roaming the property. Make sure nothing happened to him."

Monroe nodded, cast a glare at Bogart, and then hurried from the room with his assault rifle. Ross looked back at Bogart, who remained kneeling on the floor alongside the bed while clutching the mattress for support.

"Your assignment is over," Ross snarled. "We're dropping you off in town, and I don't ever want to see you again."

"I messed up, I know," Bogart said in an apologetic tone. "But I can fix this."

"I told you that woman was up to something," Ross lashed out. "I told you she needed to be watched. Kirk said she called someone yesterday afternoon. You knew the score, and you blew it! If any of my men are dead because of your fuck-up, you're going to wish you never met me!"

Ross turned and left the room. Bogart allowed his hand to fall from his bleeding temple. He frowned while pulling himself up from his knees and collapsed into a sitting position on the bed. He lowered his head and clasped his hands between his knees.

"I'll make this right," he muttered softly.

Chapter Twenty-nine

*T*he helicopter touched down just three hours later toward the back of the partially renovated lodge. Ross, Monroe, Kirk, and Zack hurried for the helicopter, each carrying a duffel bag. They tossed their gear into the storage compartment as the helicopter's rotors slowed. Jackie climbed out of the front, tossed her headset on the seat, and glared at the already grumpy men.

"How the hell did you lose both witnesses?" she demanded then considered. "*And* a team member? I haven't seen Holden this angry since, well, since I left him handcuffed to a bed."

All four men cast glares at Bogart as he approached with less enthusiasm. Ross looked back at Jackie.

"It's a long story," Ross muttered through gritted teeth. "Was Holden able to locate any private planes taking off in the time frame I'd given him?"

"There was one heading to Chicago in your time frame. He's almost certain that's them," Jackie announced as she attempted to collect her emotions. "Holden has men at the major airports and at several private fields. If they're expecting a welcome party, the plane is small enough to land just about anywhere, and you're shit out of luck."

"How much of a head start do they have on us?" Monroe asked as he approached.

"They took off two hours ago. They must have had a plane waiting at the same private airfield where I landed," Jackie informed him. "The guy who lent me the helicopter confirmed a plane took off shortly before I arrived. If they are heading to the Chicago area, they'll be landing in about an hour."

"It'll take us a little more than three hours to reach Chicago from here," Ross remarked and groaned. "If Holden's men don't intercept them, they'll have a two-hour head start on us."

"Hey, I got here as fast as I could," Jackie remarked. "But I can shave a half an hour off your flight time once we reach the private plane, if I break a few laws."

"Do what you can." He looked at the others. "We need to go--now," Ross informed his men.

They climbed into the helicopter. Bogart prepared to climb aboard but lacked enthusiasm. Jackie studied his defeated look then folded her arms across her chest.

"I assume this was your screw-up."

"I don't want to talk about it," Bogart muttered then climbed into the back with the others.

Jackie shook her head and jumped into the pilot's seat.

✝

*T*he private plane no sooner landed before the steps dropped. The remaining members of Whiskey Tango Foxtrot wasted little time running down the steps with their gear slung over their shoulders. Bogart took his time walking down the steps with his bag nearly dragging behind him. Jackie followed him and studied his defeated attitude. It was possibly the first time she appeared sympathetic toward the man.

"You'd better hurry," she informed him, resuming her tough girl act. "They're liable to leave you behind."

He barely glanced at her. Any spark of the man he used to be had burned out.

"I'm already being left behind," Bogart muttered while avoiding eye contact with the attractive pilot. "I've been served my walking papers. You called it, as usual. I screwed up, and it may have cost Lee and Beck their lives."

The four men tossed their bags into an awaiting vehicle. Jackie stared at him a moment then shook her head. She left the defeated Bogart by the plane and approached the men to say her goodbyes. Jackie stopped before Ross and handed him the car keys.

"Thanks for setting up everything for us," Ross announced while accepting the keys from her.

"Yes, it's a cycle of never ending favors," she informed him with little emotion. Jackie drew a deep breath then casually indicated

160

Bogart by the plane. "You know, Bogart is a bigger asset than you give him credit. I don't know what he did to fall from your good graces, but I'm willing to bet you didn't give him the benefit of the doubt either."

Ross tossed his head back and groaned lowly. "Jackie, don't defend the guy."

"Just because he drives me insane, that doesn't change the fact that the man saved my ass," she informed him. "He'll eat you out of house and home, but he's loyal and trustworthy. He's also a good conman." She studied Ross, who just stared back at her with a look of disinterest. "You *need* a good conman."

Ross took Jackie's hand in his and gently kissed the back of it. He then patted her hand and smirked. "You, my dear, are a major pain in the ass." He released her hand then looked at Bogart by the plane. "Let's go!" Ross gruffly indicated for Bogart to get in the vehicle.

Bogart appeared surprised by the order directed at him. He grabbed his bag and hurried for the car. Bogart secretly smiled at Jackie then joined the others. Jackie watched them drive away and sighed softly.

"Thank God," she muttered softly. "I was afraid he'd follow me home again."

†

*L*ee slowly woke and looked around the moderately familiar yet somehow unfamiliar living room. She could see the glass balcony doors overlooking the familiar corner of Chicago. She recognized that view, except this view was from a higher angle. Lee then realized she was in Sal's penthouse suite. She'd only been in his suite a few times for various reasons in her short career with the company. She struggled against the plastic zip ties binding her wrists in front of her. Lee had a limited working knowledge of zip ties, but she knew there was no way she was slipping out of them or cutting them without very sharp tools. She looked around the room and saw a man standing guard just inside the door. He wasn't familiar to her, although he was rather intimidating.

It didn't take long for Lee to remember briefly coming face-to-face with Jericho in the woods. The sun was shining through the glass balcony doors, indicating she'd been out several hours. She glanced at the elegant grandfather clock just across the room. It was eleven o'clock in the morning Chicago time. Thoughts of Tonya crossed her mind. She didn't know what happened to her friend. Perhaps Tonya escaped, but there was no telling at this point. She didn't even know if the men from Whiskey Tango Foxtrot made it out alive. Lee was almost positive the man by the door wasn't going to offer her any information on her friend or the team who laid down their lives to protect her. She did find it interesting that they took her alive. Why not kill her? Of course, if they didn't kill her, perhaps that meant they wouldn't have killed Tonya either.

Despite preparing for the worst, she was going to stay positive and believe the others were alive. She needed to stay focused, and getting herself upset over the possible death of her friend wasn't going to help her situation any. She then heard Jericho's familiar voice. Lee strained to listen. It sounded like it was coming from one of the nearby bedrooms.

"They're going to be looking for her," Jericho's voice announced faintly from the other room. "We can't afford to have anyone accidentally finding that man in the mansion basement. It's going to be a madhouse by late afternoon. I want the four of you to go out there. Remove the prisoner and find Tonya before the guests start arriving."

Lee's mind was racing with her newly found information. Was Tonya being held at the mansion? Was that *other* man Gil? What day was it? It was Saturday! Today was Sal's birthday party being held at his mansion. All her co-workers would be there along with around two hundred guests. Jericho entered the living room while replacing his cell phone to his jacket pocket. He looked at her, saw that she was awake, and smirked.

"Well, look who's awake," he announced cheerfully.

"What am I doing here?" she demanded. "What is it you want from me?"

"You mean, why didn't we kill you and make our lives that much easier?" he asked then snorted a soft laugh. "You really don't know the information you hold, do you?"

"If I had any information, I would have given it to Agent Falcone," she informed him. "What makes you think I know anything?"

"Before Wiley died, he gave you something of great value," Jericho informed her.

"A flash drive, or so you seem to think," she announced simply. "I certainly don't have it."

"Yes, he gave you a flash drive disguised as lipstick, but there was nothing on it," Jericho replied.

Lee stared at him with surprise. "You mean that gold tube--?"

"Yeah, the one you so kindly tried to jam in my eye," Jericho snarled. "Wiley was a smart man. Smart enough to discover the money we'd been filtering through certain accounts. He was also smart enough to hide that money in the cyber world so we'd never find it. Planting that flash drive on you was too easy. There was nothing on it but a bunch of family photos. He must have given you something else."

"He didn't give me anything," she insisted.

"He was going to meet you that night at the diner," Jericho remarked. "Whatever he gave you, he intended to recover that night at the diner. Think real hard. What did Wiley give you?"

Lee didn't want to think *real* hard. She didn't want to do anything he told her to do. She knew Wiley hadn't given her anything; although, she hadn't realized he'd slipped her the flash drive either. Her curiosity got the better of her, and she gave her last encounter with Wiley some consideration. The contents of her purse had been scattered across his office floor. Wiley helped her collect her belongings. Apart from the lipstick flash drive, that she hadn't realized he'd slipped her, she couldn't think of anything added to her purse.

"I'm sorry," she announced firmly. "If he gave me something, I have no idea what it was."

"That's okay," Jericho announced cheerfully. "You have all night to think about it. No one's going to come here looking for you. If they go anywhere, it'll be the mansion. All they'll find there is a party in progress."

There was a knock on the door. The guard looked through the peek hole then opened the door. Another man entered and approached Jericho, who stood when he saw him.

"Did you get it?" Jericho eagerly asked.

The man revealed a paper bag and gave it a shake. "Several doses of the good stuff for our special guest," the man replied.

The man approached the coffee table and removed a vile containing liquid and a hypodermic needle. Lee suddenly tensed. The man grinned at Lee.

"Don't worry," he informed her. "This is the good stuff. Not that shit from the street. You're going to feel *real* good. Your mind will be open to anything and everything." The man eyed Jericho and grinned. "I'm thinking party time."

Jericho rolled his eyes and shook his head with obvious disgust. "You can do whatever you want with her *after* you get the information we need."

Lee stared at the needle the man held and felt alarm sweeping through her body. She wasn't entirely sure what was in the vile, but she didn't want any part of it or the man, who seemed eager to play doctor.

"Doping me up isn't going to give me information I don't have," she quickly announced but knew it wasn't going to change their minds.

"Are you sure of the dose?" Jericho asked the man.

He drew some of the solution into the needle then eyed Jericho. "Yeah, I got the information from a friend of mine at the hospital. The first shot will relax her, but it'll take twenty to thirty minutes. My friend said to make sure the room was quiet and dark for the best results. Once she's good and relaxed, the second dose will open her to suggestion and free her mind."

Jericho approached the balcony and closed the blinds, darkening the suite. Lee attempted to move away from the man with the needle. Jericho and the guard grabbed her, pinned her to the sofa, and allowed the second man to inject her in the arm with the needle. She attempted to fight them, but with her wrists bound and the men holding her down, fighting was useless. They held her immobile as the man inserted the needle into a vein in the crook of her arm. She jumped from the pinch, and her heart raced at the thought of the drugs entering into her bloodstream. Once he removed the needle from her arm, they released her. At first, she didn't feel anything. Within minutes, her ears started ringing and the room became fuzzy.

"Now, we wait," the man informed Jericho.

Chapter Thirty

Gil sat casually relaxed on the chair within the dank basement room at Romano's estate while playing a game on his cell phone. There was no reception available in the basement, so the game was his only form of entertainment. He glanced at his watch, appeared bored, and groaned softly.

"One more night, Ross," he muttered. "If I don't hear from you, I'm out of here."

The sound of Darth barking in the corridor alerted Gil of approaching company. He lunged across the room, replaced his cell phone on the table, and returned to his chair. He attached the handcuff on the chair to his wrist. Male voices were heard in the hallway, although they attempted to keep their voices down.

"Find Tonya," the man ordered. "We'll take care of this one. The boss doesn't want him disrupting the birthday celebration this afternoon."

Gil listened to the conversation, considered his options, and immediately unlocked the handcuff with his pick, so it only appeared to be latched. The door opened and two men entered along with Darth. One of the men stood by the closed door while the first approached Gil, who looked up at him with little emotion. The man smirked at him as he removed his gun affixed with a silencer from his hidden shoulder holster.

"I'm afraid your time is up," the man announced and aimed the gun.

"Don't I get any last words?" Gil asked casually.

The man lowered the gun and appeared humored by the request. "Sure, why not?"

Gil stared into the man's eyes and calmly spoke in German. The man before him appeared baffled until he heard Darth snarl. He turned just in time to see Darth attack the man standing by the door. Gil kicked upward; knocking the gun from the man's hand, then sprang from his chair and punched him several times until he collapsed to the floor. Darth had the man by the door on the floor and violently shook him by his arm, keeping him off balance. Gil said something in German, allowing Darth to release the man's arm. Gil then punched the man in the head, knocking him unconscious with a single blow. Gil straightened and looked at Darth.

"You make an excellent partner," he announced. "Now, we need to tie up these two. It sounds like we have a damsel in distress to save."

†

*G*il, along with his canine counterpart, slipped into the kitchen only a few minutes later. He suddenly stopped to see that the kitchen was alive with activity. There were caterers in white chef jackets and wait staff in black jackets rushing in every direction attempting to arrange everything for the party. Gil stopped one of the female caterers and offered a tiny, embarrassed smile.

"I seem to have misplaced my jacket," he announced. "I laid it down, and now it's gone."

"Someone left one on the chair by the table," she announced and indicated the kitchen table.

"That must be it," he replied cheerfully while smiling sweetly. "Thanks."

She returned the smile while admiring his broad shoulders and athletic build.

"Anytime," the female caterer replied.

Gil appeared flattered by the way she gave him a quick once over. He then hurried to the table, grabbed the discarded jacket, and slipped into. He picked up an empty silver tray. Guests were already starting to arrive and flooded the backyard set up for an extravagant, garden party. Gil carried his tray and headed into the hallway. He approached the foyer then stopped when he saw Sal on the stairs. Sal was staring at the front door with a transfixed look and then hurried down the steps to greet his guest. Pinto stood inside the doorway, dressed casually elegant for the garden party. She attempted a smile as Sal approached her. He appeared awkward a moment while seemingly deciding if hugging her would be appropriate. He opted to hold his arms open. Pinto smiled gently and allowed him to embrace her. He pulled back and secretly wiped the tear from his eye.

"I didn't think you were coming," Sal said softly with a quiver in his voice.

"I had a change of heart," she announced while appearing stiff and awkward. "I felt as if I needed to be here."

"Let's go to the study," he announced, "so we can have some privacy."

They headed in the opposite direction. Once they were gone, Gil slipped through the foyer and headed up the stairs with Darth on his heels.

✝

*T*he black SUV pulled up alongside a white catering van as well as a black sedan in a vacant lot. Holden casually leaned against the van and watched as the five men piled out of the SUV and approached him. Ross eyed the white van with a caterer's logo on the side.

"What's with the van?"

"I was able to commandeer a van from the catering company serving Romano's party today," Holden announced. "This should be your ticket onto Romano's estate."

"I'm guessing you weren't able to stop them at the airport," Ross remarked.

"They must have landed at an abandoned airfield," Holden announced. "We couldn't cover all of them, but my men have confirmed that a woman matching Mac's description entered Romano's estate. Without proof that she had abducted anyone, I couldn't obtain a search warrant. I need proof."

"No, you need us to go in there and rescue your witness," Kirk remarked.

"Well, you were the ones who lost her in the first place," Holden snarled.

"We'll get her back," Ross assured him.

"There's more," Holden announced. "Romano's right hand man, Finn, has been casing the office building."

"Casing?" Monroe suddenly asked. "Why would he be casing a building he has unrestricted access to?"

"That's a good question," Holden replied. "I'm guessing he's waiting for someone. My men reported his car was last seen entering

167

the parking garage, so I'm guessing whatever he was waiting for has arrived."

"So Lee could be at the office building or at the mansion," Ross remarked.

"Exactly," Holden replied. "I have a few men ready and waiting for my command at both locations, but I need proof before we storm either building."

"You don't need proof," Zack replied casually. "All you need is reports of gunfire, and you're golden."

"Yeah, well, let's call that 'plan B'."

Zack grinned. "I like 'plan B'."

Ross turned toward his men. "I want Zack and Monroe in the catering van at the mansion. Dress appropriately and try to blend in. There will be a lot of party guests." He glared at Zack. "This isn't a clean sweep. If there's any gunplay, you'd better be sure of your target." He then looked at Kirk and motioned for him to follow. "Kirk, you're with me at the office building."

Bogart tensed and stared at Ross. "What about me?"

"You're with Holden," Ross replied.

Holden and Bogart began to protest simultaneously.

"There's no way in hell--" Holden bellowed.

"I can make this right," Bogart insisted. "Let me prove I can do this."

Ross groaned softly then motioned him with Zack and Monroe. "Don't make me regret including you."

Chapter Thirty-one

The white catering van pulled up to the closed front gate of Romano's mansion. A heavyset security guard immediately approached the van. With a skeptical look on his face and a quick once over of the van, the security guard eyed Monroe sitting behind the wheel. He consulted his clipboard then looked back at the driver and raised a clever brow.

"A little late, aren't you?" the guard asked in a gruff tone while eyeing Monroe and Bogart's chef jackets.

"There was some confusion with the dessert," Monroe announced. "But we have it straightened out now."

"I'll have to see your identification badges," the guard remarked without looking away from Monroe or Bogart in the passenger seat. He was a stern man and wasn't about to back down.

Monroe patted down his jacket then made a face, expressing his surprise. He groaned softly and looked at the guard.

"I left it inside," Monroe announced. "I can get it and bring it back out to you--"

"No," the guard informed him. "I'll call up to the kitchen and have one of the other caterers vouch for you."

The guard was about to turn away from the window when Bogart extended a small platter of puffy pastries. He grinned boyishly.

"Creampuff?"

The guard looked at the small creampuffs on the tray and attempted to hide his smile as he took one.

"Well, maybe one," the guard announced then bit into the pastry. He smiled his approval. "Delicious."

"I doubt there'll be any left by the time you're able to join the party," Bogart announced.

"Join?" the guard demanded. "I'll be lucky if they bring a doggie bag out for me. We're not allowed to attend. I guess we're not special enough."

"Of course not," Bogart muttered while shaking his head. "You just protect the entire estate, that's all." He handed the guard the tray past Monroe. "Here, you take these. You've earned them. We'll collect the tray on our way out tonight. No one will notice a dozen are missing."

The guard accepted the tray and grinned. "That's kind of you." He approached the guardhouse and pressed a button, opening the gate. "Go on; get to work."

Bogart smiled and gave the guard a thumbs up. Monroe put the van into gear and drove through the gate. They pulled around back and parked alongside the other catering vans. Zack jumped out the back door dressed in a stylish, expensive suit. He immediately fiddled with the tie. Bogart and Monroe jumped out and shed their chef's jackets to reveal their suits as well.

"Let's mingle, boys," Monroe announced and headed toward the party in the backyard. "Zack, you know what to do--"

Both men looked back but Zack was already gone, his tie discarded on the ground. Monroe shook his head.

"I swear, he's a shape shifter," Monroe remarked. "Once we have eyes on Jericho, you'll keep him occupied while I slip into the house."

"And if Jericho doesn't show?" Bogart asked. "He is, after all, a wanted man."

"We'll scan the crowd," Monroe announced. "If we don't see him in ten minutes, we'll split up. You'll take the basement, and I'll take the second floor."

"Where's Zack going to be?" Bogart asked.

"Who knows," Monroe muttered. "He's probably in Moscow by now. Keep an eye out for Mac. She's the only one here who'll be able to identify us."

"Maybe you," Bogart informed him then grinned. "She and I have plans to hookup sometime." He appeared starry-eyed. "A boy; a girl; a chance meeting at a garden party--I can work that angle on so many levels."

"Fine, if we run into Mac, she's all yours," Monroe remarked and headed into the crowd.

Something caught Bogart's attention, and his expression suddenly dropped. He grabbed Monroe's arm and pulled him back, startling him.

"I think we may have one more obstacle," Bogart announced softly then indicated the terrace with his eyes.

Pinto walked with Sal across the patio and toward the crowd of people. Sal held her hand linked onto his arm with pride and introduced her to his guests. Monroe stared at her a moment then looked at Bogart and shielded his face.

"What's she doing here?" Monroe muttered.

"I don't know, but she could blow our cover," Bogart announced softly. "She knows we have a hard-on for her father and plan to interrupt his illegal operations. If she's made nice with him, she might tell him about our meeting with her."

Monroe patted Bogart on the shoulder. "Good luck avoiding her," he announced. "I'm heading inside."

Before Bogart could protest, Monroe was already halfway to the house.

†

*G*il and the dog quietly hurried along the second floor hallway.

He stopped before each door, listened a moment, and then peered inside every room. All the rooms were empty and unlocked. He reached the door at the far end of the hallway and tried to open it. It was the only locked door. He looked at Darth, who stared up at him.

"I think we have a winner," he said softly to the dog.

The dog let out a low woof in response. Gil removed his lock pick device and worked on the door lock. Darth waited patiently outside the door with his nose just below the lock. The dog was anxious to enter. Gil slowly opened the door, allowing Darth to slip in first. He then entered behind the dog and looked around the room. Darth ran across the room to Tonya, who was bound with duct tape to a large, decorative chair with duct tape over her mouth to keep her quiet. She saw Gil and attempted to call out to him. Gil shut the door behind him and hurried across the room toward her. He gently removed the duct tape from her mouth.

"Are you okay?" he asked while working on removing the duct tape tying her wrists to the arms of the chair.

"I'm fine now," she replied and watched him work on the tape binding her. "They said you'd been captured."

"Being a prisoner is subjective," he replied. "It all depends on what side of the bars you're standing."

He removed the duct tape from her right wrist then heard the door open. Gil quickly straightened and turned along with Darth. Zack stood inside the room and stared at Tonya with surprise then looked at Gil.

"Leave her," Zack announced firmly.

"Yes, sweetie," Mac hissed from where she stood just behind Zack. "Leave her."

Zack spun around, prepared for a fight with Mac. Although already prepared to block the punch he knew was coming, she was faster than he was. She kicked Zack in the side and sent him off balance. Zack recovered before Mac could get in a second kick, and he responded with his own kick, striking her in the abdomen. She was sent bounding into the nearby dresser with a thunderous crash. Barely fazed by the hard hit and sudden stop, Mac lunged for Zack with a flying roundhouse kick. Zack blocked the kick, but he was still thrown across the room. He struck the wall hard enough to knock framed pictures to the floor. He dodged her flying foot that came close to striking him in the face and punched her in the thigh, nearly dropping her.

Gil removed the duct tape from Tonya's ankles while she worked on the tape on her left wrist. Gil pulled her to her feet and hurried her from the room past the fighting couple. He hurried her along the second floor corridor and into the bedroom across the hall. Tonya ran for the bathroom with Darth on her heels. She said something to the dog in German. Darth ran into the bathroom. Tonya shut the door, locking the dog inside. Gil turned from the bedroom door, saw her by the bathroom, and heard Darth barking from behind the closed door. As he approached, Tonya revealed a candlestick and struck Gil on the head, knocking him to the floor. She looked down at the unconscious man while Darth barked, snarled, and scratched at the closed bathroom door.

"Sorry, Gil," she announced and casually tossed the candlestick aside. "It's nothing personal."

Chapter Thirty-two

*W*ithin Sal's penthouse suite, Lee was sprawled across the arm of the sofa with her head leaning back against the headrest. She wasn't sure where she was anymore, although she was no longer tied. In the dimly lit living room, she could only hear the faint sounds of the city beyond the nearly soundproof balcony doors. Her body felt heavy yet oddly light with a tingling sensation, which she couldn't decide whether or not it was pleasant. She could hear someone screaming her name, although she didn't know why. She didn't know where it was coming from, but the man's voice brought her out of her daze and into reality. As she looked across the hazy room, she saw Beck, with his hands bound behind his back, fighting two men who attempted to pull him toward the main door. He looked directly at her while screaming her name. Despite being restrained, he put up a good fight.

"Lee!" he shouted. "Lee, run!"

She didn't know why he was telling her to run. She was running. It was a beautiful summer day, and she was running through a meadow covered in flowers. She smiled at Beck and waved. He stopped struggling while staring at her with alarm. He then looked at Jericho across the room.

"What did you do to her?" Beck demanded. "If you hurt her, I'll kill you!"

"Shut him up," Jericho announced.

The first man placed a cloth over Beck's mouth and nose, while attempting to subdue him. He struggled against the drug-soaked cloth then slowly sank to the floor.

"Load him in the van," Jericho ordered his men. "I'm taking him to the mansion personally. I don't know what his friends are up to, but if they don't back off, we'll kill him." Jericho turned to the man sitting quietly in the chair near the glass balcony doors. "I'll leave a man outside the door. The rest will be in the lobby and the parking garage. Do you think you can get her to remember what Wiley gave her?"

"I'll get it out of her," he casually announced. "Remember our deal. I get her before you eliminate her."

"Yeah, whatever," Jericho muttered, seeming disinterested. "The information first."

Jericho left with the two men, who carried Beck from the suite. Lee waved to Beck while hanging over the back of the sofa. As she turned on the sofa, her capture was now sitting alongside her with a sly grin on his face. He placed his hand on her leg and rubbed her inner thigh.

"You and I are going to have a little fun while we wait for the happy drugs to kick in," he announced and moved closer to her.

He placed his hand to her face and kissed her aggressively on the mouth. Lee pushed against him as her arms tensed. She was somehow stronger than she thought. Her emotions took over and she started screaming while thrashing her fists against his chest in an uncontrolled fit of rage.

"Get away! Get away!" she screamed in a shrill voice she didn't even recognize as her own.

The room was becoming clearer as her senses were aroused by her surroundings. The faster her heart pounded, the more invigorated she felt. He attempted to keep her flying fists from striking his chest. She screamed and ran her fingernails across his cheek, leaving four deep scratches, and drawing blood.

"Get away! Get away!"

The man jumped up from the sofa while clutching his bleeding cheek. He stared at her with surprise. She was now enraged while glaring at him like a wild woman.

"Maybe we'll let the drugs work a little while longer," he remarked then grabbed the discarded syringe on the coffee table. "Then it's a slightly stronger dose to seal the deal."

Lee attempted to control her breathing while glaring at him. She could hear a growling sound then realized it was coming from her. She had a strange urge to bite the man and kept her eyes locked on him as he crossed the room. He finally moved out of her line of sight, allowing her to relax again. Her breathing slowed, and she once more ran through the meadow.

✝

A black sedan was parked halfway across the parking garage on the main level. A federal agent sat behind the wheel and kept watch of the entrance to the building. He appeared mostly bored and rubbed his temple. The agent groaned softly, removed his cell phone, and pressed a single number. He immediately smiled when the caller answered.

"Hey, honey," he said warmly into the phone. "I'm going to be another few hours." There was a brief pause as he listened in response. He chuckled softly. "Just Holden and his paranoia. He has me casing a parking garage. I don't know what he's expecting to happen here. The place is dead."

The exit door opened, catching the agent's attention. His expression turned serious a moment. He attempted a smile while returning his attention to his phone call.

"I'll see you in a few hours, okay? Love you," he announced then disconnected the call.

He watched the man exit through the open door. Despite the baseball cap, it was evident the man was Jericho.

"Well, I'll be damned," the agent proclaimed softly.

He reached into his pocket for his cell phone. Something moved past his driver's side window. The agent looked at the window alongside him. A black blur stood before the window, but all the agent saw was the silencer of a semiautomatic aimed at him. The nearly silent shot pierced the glass, striking him in the head. Blood spattered against the inner passenger side window.

✝

*L*ee ran across the meadow, feeling free and almost weightless. She then saw the silhouette of a man across the field. To her surprise, he was wearing a cowboy hat and cowboy boots. He was the man of her dreams, and he'd come for her! She ran toward him with childish glee. She fell into his arms, and they rolled around the meadow together. It felt good being in his strong arms as she lie in the meadow. Lee met his gaze and found herself staring at Ross. He leaned in closer and kissed her passionately. She eagerly returned the kiss. Lee opened her eyes and realized she was kissing the man with the scratches on his face. He lowered her to the sofa while aggressively kissing her. She attempted to fight him and the hands

175

that firmly traveled her body, but she felt weak. His weight was enough to keep her pinned.

The familiar sound of a gun cocking echoed through the nearly silent room causing the man to freeze on top of Lee. He broke off the kiss and slowly turned his head toward the barrel of the gun aimed at his temple just inches away. Lee looked as well. Finn stared with an unpredictable sneer on his face while looking down the barrel of the gun at the man. He cracked his neck and rolled his shoulders without breaking his evil stare at her capture.

"Now I know you weren't thinking about molesting the young lady," Finn announced in an almost playful tone, although the look on his face was anything but playful. His look was psychotic.

"I wouldn't dream of it," the man replied and slowly moved to his knees near Lee's legs.

Finn rounded the sofa while keeping his gun aimed at the man with the scratches on his face. He casually eyed the syringe then looked back at the man and grinned.

"Having a little party?" Finn asked then indicated the syringe. "Join in, my friend. Let's all party."

"What?"

"You heard me," Finn announced in a firm tone with less of a smile. "Join the party. What's good for the goose and all that bullshit." He again indicated the syringe with a look. "You can either stick that needle in your vein, or I can put a bullet in your temple." His playful grin turned into a sneer as he tightened his finger on the trigger. "Do it, friend."

The man took the syringe and injected it into his arm. Finn immediately frowned and shook his head.

"Now we both know that ain't nearly as effective a route," Finn announced.

The man casually tossed the syringe aside, having dispensed the contents into his muscle rather than his vein. The drug's effect would be slower and less potent injected into his muscle. His smirk mocked Finn. Finn again cracked his neck and rotated his shoulders. A strange, twisted smile crossed his face.

"Good thing I'm a resourceful man," Finn announced then sneered and struck the man alongside his head with his gun.

The man dropped backward onto the sofa, his head bleeding from the hit. He was obviously out cold.

"Enjoy your little nap, friend," Finn announced then looked back at Lee with a pleased grin.

Lee was already stumbling toward the penthouse door. Finn slung his head back and groaned while rolling his eyes.

"Seriously? You're running away from me?" he demanded then reconsidered while watching her stumble to maintain her balance. He appeared slightly humored. "Well, *meandering* perhaps." His expression then turned irritable. "I just saved your life, little darling. A heart felt thank you seems appropriate."

Finn casually strutted behind her while grinning. She attempted to open the door, but he easily pushed it shut. Lee leaned forward on the table near the door for support while Finn hovered over her from behind with a cheap grin on his face.

"How about we stop playing games," he announced and leaned over her shoulder. "Admit you're hopelessly in love with me, so we can move on to the next stage in our unusual relationship."

Lee spun around, and with all her strength, struck him in the head with a decorative candlestick. Finn clutched his bleeding head and fell to his knees. Lee opened the door and stumbled into the hallway, nearly tripping over the unconscious guard just outside the penthouse. She clung to the wall and managed a slow jog toward the elevator. She pressed the button and attempted to maintain her balance while darting looks between the lit floor numbers and the open penthouse door.

"Damn it, Lee," Finn was heard shouting from within the penthouse. "You're starting to piss me off!"

Finn stumbled from the penthouse with blood streaking the side of his face. The elevator door opened. Lee nearly fell inside the elevator as Finn ran for her. She repeatedly struck the 'close' button. The door closed just as Finn reached it. Finn slammed his hand against the closed elevator door and then ran for the stairs. No sooner had Finn vanished down the stairs when an electronic hum came from the stairs on the opposite end of the penthouse corridor. Ross and Kirk appeared from the stairwell with their semiautomatics leading the way. They approached the penthouse door and paused just outside. Both suspiciously eyed the unconscious man on the floor. Kirk inserted an official penthouse keycard into the lock. The green light lit. Kirk pushed open the door with his back and entered the penthouse with his gun aimed and ready to fire. Ross filed in after him.

Ross discovered the unconscious man lying on the sofa and the discarded needle on the coffee table. Both men fanned out in opposite directions and searched the large penthouse. When their search revealed the place was empty, Ross approached the unconscious man and looked at the unmarked vile. He frowned with disgust.

"Whatever happened here," Ross informed Kirk, "it looks like we only missed it by a few minutes."

"Did the guy overdose?" Kirk asked while indicating the man but kept his gun and his attention on surveying the penthouse for possible intruders.

"No, I don't think so," Ross replied. "Someone clocked him. I'd like to believe it was Lee. The mystery drug has to be something they wanted to use on her to open her mind perhaps. She may have gotten away, but we don't know if she's been sedated or who's after her."

"Damn it, Ross," Kirk snarled. "She could be anywhere in the building if someone is chasing her."

"Yes, I know," he replied. "I need you to wait by the parking garage exit. Hopefully, we didn't miss her already. I'm going to the floor she worked on. If she's being chased, there's a good chance she'd head someplace familiar." He tapped his earpiece transmitter. "Maintain contact."

Kirk nodded. Both men hurried for the penthouse door, jumped over the unconscious guard, and ran in opposite directions.

†

*L*ee sank against the wall of the elevator and held her breath a moment as she scrambled for a plan. She was having a difficult time thinking clearly, as the drugs clouded her thoughts. She pushed buttons six through lobby, so Finn wouldn't know what floor she actually departed the elevator. When the door opened, she hurried from the elevator onto the fifth floor. Lee paused a moment to hold her head, and waited for the hallway to stop spinning. As she looked around, she swore the walls were breathing. It was a frightening image, but she knew it wasn't real. She hurried along the hall as best she could and entered the first unlocked door she reached.

She shut and locked the suite door behind her and looked around at what appeared to be the lobby of a realtor's office. She stumbled across the lobby and entered the first office on the right. She shut and locked the door behind her, collapsed behind the desk, and again held her head. She didn't know how to make the room stop spinning. Once her vision cleared, she grabbed the nearby phone and pressed 911 onto the keypad. As she placed the phone to her ear, she realized there was no dial tone. She groaned and pressed several different buttons in an attempt to get an outside line. When she couldn't obtain one, she became frustrated and slammed the phone down. As she looked up and stared at the sprinklers above her, a

178

thought occurred to her. She returned to the office door and entered the hallway. She scanned the hallway then saw the fire alarm pull station only a few yards down the hall. Lee gathered her strength and hurried down the hall while clinging to the wall. It almost seemed as if the hallway was getting longer and the fire alarm was moving further away. She was determined to reach it. Help would come.

Chapter Thirty-three

*R*oss walked along the nineteenth floor corridor. The floor was quiet and seemed abandoned for the weekend, as was the rest of the building. Ross appeared defeated after finding no trace of Lee and tapped his earpiece.

"I've got nothing, Kirk," he announced while looking around. "I don't think she's been here."

"I'm just inside the parking garage," Kirk responded through Ross's earpiece. "I don't think anyone's left since we arrived. Seems quiet."

"Maybe we missed them," Ross announced as he cast his back against the wall. "You stay in the garage. I'm going to sweep the building. If she's here, we'll find her."

The fire alarm sounded, alerting Ross. He looked at the ceiling a moment then appeared encouraged.

"What's that?" Kirk asked through Ross's earpiece.

"That's Lee calling for help," Ross replied. "I know how to find her, but so will the guys hunting her."

Ross ran along the hallway and entered the computer closet. He hurried to a box on the wall and saw the potential fire was coming from the fifth floor in one of the suites.

"I have her," Ross announced then hurried from the computer closet and for the elevators past the receptionist's desk. "She's on the fifth floor."

"Should I meet you there?" Kirk asked.

The lights above the elevators indicated both were moving. He pressed the elevator button, hoping to slow the bad guys' approach and then ran for the stairs.

"No, you wait in the garage in case I lose her," Ross informed him. "She's got company closing in on her."

Ross hurried through the fire doors and ran down the stairs, hoping somehow to beat them to the fifth floor.

✝

*O*nly a moment or two had passed when the alarm suddenly silenced. Lee lifted her head from where she sat on the floor beneath the fire alarm pull station and stared at the ceiling. What had happened? Who turned off the alarm? She wanted to stand, but she didn't have the strength to pull herself to her feet. She crawled across the floor to a small table in the lobby and attempted to pull herself up. She heard a tremendous crack as the suite door was kicked open. Lee expected to see Finn, but it was another unfamiliar man with a gun in his hand. He kept the gun aimed at her as he approached.

"No sudden moves, sweetheart," the man announced. "The boss wants you alive."

The man suddenly cried out and fell to the floor near her feet. She let out a startled scream then looked up to see Finn sneering at the man while cracking his neck. He then glared at her and pointed a warning finger.

"You are your own worst enemy," he announced sharply then extended his hand to her.

She jumped away from his hand, although she knew she couldn't stand on her own and he'd be on her any second.

"We don't have time for this, little missy," he hissed and grabbed her arm.

Finn pulled her roughly to her feet, throwing her off balance. She fell into him. He caught her around the waist and hurried her toward the open suite door. She attempted to fight him, but it did little more than slow him down. Finn slammed her backward against the doorframe, pinning her body with his, and kept her from falling. He stared into her eyes with irritation.

"That little fire alarm stunt of yours just gave the others your exact location," he snarled. "Any moment, six heavily armed men are coming right here to end life as we know it. Now stop being a pain in my ass and let's get the hell out of here." He searched her frightened eyes. "At the moment, I'm all you've got. You need to trust me."

She stared back at him, not liking his body pressed against hers, but she almost had no choice. Lee slowly nodded. He moved away from her and caught her around the waist before she could sink to the floor. He half pulled and half carried her to the fire stairs. As they stepped into the stairway, the elevator dinged. Finn silently pulled the door closed and looked at Lee, who now clung to his shoulder.

"You're not going to like this," he announced, "but we're pressed for time and low on options."

Finn lowered himself before her and swiftly tossed her over his shoulder while clutching her just above the knees. She let out a startled gasp. He ran down the steps with her over his shoulder and his gun clutched firmly in his free hand. He glanced at her backside near his face only once and grinned at the sight.

"Pity we couldn't do this more often," he teased while taking the steps at a face pace.

Lee resisted the urge to scream as she watched the blurry steps behind them and bounced around on his shoulder. Every moment felt as if she was going to fly headfirst onto the concrete steps. As they reached the landing on garage level, the door burst open to reveal a man with a gun. He aimed his weapon at Finn. Finn shot the man in the chest, leaped over his fallen body, and out through the garage level door with Lee still over his shoulder. As he ran across the parking garage, his pace increased and her bouncing on his shoulder became almost unbearable. She was certain he was going to drop her.

When he reached his sedan, he barely stopped before slinging her off his shoulder and to her feet. She was unable to maintain her balance and felt dizzy to the point of passing out. She fell roughly against the car and immediately felt the surge of pain through her upper back. Finn opened the door, grabbed her without warning, and practically threw her into the passenger seat. Another man appeared from the doorway and fired at Finn as he approached the driver's side. Finn fired back with a barrage of bullets, forcing the man to take cover behind another car. Kirk appeared from several cars away and fired at Finn as well. Finn fired back at Kirk then jumped into the car with Lee. He started the car and burned out in reverse, skidding in a half circle before jetting forward with tires squealing. The man leaped out from behind the safety of his car and fired at Finn as he drove through the parking garage at high speeds. Kirk saw the man several cars away and aimed his gun at him.

"Drop the weapon," Kirk yelled.

The man turned and fired at Kirk. Kirk took cover behind another car then returned fire. Kirk tapped his earpiece.

"Ross, one of Sal's men has Lee. He's getting away in a black sedan. License plate delta alpha 3296," Kirk announced. "There's a shooter near the south stairs."

†

*R*oss stepped over the dead man in the realtor's office doorway and touched his earpiece while entering the hallway.

"I'm on my way," Ross announced as he hurried for the elevators. He removed his cell phone and pressed a button while waiting for the elevator. "Holden, one of Sal's goons has Lee. Black sedan. License plate delta alpha 3296 leaving the parking garage. Apprehend with caution."

The elevator dinged and the doors opened. Ross returned his phone to his jacket pocket, aimed his gun at the open elevator doors, and checked to see that it was empty. A man suddenly appeared from the far stairwell and fired at Ross. Ross fired back then dove into the elevator. He pressed the first floor button.

"I don't have time for gunplay," he muttered.

The man ran for the elevator as the doors were closing. He aimed his weapon. Ross fired first through the nearly closed doors. The man went down just as the doors shut.

†

*M*eanwhile, Finn continued to drive recklessly through the parking garage. Lee screamed while clinging to the center console and the passenger door as they flew around a sharp curve. They were speeding toward the exit. The wooden arm remained down across the exit and the chain-link fence was mysteriously lowering. Lee screamed with horror while Finn cried out with an excited howl. The sedan smashed through the wooden arm, shattering it, and just barely made it beneath the lowering fence. The car careened onto the street and took the sharp curve, sending the car in a semicircle, leaving behind a massive skid mark. Finn stepped on the gas and jetted along the road away from the office building. He looked into the rearview mirror then at Lee, who stared out the windshield with a horrified look on her face while clinging to the car.

"Now *that* was fun," Finn cried out enthusiastically. "Admit it, honey bunny; this is the best date you've ever been on."

Lee slowly turned her head and stared at him with her mouth hanging open. He laughed, obviously humored by her expression.

"Where are you taking me?" she finally demanded.

He appeared disappointed. "Not even a thank you? For a well-bred young lady, you're terribly rude."

"I'll thank you when you don't get me killed," she replied nearly out of breath from the drugs and the surge of adrenaline. "Where are you taking me?"

"I'm taking you someplace safe," he announced. "You're welcome."

A car suddenly appeared before them from a cross street, cutting off their route. Lee screamed.

"Seatbelts, please," Finn announced and turned the wheel sharply to avoid the car.

Men fired out the car's side window at them as the sedan squealed while turning. Finn stepped on the gas and sped along a side street while Lee frantically attempted to connect her seatbelt. The car chased after them.

†

A police car pulled into the parking garage past the shattered wooden arm. Both officers surveyed the damage as they drove past then pulled up to the entrance of the building. As they got out of the car, the driver removed his sidearm while the officer on the passenger side removed the shotgun. He pumped the shotgun, causing the distinctive clatter to echo throughout the nearly silent parking garage. As they approached the door, they saw a dead man lying behind the first car not far from the entrance.

"Ah, hell," the first officer muttered and quickly scanned the area with his shotgun leveled.

"I'll call it in," the second officer announced and reached for his shoulder radio.

The second officer suddenly fell to the concrete floor, startling the first officer. He looked at his fallen partner then turned in the direction of possible fire. Before he could even get a shot off, two nearly silent shots struck him and tossed him to the garage floor.

†

Several police cars now joined in on the race across the city, chasing after Finn's speeding car. Lee peered into the side mirror several times and each time witnessed yet another police car crash into a parked vehicle along the narrow alleyway. Her stomach had been fluttering and her heart pounding since she got in the car with Finn. Lee wasn't sure how long they were racing around the outskirts of the city attempting to lose the men shooting at them. She didn't even know where they were by that point. Finn pressed a button on the steering wheel.

"Talk to me," announced the familiar male voice over the car's speaker.

"Extraction of sweet cheeks was a success," Finn announced and ducked as the rear window shattered from a bullet. Lee screamed. "But we've got some rival suitors looking to claim her sweet, little ass."

"Where are you?" the voice Lee now recognized as Sal suddenly asked.

"Five minutes from your little soiree."

"Come in the back entrance," Sal said over the speaker. "I don't want my guests disturbed. Your friendly neighborhood fed just sent the agent at the back gate in search of you. You have a clear path."

"Yes, sir," Finn announced as he concentrated on his driving. "But you'd better have that gate open when we get there, because we're coming in hot."

"I'll have someone standing by."

Finn looked at Lee and grinned enthusiastically while raising his brows. "Expect a very sharp turn."

Lee again braced her hands on the door and center console. She saw the rear entrance of the estate just up ahead. The car chasing them was on their rear and continuing to fire at them. The gate started to open as they approached. The sedan skidded into a turn and jetted for the mostly open gate. Lee screamed, convinced they weren't going to make it. Sparks flew as the car scraped the gate. Once they were through, the gate began to close. The car behind them slammed on its brakes while making the turn and stopped before the mostly closed gate. Before the security guard could react, the car outside the gate peeled out in reverse and drove away. A few minutes later, the fed's SUV returned to the back gate. The agent stepped out of the vehicle and looked at the slightly bent gate then the guard, who simply stared back. The agent shook his head and removed his cell phone. He pressed a button and placed the phone to his ear.

"We lost the sedan, but I have a bad feeling they made it onto the estate grounds," he announced.

Holden cursed through the phone from the other end. The agent disconnected the call and groaned softly.

Chapter Thirty-four

Monroe entered the grand foyer inside Sal's mansion while casually looking around. When no one was looking, he swung around the banister and hurried up the stairs, taking them two at a time. He tapped his earpiece while glancing into several rooms along the second floor hallway.

"Zack, what's your location?"

There was no response. Monroe cursed softly under his breath and continued his search. A strange grunting sound came over his earpiece, causing him to stop in the hallway.

"Zack?" Monroe announced as his brows knitted. "You okay, buddy?"

Monroe kept his finger to his earpiece and turned toward the stairs to make sure no one had followed him.

"Zack, where are you?" he demanded in a whisper.

In the hallway several doors behind Monroe, Zack flew backward from a bedroom doorway and crashed into another room. Monroe turned and looked down the empty hall with a bewildered look, having heard a thump. He turned back toward the stairs and touched his earpiece.

"Damn it, Zack, answer me!"

Mac crossed the hallway behind Monroe and stormed into the room after Zack with a determined gait. There was another garbled groan through the earpiece. Monroe looked around then shook his head.

"You better not be playing games," he muttered aloud to himself then continued down the hallway.

As Monroe approached the bedroom down the hall, he heard the muffled sound of a dog barking. He appeared curious and hurried into the nearby bedroom on the left. Monroe suddenly stopped in the doorway to see Zack and Mac on the floor twisted together like a pretzel. There was a lot of grunting, and it was impossible to tell who was winning. Monroe stared at the couple a moment as if uncertain what to think until he saw the woman's face. His eyes widened with horror.

"Mac!"

Monroe reached inside his shoulder holster and removed his gun. In the second it took him to aim his gun, Mac had freed her leg from her bizarre hold on the immobile Zack and kicked the gun from Monroe's hand. Monroe chased after his flying gun and nearly tripped over Gil, whom he found gagged and tied with expensive silk neckties. He muffled a scream to Monroe while thrashing around on the floor. Monroe leaped to Gil's side and swiftly removed the gag then immediately worked on the neckties binding his wrists behind his back. Gil gasped then appeared angry.

"It was Tonya," he snarled with a look of mayhem in his eyes. "The little bitch hit me with a candlestick."

"Yeah, she pretty much fucked us all," Monroe muttered while working on the tight knot.

Zack was tossed over the bed with a bounce and struck the floor near them. He appeared slightly dazed then slowly moved into a crouched position and looked at his two friends, who just stared at him.

"Seriously?" Monroe demanded. "Are you going to let a girl kick the crap out of you?"

"Hey, feel free to step in anytime," Zack snarled back. "That demented demon bites!"

"What the fuck?" Gil lashed out hotly and appeared annoyed with Zack. "So do you!"

Zack suddenly grinned and raised his brows slyly. "Yeah, I got her good too."

Mac casually stood by the foot end of the bed and folded her arms across her chest while staring at them. She sneered at Zack with limited patience.

"I wasn't finished with you," she snapped in an icy tone while tapping her manicured fingernails on her arm.

Zack grinned at his friends. "Excuse me," he announced playfully. "Round two of foreplay."

He jumped to his feet, catapulted around the tall bedpost, and struck her in the chest with both feet. Mac flew backward and into the closet door, nearly knocking the wind from her. Both men watched with amazement and shook their heads. Once Gil's hands were free, he worked on untying his ankles while Monroe reclaimed his gun. Gil jumped to his feet, swayed slightly from his head injury, and then hurried to the bathroom door. Neither seemed particularly concerned for Zack's welfare.

"We need to get Tonya," Gil announced as he opened the bathroom door.

Darth ran out of the bathroom to join him. He greeted the dog with an affectionate ear scratch then turned to Monroe, ignoring the fighting man and woman by the closet.

"She couldn't have gotten far," Gil informed him. "They had her tied up, so she's no more welcome here than we are. She'll be looking for a way to sneak out."

"We don't know what her deal is," Monroe informed him in a firm tone. "She alerted Sal's men to ambush us at the lodge and abduct Lee."

Mac tossed Zack roughly to the floor with a thud not far from them. She straightened and glared at the two men, who now looked at her.

"She's not working for Sal," Mac informed them while giving each an irritated look. "She double-crossed Sal. She's the one who wants Lee, and she needs her alive."

Monroe and Gil stared at her with some disbelief.

"I thought they wanted her dead, because she was a witness," Monroe remarked.

"Tonya thinks Lee knows what Wiley did with the fifty million she stole," Mac informed him. "She has fifty million little reasons to keep Lee alive. I want the bitch as badly as you do. That's my boss's money."

"You attacked us at my beach house and at the lodge," Monroe informed her in an accusing tone.

"I didn't attack you," Mac snarled at Monroe. "I was sent to protect Lee and keep an eye on Tonya for suspicious behavior. Tonya must have contacted Jericho's men, who blew up your beach house. I guess that was before they realized they needed Lee alive for whatever information they thought she had." Mac folded her arms across her chest and glared at him. "I went to Colorado to talk to Sal's daughter on his behalf. I wanted to reason with the girl. She let it slip that people believed her father wanted Lee and Tonya killed. I realized it had to be your team. Sal's sources confirmed that a private plane was on its way to Colorado. I took a chance that it might be Jericho and staked out the only private airfield near that town."

The men exchanged looks as if deciding whether or not to believe her.

189

"I followed Jericho and his men to the lodge," Mac continued. "I intended to get Lee to safety, but they'd already gotten to her first, so I took the next best thing. Tonya."

Zack slowly moved to his feet and looked from his friends to Mac. "If you're telling the truth, why are we fighting?"

She glared while giving him a quick once over. "Because, you were too thickheaded to listen to me."

"You jumped me," Zack snapped with annoyance. "Not the other way around."

"I'm sure you deserved to be hit for something," she informed him.

Zack sneered and was about to lunge for her.

"Okay, wrap it up you two," Gil snarled at them. "You can kill each other later. Let's just find Tonya and work out what to do with her after we've captured her."

Mac smiled sweetly at Gil while cocking her head. "I'm good with that." She then looked at Zack and raised her brows seductively. "I think we determined I won that round, so let's all be friends."

Zack sneered and took a threatening step toward her. She maintained her smile and didn't even flinch to his advance, almost welcoming it.

"Let it go, Zack," Monroe growled. "Let's find Tonya. Find her and we'll find Lee."

"Lee's on her way someplace safe," Mac informed them. "She's in good hands." She then considered the comment and smirked. "Well, slightly tainted, moderately good hands."

Monroe tapped his ear then hesitated and looked around with surprise. "I lost my comlink." He looked at Zack. "Contact Bogart on yours."

"Bronco Betty destroyed mine when she kicked me in the head," Zack muttered.

"Bronco Betty?" Mac snarled.

Monroe groaned, removed his cell phone from his pocket, and pressed a single button as they headed for the bedroom door. Bogart's cheerful voicemail message began.

"Damn it, Bogart's phone went to voicemail," Monroe growled. "He's completely useless."

"He's still alive?" Gil asked and appeared curious. "Huh, I thought Kirk would have killed him by now."

They left the bedroom.

t

$\mathcal{B}$ogart stood among a group of four young women, who had mysteriously gathered around him, each taking turns to flirt with the handsome man. He suavely held his champagne glass and entertained them with humorous stories all while keeping careful watch of Pinto's movements. He glanced toward the servants' wing of the mansion and saw Finn and another man escorting Lee, in her weakened condition, into the mansion through the servants' entrance. His expression dropped slightly. He looked at his audience of four attractive women and smiled charmingly.

"If you ladies will excuse me," he announced. "I need to visit the little boy's room."

All four women were pleased with his charming way of excusing himself. Bogart walked away from the women and touched his earpiece.

"Zack, Monroe," he announced softly, so not to attract attention. "Do you read me?"

There was no response. He became frustrated while continuing his approach toward the patio entrance.

"Damn it, where are you guys?" he bellowed a little louder, although he seemed to catch the attention of several guests, who suspiciously eyed him.

There was still no response. Bogart smiled at the man who gave him a strange look to the conversation he was holding possibly with himself. As Bogart hurried into the mansion through the glass doors, Pinto stared across the garden and watched him with surprise. Her look was curious. She then scanned the crowd of guests, as if looking for something or someone.

Chapter Thirty-five

*F*inn and another man guided Lee into one of the empty bedrooms in the staff wing of the mansion. They assisted her to the double bed and helped her into a comfortable position against the headboard. Lee held her head and resisted passing out. Her head was now pounding in rhythm with her heartbeat. The other man whispered something to Finn then left the room. Lee glanced alongside the bed and saw a baseball bat between the bed and the nightstand. She contemplated if she could reach the bat in time, and if she had it in her to strike Finn with it. She shut her eyes and drew a deep, shaken breath. She didn't have it in her; not right now.

Finn locked the door behind him then approached Lee on the bed. She kept close watch on his every movement all while thinking about the baseball bat just two feet from her. She felt distrusting in her vulnerable condition, but she wasn't sure what she wanted to do about her situation or even if there was anything she could do. Lee felt she owed Finn the benefit of the doubt, at least until he gave her enough reason not to trust him. He sat on the edge of the bed near her feet while facing her.

"Feeling better?"

"No, not really," she replied softly while staring at him. "What do you want?"

He threw his head back, looked at the ceiling, and groaned softly. Finn looked back at her and stared into her eyes with a look of possible annoyance or disappointment.

"Haven't you been paying attention, darling?" he almost demanded. "I'm here to help you."

"You work for Sal," she announced. "Sal's people attacked the lodge."

"No, Jericho attacked the lodge," he informed her. "Jericho and that little blonde twit you call a friend."

She stared at him with a strange, startled look. "What are you talking about?"

"Tonya," he informed her sternly. "She's the one who orchestrated this entire cluster fuck." Finn tensed then gently cleared his throat. "Pardon my language." He leaned closer causing her to tense. "Tonya and Jericho were skimming money from Sal's business and transferring it into some other account. Call it cyber money. Before they could transfer their cyber money into their own private account, Wiley discovered the discrepancies. Discrepancies to the tune of fifty million dollars."

"You're wrong about Tonya," Lee informed him. "Her life has been on the line the same as mine."

"Has it really?" he asked almost tenderly. "After your little talk with Sal, we discovered Tonya was in on the scheme with Jericho. You could almost say she was the brains of the entire operation. So we've had an interest in bringing her in for, shall we say, questioning." He straightened proudly. "The initial attack on the lodge that ended in your abduction was orchestrated by Jericho with help from his girlfriend, Tonya. We had been unsuccessful in tracking you two after the fed's little 'change of plans', but we were able to locate Jericho and track his movements. Knowing he'd eventually lead us to Tonya, we kept eyes on him. Mac has the little blonde princess under lock and key in an upstairs bedroom. You're not safe until we stop Jericho and the muscle he lured away from Sal. Once he hears you've escaped, he'll be looking for you. Whatever Wiley gave you, he wants."

"Why does everyone assume Wiley gave me something," she demanded with annoyance. "He didn't give me anything other than that flash drive. That's all. Jericho told me there was nothing on it but family photos. The flash drive was just a ruse to cover Wiley's tracks."

"No, darling," he announced. "There's more to it than that. You just haven't unlocked that little mystery. We need the information stored in that pretty, little head of yours in order to get Sal's money back. In the meantime, it's our goal to make sure that pretty, little head of yours remains intact and out of Jericho's hands." He suddenly grinned. "See, we're the good guys."

"I find that difficult to believe," she replied while studying him, although her mind seemed to process the information he'd given her regarding her friend. "Tonya is my friend," Lee announced with more conviction. "She's a victim in this too."

"Then explain how Jericho's men found you in your safe haven?" Finn demanded.

"Mac," she announced boldly. "We saw Mac in that little town not far from the lodge. She must have spotted us and called for backup."

"Darling, I am Mac's backup," he announced. "Mac is no more a bad guy than your friendly former Navy SEALs. I'll admit, she's a bitch in every sense of the word, but she's playing on my team. I saved you from those men. Sal's always had a weak spot for you. I suppose you reminded him of his daughter. Even if he didn't need what's locked inside that pretty head of yours, he'd still have sent me to recover you from the hands of all that's evil."

She stared at him, uncertain what to believe. "Let's suppose you are telling the truth," Lee announced. "What do I know that will help recover the fifty million dollars?"

"A password, perhaps. An account number," he announced. "Wiley did something to knock out the entire computer system to keep the money from being transferred. The ComServe guy and our security guard both disappeared without a trace; and ComServe just got permission to tear the entire hard drive apart." He straightened proudly. "Wiley involved you when he slipped you that bogus flash drive. Whether you know it or not, you were Wiley's back-up plan. Who knows more about the bank accounts than Wiley? That would be you, darling."

The comment hit Lee hard. Had Wiley involved her on purpose? Did he mean for her to solve his riddle of the missing money in the event of his death?

"Once it's learned that Jericho doesn't have access to the money, his newly found friends will turn on him, and he loses his army," Finn assured her while staring into her eyes. "He'll be forced out of hiding by the same people who've been helping him. Your fed buddy can then throw the cuffs on him and lock him away forever."

"I'm telling you, Wiley didn't give me anything," she insisted and almost pleaded with her eyes. "If I knew what you were looking for, I'd tell you."

"Think back to that afternoon when you were in his office," Finn remarked gently. "There has to be something. Something out of character; something *off* about him."

Lee sank into thought and recalled her last moments with Wiley in his office before she left. She spilled her purse. That was when he must have slipped the lipstick flash drive into her bag. Something odd then struck her. Finn studied her and appeared curious by her expression.

"You remember something?"

She stared at Finn a moment as her mind reeled with information. "What if the photos on the flash drive were the key?" Lee suddenly asked.

Finn stared at her with bewilderment and tilted his head. "But they were just photos of his family."

"I can't be sure without actually seeing the files on the computer, but I think we're looking for accounts with the names of his wife or children."

"And that could be the file which he transferred the money," Finn announced enthusiastically. He jumped up from the bed and started pacing the room while rubbing his chin as he sank into thought. "Unfortunately, we have no way of accessing the computer right now. We can't do anything until the computer is up and running."

Lee then considered when the computers first went down that afternoon. She had entered the computer closet and found Wiley working on the problem.

"He wasn't trying to fix the system," she muttered aloud. "He was shutting it down."

Finn turned and looked at Lee. She looked up and met his gaze as a smile crossed her face.

"It's not broken, it's been disabled," Lee announced. "That's why the tech guy had to be removed. Jericho knew he didn't have the last piece of the puzzle, so he didn't want anyone going into the system and finding the money before he did."

"You think it's just a matter of flipping the 'on' switch?" Finn asked with surprise.

"No, not quite that simple," she replied. "Wiley was an accountant, not a computer genius. He probably disabled the motherboard. Remove a few necessities, and it's a one hundred pound paperweight."

"So while everyone has been fixated on a program error, it's been the hardware all along?"

"Exactly," Lee announced while smiling.

Finn grinned and shook his head. "You are a genius, darling," he informed her. "We're going to have such smart children."

Lee stared at him with surprise as her mouth fell open. He didn't bother commenting on her look, just laughed.

"I'll tell Sal what you discovered," Finn announced cheerfully. "We'll get another tech guy over there to check the motherboard and find that missing money." His look then turned serious and surprisingly compassionate. "Don't you worry about a thing. You'll be safe here until we get our hands on Jericho and his men. I won't let no body hurt you."

There was a commotion in the hall. Finn removed his gun and hurried for the door. Lee slowly moved to her feet, snatched the baseball bat, and carefully hid it behind her back. She stared at the door with concern, not knowing who was on the other side. Finn listened a moment then opened the door. Lee revealed the bat, clutching it in a defensive manner. The man who had earlier assisted her into the staff wing with Finn tossed Tonya into the room and entered behind her. Lee relaxed her grip on the bat and stared at Tonya with surprise. Tonya saw Lee and nearly broke down into tears.

"Lee, thank God!"

She attempted to run for Lee, but Finn caught her around the waist and slung her backward and into the awaiting man, who caught her. Finn glared at her and cracked his neck.

"Ain't no one buying your act, missy," he growled in a threatening tone. "Peddle those crocodile tears elsewhere." He gave a stern look to the man standing behind her. "Take her to that locked room in the basement. Toss her a blanket or something until we're ready to turn her over to the authorities."

The man firmly took hold of Tonya's arm. Tonya stared at Lee with fear in her eyes.

"Please, Lee. Don't let them do this," she begged softly. "You don't know what Finn intends to do to me. You know the sort of man he is and what he's capable of doing." Tonya's eyes pleaded with hers. "Do it, Lee. Do it now."

Finn casually glanced back at Lee only two steps away from him. He eyed the baseball bat clutched firmly in her hands and then met her gaze. He replaced his gun to his shoulder holster and raised his hands slightly.

"You need to pick a side, darling," Finn announced casually to Lee. "I trust you, but I can't make you trust me. If you truly want to crack my skull, take your swing. If you're going to break my heart, you may as well break my head too."

Lee looked from Finn to Tonya, who pleaded with her eyes. It was possibly the first time she saw evil in her friend's eyes. Tonya wanted her to crack Finn's skull, and Lee had to ask herself why. Lee met Finn's gaze.

"I can't believe I'm saying this," Lee announced then tossed the bat aside. "But I trust you, Finn."

He grinned with pleasure then winked at her. "I always knew you had a thing for me."

Finn turned toward his man holding Tonya's arm. Tonya stared at Lee with possible surprise or even horror. Her look suddenly turned angry and the evil woman emerged. Tonya kicked the man in the shin then rammed her elbow into his ribs. She grabbed his semiautomatic from his shoulder holster and spun toward them with the gun aimed. Finn drew his semiautomatic, but Tonya was already taking aim. She fired the nearly silent shot, hitting Finn in the shoulder. Finn dropped the gun and clutched his bleeding shoulder with agony as he fell against the nightstand. As the man behind Tonya lunged for her, Tonya shot him in the chest. Lee gasped as she watched the man fall to the floor, undoubtedly dead. Tonya then aimed the gun at Lee and the moderately disabled Finn, who held his bleeding shoulder. Lee stared at her friend with horror while Finn glared at Tonya with evil, hateful eyes. Tonya's sneer told Lee every word Finn had said was true, and she had no doubt Tonya intended to kill her too.

"Some friend you turned out to be," Tonya snarled, revealing an angry, hateful person. "Now that I know how to find the file containing my money, I no longer need you." She then sneered at Lee with loathe. "And for the record, you're the least fun person I've ever known."

Lee stared at the gun aimed at her and felt her heart pounding as Tonya's finger tightened on the trigger. As the near silenced shot fired, Finn tackled Lee to the floor. She felt a surge of pain throughout her body from the hard tackle and the rough landing. For a moment, she wasn't convinced she hadn't been shot. She remained immobile on the floor beneath Finn. Lee slowly opened her eyes and saw Finn staring across the room with indescribable horror on his face. As Lee looked across the room, she saw Tonya take two quick steps toward them. Finn gasped as he cradled Lee's head with his arms and head, attempting to shield her and partially obstructing her view of the gun now aimed at them. Bogart suddenly leaped through the doorway and tackled Tonya onto the bed. The gun flew from her hand as they struck the bed. Both bounced and flew off the other side. Lee's heart was pounding from her near death experience and the fear that it wasn't yet over.

"Finn, your gun," Lee cried out from beneath him.

He didn't respond and his breath was shallow in her ear. Lee could feel something wet soaking her abdomen. She attempted to move the man on top of her, but she was trapped beneath Finn's body while wrapped in his arms. Tonya and Bogart struck the floor harshly on the opposite side of the bed and fell apart. Tonya moved to her knees and punched Bogart in the groin. He clutched himself and let out a low, painful groan. Tonya sprang to her feet and ran from the room. Bogart slowly crawled across the floor around the foot end of the bed while clutching himself. As he crawled toward Lee, he grabbed Finn's discarded gun but Tonya was gone. Lee was finally able to roll Finn off her and onto his back. Finn gasped several times but didn't move from where he landed. Lee scrambled to her knees and hovered over him. In addition to the shoulder injury, he had taken a bullet to his back, which penetrated through his midsection. Lee stared at the large amount of blood covering his abdomen, not realizing his blood soaked through onto her also. As his eyes opened, he looked at her and smiled in his usual, moderately creepy manner.

"Told you I'd save you," he gasped softly while maintaining his grin despite his tremendous pain.

"Call an ambulance," Lee shouted to Bogart.

He nodded and removed his cell phone. Lee took Finn's blood covered hand in hers. He clung to her hand, raised it to his lips, and kissed the back of it with affection. He then smiled at her and shut his eyes.

"Lee, darling," he gasped softly while smiling. "You've always been the only girl for me."

Lee fought her tears and clung to his neck. He gently patted her shoulder, took a deep, shaken breath, and then exhaled softly. His hand slipped from her shoulder. She pulled back, looked at his motionless body, and sobbed softly.

Chapter Thirty-six

$\mathcal{J}$ericho paced the empty, second bay of the eight-car garage while his two men guarded the side door and their prisoner. Beck's hands were tied behind his back, and he had duct tape across his mouth, although he seemed to be talking endlessly despite the tape. Six of the eight bays contained expensive sports cars. Each double, wooden garage door was designed with an old-fashioned, Spanish Colonial flair. Jericho was becoming impatient while alternating looking at his watch and out the high, glass windows on the garage door.

"What's taking them so long?" Jericho growled to his men as he turned. "They should have returned with the other prisoner from the basement by now."

"Want me to check on them?" one of his men asked.

"No," Jericho announced. "I'm going down there myself."

"That's risky," the man replied. "What if you're seen?"

"There are over two hundred people in the garden," Jericho remarked. "I doubt anyone will notice me. I'll take the long way, so there's less chance of being seen."

"What about him?" the man asked and indicated Beck.

Beck muffled a casual response through the duct tape covering his mouth. Despite his calm demeanor, his muffled words almost certainly included a rash of carefully strung together curse words. Jericho glared at Beck then frowned.

"He's coming with me," Jericho muttered.

"That's not a good idea."

"No, it's not, but if something's happened to Tonya, I may need him as collateral," Jericho replied.

"Want us to come along?"

"Both of you need to wait here," he announced sternly. "If Tonya's inside, I'll send her here. If things go sideways, you get her out."

Both men nodded. Jericho grabbed Beck's arm and pulled him to his feet. Beck casually muttered another comment possibly insulting Jericho's mother.

✝

As Jericho and Beck approached the basement holding room, Beck continued his rant beneath the duct tape. Jericho groaned, stopped him, and ripped the tape from his mouth. Beck let out a slight yelp then licked his sticky lips.

"I'm not talking," Beck announced boldly and was silent for the first time.

"That'd be a first," Jericho snapped. "Considering you haven't shut up since you came to."

Jericho unlocked and opened the door, shoving Beck into the concrete holding room. Beck stumbled slightly then caught his balance despite his hands being tied behind his back. Both stopped just inside the room and stared at Jericho's two men, who were tied and gagged, as they writhed around on the floor. Beck's lips curled into a tiny smirk, which he immediately hid from his abductor. Both bound men attempted to shout for their freedom.

"You idiots," Jericho screamed.

Jericho removed a knife from his boot, cut through their duct tape bindings, and continued his rant as they pulled the tape from their mouths and untied their feet.

"How did you let him get away?" Jericho demanded. "How long has he been running around free?"

"Long enough," the first man muttered. "I'm sure he's long gone by now. Probably bringing the police down on us this very minute."

Beck chuckled softly and could barely contain his humor for their situation. All eyes were on him, although they didn't share his humor. Beck again felt compelled to talk.

"Oh, I think the police are the least of your worries at the moment," Beck announced while grinning. "I'm surprised the place isn't crawling with feds right about now." His look mocked them. "And even the feds would be a picnic compared with the storm heading your way."

Jericho sneered at Beck then looked at his slightly battered men. "What about Tonya?"

"I don't know, but we're sure she's here somewhere," the man remarked. "The others were supposed to search the house for her, but they haven't reported back yet."

Jericho sank into thought then glared at Beck, who maintained his sly grin. "You don't know how lucky you are that we need you, or I'd kill you where you stand." Jericho looked at the man with the bleeding dog bite wound on his arm and indicated Beck. "Take this one through the staff wing and back out to the garage. Don't let anyone from the party see you," he threatened. "If we're not out in twenty minutes, take him to the safe house."

Jericho handed the man a snub-nose revolver hidden in his belt holster. The man took the gun and forced Beck from the room. Jericho nodded the other man toward the door.

"We need to find Tonya," Jericho announced sternly. "Hopefully, our man has gotten the information we need from the other one in the penthouse. Just in case, we're making a little side stop to Sal's bedroom. He should have enough cash and jewelry in that wall safe to get us across the border."

✝

*A*gent Falcone's official SUV pulled up to the front gate of the mansion with a light flashing from the dashboard, catching the security guard's attention. He stopped by the gatehouse and flashed his badge to the guard.

"Special Agent Falcone with the FBI," he announced in his gruff, official tone. "I need to speak to your employer."

"I'm sorry, Agent Falcone, but you've come at a bad time," the guard announced. "He's entertaining two hundred friends, family, and employees for his birthday celebration. You'll have to come back another time."

"Either you let me in and notify your boss, or I can come back with a search warrant," Holden remarked.

Behind the gatehouse, Kirk was seen with his back against the stone wall. Holden eyed Kirk by the wall then glared at the guard standing by his vehicle.

"I'm afraid you'll need that search warrant," the guard informed him.

Holden watched as Ross ran up to Kirk, leaped onto his bent knee, and caught the upper edge of the wall. Once he was on the wall, he extended his hand down to Kirk. Kirk moved away from the wall, took a running start, and half scaled the wall while grabbing Ross's hand. Ross pulled him the rest of the way up the wall. Both men disappeared over the top and onto the property. Holden glared at the guard.

"I can assure you," Holden informed the man, "when I return with that warrant, there will be twenty agents storming the estate and ruining his little party."

Holden put the SUV in reverse, backed away from the gate, and drove away from the mansion.

†

*R*oss and Kirk kept close to the wall on their approach to the mansion then remained hidden behind several trees until they reached the side of the house. Ross dropped his backpack on the ground behind the hedges and tapped his earpiece.

"Anyone copy?"

There was no response. Kirk removed two suit jackets from the bag, smoothed out the wrinkles and tossed one to Ross. Ross slipped into the jacket while Kirk put on his jacket.

"Copy you," Bogart's voice announced over Ross and Kirk's earpieces.

"Bogart?" Ross demanded and withheld his groan. "Where are the others?"

"I'm with Gil, Monroe, and Zack," Bogart informed him through the earpiece. "We have Lee." He then hesitated. "And an unlikely ally."

"Is Lee safe?"

"Yeah, we're all just spiffy," Bogart snorted. "Lee said Jericho brought Beck here, but we ain't seen him. Tonya's also running around somewhere. According to Lee, Tonya has everything she needs to access the computer server at the office building. Once she hooks up with Jericho, they're out of here."

"Holden and his men are watching the exits while awaiting their search warrant, and he has men staking out the office building," Ross announced while hiding the empty bag beneath the bushes. "Monroe's call about Lee being held at the mansion should be enough to gain that search warrant. Kirk and I are on our way inside. You and Monroe stay with Lee and keep her out of sight. Zack and Gil need to sweep the lower level. Kirk and I will take the second floor."

"You've got it, boss man."

Ross groaned and rolled his eyes. Kirk and Ross straightened their jackets and headed around the side of the house to join the party.

†

*T*he man with the dog bite wound on his arm forced Beck into the staff wing corridor and toward the side entrance for their departure. There was a shadow moving behind them. The man stopped Beck and looked down the hall the direction they had come. There wasn't anyone there. Beck looked as well, although he now appeared more confident about his situation.

"You know," Beck announced casually. "If you were smart, you'd let me go and worry about saving your own ass. My friends have bigger fish to fry than you. If you made a run for it now, you'd have an unbelievable head start. Your odds of making it out of here alive improve considerably."

"Shut up," the man snarled and gave him a slight shove to keep him moving.

Beck turned partially as he walked and glanced at the man while casting a look down the corridor behind them. Someone moved within one of the staff room doorways. Beck hid his smile and studied the man.

"One of my friends is slightly unbalanced," Beck casually informed him. "He knows more ways of killing a man then you probably realize existed. I mean, this guy is good. He'll snap your neck before you even know he's standing behind you."

Beck again glanced behind the man, causing him to glance back out of reflex. There was no one there. Beck suddenly kicked the man in the abdomen and sent him flying backward. The gun flew from his hand and slid across the hallway. Beck shifted from foot to foot and awaited the silent attack that was certain to come.

"Now, Zack!" Beck cried out and looked around.

There was no one there. Beck appeared slightly alarmed as the man scrambled to his feet and went for the gun. Beck, with his hands still tied behind his back, lunged for the rising man and bowled him over, unfortunately, taking both of them to the floor. The man punched the defenseless Beck, slid across the floor, and snatched his discarded gun. He aimed the gun at Beck from his position on his knees just a few feet away. Beck rolled partially onto his back and stared at the gun.

"The hell with keeping you alive," the man snarled and tightened his finger on the trigger.

A vase suddenly shattered over the man's head, sending him to the floor. Beck appeared stunned and looked up. Pinto gasped and placed her hand over her mouth with alarm.

"Oh, God," she suddenly cried out. "Is he dead? Did I kill him?"

Beck stared at her with his mouth hanging open and appeared unable to speak. He let out an uneasy laugh and shook his head without taking his eyes off her.

"No, he's still alive," Beck announced and indicated the unconscious man. "There's a knife in his pocket."

Pinto squeamishly knelt alongside the unconscious man and felt around inside his pants pockets. She removed the pocketknife, opened it, and hurried to Beck. With some effort, she cut the plastic zip ties binding his wrists behind his back.

"What are you doing here?" he finally asked as she freed his hands.

"After you and your friends left, a woman showed up at the club," she informed him while on her knees behind him.

Beck moved to his knees facing her. "What woman?"

The man groaned and started coming too. Beck leaned over and punched the man in the face. He collapsed back to the floor. Beck looked back at Pinto as if nothing had happened.

"A woman named Mac. She said she worked for my father," Pinto explained. "Something I said about my father possibly being involved in the attempt on Tonya's life distracted her, and she took off. I was worried I said something wrong, so I tried to call you to warn you of what happened, but I only got your voicemail." She hesitated, inhaled deeply, and straightened proudly. "I came here, because I needed to find out if what you said was true, you know, about my father."

"As you can see, I was telling the truth," Beck casually informed her.

"I don't think so," Pinto boldly announced. "I asked him about Lee and Tonya. He said he caught Tonya stealing from him, so he fired her, but he had nothing bad to say about Lee. In fact, he seemed concerned for her. He told me she was coming to the party, and that Finn was bringing her, so she'd be safe. I think he was telling the truth. I saw her arrive, and then your friend, Bogart, went to check on her."

Beck appeared concerned and quickly stood. He extended his hand to her. She accepted his hand, allowing him to pull her to her feet.

"We need to find Lee," he announced firmly. "It's very important, Pinto. Her life is on the line."

"My father won't hurt her," Pinto insisted, sounding irritated, and handed him the knife. "He said I could talk to her once she had a chance to get some rest."

"Fine," Beck announced firmly. "She's rested long enough. Let's go see her. We'll find your father, and you need to insist he takes you to see her."

"Fine," she retorted. "I will."

Beck then indicated the unconscious man. "We'll need to tie him up first."

Chapter Thirty-seven

Monroe hurried the visibly shaken Lee into a nearby staff bedroom. Bogart entered behind them and quickly locked the door. They'd heard someone in the hallway not far from them and needed to take cover just in case. Lee held her forehead as her head hung down. She sniffed and fought her tears then looked at the blood on her hands and shirt. The color drained from her face as she started to tremble. She then ran into the nearby bathroom. Monroe exhaled softly and followed her.

"I wouldn't do that," Bogart casually warned.

"She's upset, Bogart," Monroe snapped while glaring at his friend. "Stop being an ass."

As Monroe stepped into the bathroom doorway, Lee heaved into the toilet. Monroe quickly turned and walked away from the bathroom, seeming moderately queasy himself.

"Told you," Bogart announced with a knowing smirk. "When a woman turns that shade of white, she's either passing out or purging. Trust me, I've been purged upon many a time."

Within the bland staff bathroom, Lee flushed the toilet then held her forehead and her stomach. She approached the sink and frantically attempted to wash the blood from her hands. Halfway through the process, she saw the large amount of blood soaked into her shirt. She held back her sob and feverishly unbuttoned her shirt with trembling hands. The blood had already dried, pasting the shirt against her skin. Lee ripped the shirt off, not expecting it to hurt as much as it did. She cast the blood-soaked shirt aside then leaned on the sink and held back her sobs. She saw a clean shirt extended toward her out of the corner of her eye. Lee glanced at Monroe and straightened, not caring that he had full view of her in only her bra.

He seemed more interested in the large amount of blood that had soaked through onto her abdomen.

"I found this in the closet," he announced gently.

She uncertainly accepted the shirt while seemingly in her own world. She never would have believed she'd be so upset over Finn's death, but she never would have expected the man to sacrifice his life to save hers either. Monroe turned to leave.

"I treated him so badly," she announced softly.

Monroe turned back toward her and stared at her a moment. "It wasn't your fault, Lee," he assured her. "He valued your life above his own. The team and I have done the same for one another on many occasions. None of us has ever regretted it."

She wiped her eyes with a trembling hand, sniffed, and straightened proudly. "Tonya was supposed to be my friend," Lee announced sternly. "She was supposed to be my friend, and she tried to kill me. Finn is dead because of her. If I had a gun and her in front of me--"

"Let us handle Tonya," he announced firmly. "That's not something you want to ever live with."

She frowned and slowly nodded. Lee slowly slipped into the button shirt and grimaced slightly. She'd been tackled several times over the course of a few days, and she couldn't deny her body was protesting. Monroe's eyes again strayed to her abdomen and his expression dropped slightly.

"Oh--" he mumbled softly.

Lee followed his gaze and looked to the blood covering her abdomen. She couldn't believe all the blood that had soaked through her shirt. She looked back at Monroe and frowned.

"Yeah, I'll shower when this is all over."

Monroe cringed and took a step toward her. "It's not that," he announced. "Hold still."

Lee was puzzled as she watched Monroe reach for her abdomen. Bogart stepped into the bathroom just in time to witness Monroe plucking the bullet from the small wound on Lee's abdomen. She yelped with surprise. Monroe smiled weakly and showed her the blood covered bullet. She looked from the bloody bullet to the small, bleeding wound on her abdomen.

"Seriously? I've been shot?" she almost demanded.

As Bogart stared at the bloody bullet fragment, all color drained from his face and his eyes rolled back as he collapsed to the floor. Both looked at Bogart out cold on the floor. The main bedroom doorknob jiggled, alarming Lee and Monroe. Monroe indicated for her to wait inside the bathroom. He dragged Bogart by his feet into the bathroom, stepped over him into the bedroom, and shut the door behind him. Lee stepped over Bogart's unconscious body and approached the bathroom door. She opened it a crack and looked out just in time to see Monroe remove his gun and aim it at the bedroom door. The door was kicked open with a thunderous crack. Beck stood in the doorway with the snub-nose revolver aimed at Monroe, who had his semiautomatic aimed at Beck. Both men relaxed at the sight of the other and lowered their weapons. Beck ushered Pinto into the bedroom and shut the slightly battered door.

"I heard a thump. Where are the others?" Beck asked Monroe. "Did they find Lee? Jericho's man was holding her in the penthouse at the office building, but Pinto said Finn brought her here."

The bathroom door opened and Lee stepped out. "Finn rescued me," she informed Beck. "Sal wasn't behind any of this."

"I told you so," Pinto snapped. "Can we find my father and call the police now?"

"Holden and his men will be storming the place any minute with a search warrant," Monroe announced. "We need to find Jericho and take him down quietly. There are too many innocent lives outside. There's no telling what Jericho is capable of if he feels trapped."

"Never mind Jericho," Lee announced. "Tonya's the one you have to worry about. We need to stop her."

"Tonya's working with Jericho?" Pinto suddenly asked with surprise.

"The bitch killed Finn and another one of your father's men," Lee informed Pinto with a hiss in her voice. "She's armed and extremely dangerous."

"She also has all the information they need to access the server and get the fifty million dollars they stole," Monroe added.

Bogart stumbled out of the bathroom while holding his head. "Thanks for just leaving me on the floor," he muttered.

"We shouldn't be standing around discussing this," Lee announced sternly. "We should be at the office building. That's where Tonya needs to go to access the company server. If she gets her hands on that fifty million dollars, she and Jericho will disappear forever."

"We're not going to the office building," Monroe insisted. "Ross said to keep you safe. They're going to handle Jericho and his men. Tonya too."

"So Tonya stole fifty million dollars from my father's company?" Pinto asked while looking from Lee to Monroe. "And she needs to access the company's server?"

"The accountant disabled the server," Lee informed her. "I'm pretty sure all she needs is to reattach the motherboard, and she can access the server. Thanks to me, she now has a good idea of the account where Wiley transferred the money for safekeeping."

"We can access the server from my father's computer," Pinto informed them. "The company tech guy set it up so he could use it from home."

"But she still needs to enable the server first," Monroe informed her. "That can only be done from the office. Holden sent some officers to keep anyone from accessing the building."

"It wouldn't hurt to anticipate her getting through," Pinto informed them. "If she manages to get past them and repairs the server, we can access the files before her, if we have the necessary information."

"We do," Lee announced.

"I suggest we take this party to the study," Beck announced.

"But Ross said--" Monroe protested.

"When Ross isn't around, I'm in charge," Beck informed Monroe. "We're going to the study."

Chapter Thirty-eight

Jericho and one of his men entered the master bedroom on the second floor. Both men crossed the elegant room in opposite directions with their guns drawn and searched the room. Jericho approached a portrait of Sal's deceased wife and pulled it away from the wall to reveal a safe with a digital lock. He entered a number combination, but the light remained red. He cursed softly. Before he could attempt another combination, Jericho's phone vibrated within his pocket. He removed his phone, looked at the caller ID, and appeared curious as he placed the cell phone to his ear.

"Yeah?" he gruffly announced. Jericho suddenly stopped, appeared surprised, and looked around. "Tonya? Baby? Where are you?" He hesitated then appeared relieved. "You have the information?" There was a pause. "No, head for the garage from the employees' wing. No one will see you there. The guys should be waiting." He listened a moment. "No, we have one of their men as a hostage. It'll be okay. I'll meet you in the garage. See you in ten minutes. Love you."

Jericho disconnected the call and looked at his man, who watched him with great interest.

"Tonya's free," he announced. "And she has the information we need to access the computer."

"The feds are waiting outside," the man announced. "They're going to be watching the exits."

"That's why we're taking one of the catering vans," Jericho informed him. "Contact the guys. Tell them to head for the garage but keep watch for more of Lee's babysitters."

The man nodded and removed his cell phone from his pocket as Jericho entered another combination into the wall safe number pad. The light turned green. Jericho grinned and opened the safe. There were several bundles of cash and boxes of jewelry. Jericho grinned and emptied the contents of the safe into his bag. He then looked at his man on the phone who hadn't spoken. The man gave him a strange look.

"No one's answering," he announced.

"Try the men in the garage," Jericho ordered while securely closing his bag.

The man made another phone call. He spoke to a man briefly then disconnected the call.

"Frank's still in the garage," he announced. "The others never showed. We have to assume our hostage escaped."

Jericho slammed his fist against the safe and approached the door. He heard someone just outside the bedroom door. He aimed his gun as the door opened. One of their men joined them but appeared out of breath.

"Leroy is dead," he informed Jericho. "They're inside the mansion."

Jericho cursed under his breath then glared at the man. "Who's left? No one's answering."

"Just Wilson and Paul," the man announced, "but they're keeping an eye on Sal out back."

"Contact them," Jericho snarled. "Tell them to meet us by the servants' wing exit."

The man nodded and removed his phone.

✝

*T*he nearly two hundred guests socialized in the backyard, enjoying the open bar and the elaborate buffet set up along the patio. One of Sal's men stepped aside to answer his cell phone. Sal talked with one of his guests then seemed to notice the man on his phone several yards away. The man disconnected the call, nodded secretly to another man, and then headed toward the house. Sal watched the second man follow. He smiled at his guest and excused himself. He removed his cell phone and pressed 'Finn' on his call list. Finn's voicemail picked up. He then tried 'Mac'. There was no answer. Sal replaced his phone then looked a couple feet away to another man. He gave a slight nod then headed for the house with the man following. The man easily caught up to him.

"Finn and Mac aren't answering," Sal informed him. "I want you to check the staff quarters where Finn was taking Lee. If you don't find them, don't bother contacting me, just call Agent Falcone and get the security guard out front to let the feds in."

The man nodded as they entered the house.

t

*J*ericho kept watch on the second floor hallway and then looked back at his two men. He nodded. Both men left the room and headed toward the back, kitchen stairs. Jericho followed behind, keeping his gun carefully hidden beneath his jacket. The backstairs would lead them through the kitchen and into the servant's wing virtually undetected except by the caterers. Once in the servant's wing, it was a quick journey to the detached eight-car garage. They were halfway to the backstairs when Ross and Kirk appeared in the hallway, cutting off their path. Kirk and Ross aimed their guns at the men.

"Drop the weapons!" Ross shouted.

Jericho turned and ran in the opposite direction as his men fired on Ross and Kirk. The nearly silent shots struck the wall not far from Kirk's head. Ross fired back and winged the first man in the shoulder, dropping him to the floor. The second man continued to fire, forcing Ross and Kirk to leap to the safety of a nearby doorway. The second man continued to shoot at them then ran down the hall after Jericho. Jericho stopped by the stairs and fired at Ross and Kirk, allowing his man a chance to meet up with him by the main staircase. Both men ran down the grand stairs. Ross ran after them while Kirk turned and ran for the backstairs. Jericho and his man thundered down the grand stairs and swung the banister at the bottom. Sal and his man entered the massive hallway and stopped when they saw Jericho. Sal's expression dropped then turned to hostility.

"Get him!" Sal shouted.

His sidekick removed his weapon as Jericho and his man aimed their weapons and fired at both men. Sal leaped to the safety of the archway while his man fired at the intruders. Jericho's man shot Sal's man in the chest, throwing him against the wall. He slid down the wall leaving a bloody streak. Jericho's man approached Sal where he remained standing just out of his line of fire. Sal slowly raised his hands in the air, having no place to run without risking a bullet in the back.

"Is this how it's going to go down?" Sal demanded.

Jericho approached, although remaining behind his armed man, and grinned slyly.

"I'm afraid so, Sal," he announced. "It's nothing personal, you know. I'm just tired of working my ass off while someone like you gets richer and richer."

"You can kill me," Sal announced without showing fear, "but there will be retribution. You'll never be able to live without looking over your shoulder in fear that someone is waiting to kill you."

"Yeah, I thought about that," Jericho announced then grinned, "but I'm willing to live with those odds." He nodded to his man. "Do it."

The man tightened his finger on the trigger. Sal was suddenly struck in the chest by a flying foot, which sent him through the air and to the floor several feet away. As the gun fired, Zack was already rolling across the floor to safety. Jericho's man took several steps closer to locate the rolling man when Mac appeared from a nearby doorway and kicked the gun from his hand. Mac went for the return kick and struck him in the face, throwing him into the nearby wall. As Jericho aimed his gun, Zack was suddenly standing in front of him. Zack grabbed his wrist and twisted it until the gun fell from his hand. He followed through with a powerful flip that sent Jericho in a full, hands-free somersault. Jericho landed harshly on his backside with a loud grunt. The bag struck the floor, opened, and scattered cash and jewelry along the foyer. Jericho attempted to scramble to his feet. Zack shook his head with irritation and then thrust his knee directly under Jericho's chin, sending him back to the floor.

"Why do they always insist on getting up?" Zack demanded then looked at Mac with the man against the wall.

Mac rammed her knee into the man's groin and allowed him to drop to the floor. Zack grinned his approval.

"Nice form," he announced.

She smiled sweetly while tilting her head, adding to her innocent appeal. "Thank you."

Ross leaned casually on the railing from the second floor with his gun dangling relaxed in his hand. He hid his smile and shook his head. As Ross headed down the stairs, Sal slowly entered the foyer while tenderly rubbing his chest and glaring at Zack.

"I suppose I should be grateful for that," Sal remarked lowly.

"You're welcome," Zack replied.

Jericho leaped to his feet and bolted for the front door. Ross casually pointed, although he didn't fire his weapon.

"Got a runner," Ross announced matter-of-factly.

Zack and Mac both turned in the direction of Jericho and the front door. Jericho threw open the door. Darth stood in the doorway with his teeth bared while snarling.

Jericho stared at the dog with some surprise. "Darth, no," he announced loudly.

Gil casually leaned against the doorframe not far from the snarling dog.

"Sorry, Jericho," Gil announced. "Darth no longer works for you."

"Ross, you there?" came Kirk's voice through Ross's earpiece.

Ross hesitated and touched his earpiece. "Yeah, Kirk, I read you."

"I spotted Tonya," Kirk announced. "She ran into the garage. I'm making my approach now."

"Hold your position," Ross announced. "There could be more men waiting to ambush you."

Ross looked across the foyer, but Zack was already gone. He shook his head then looked at Gil.

"Kirk has Tonya trapped in the garage," Ross announced. "He needs backup."

Gil nodded then looked at Darth and slapped his thigh. The dog followed him across the foyer. Mac finished zip tying Jericho's wrists behind his back and looked around.

"What happened to the littlest ninja?" she suddenly asked.

"Damned if I know," Ross remarked. "He tends to roam when he's off his leash, but he always comes back home."

"Where's Lee?" Sal asked, seeming slightly anxious.

"I got word they were chilling in your study with your daughter," Ross replied.

"You know about my daughter?" Sal suddenly asked.

"A few of the guys took in her show," Ross replied.

"I'd better check on them," Sal announced and hurried for the hallway.

"I'll join you," Ross replied casually, although he seemed slightly suspicious.

Ross grabbed Jericho and forced him into the hallway behind Sal. Mac watched them leave as she tied the second man. Once the others disappeared down the hall, Mac left the tied man and hurried out the front door.

Chapter Thirty-nine

Gil approached the detached garage with his gun securely in his hand. Kirk remained flattened against the wall with his gun against his chest. Both men eyed the side door then shared a conversation with slight eye movements. Kirk hurried past the door while keeping low, so he wouldn't be seen through the small window. He reached the other side and flattened himself against the wall then looked at Gil, who now moved up to the door on the opposite side. Gil placed his hand on the doorknob and turned it slightly. Obviously, it was locked. Darth approached the door and put his nose to it, as if waiting for someone to let him inside. The men exchanged looks. Gil approached Darth while keeping low and moved the dog off to the side while facing the door. He held Darth by his collar and spoke softly to him in German. The dog focused on the door and let out a gruff woof. Kirk stepped in front of the door and kicked it open. As the door flew open, Gil commanded the dog. Darth bolted into the garage. Gil and Kirk stormed in after him.

As they entered the garage, a car was heard burning out with the smell of burnt rubber and smoke filling the bay. They heard a thunderous crash as the sports car jetted through the stylish, wooden garage door, exploding it across the driveway. Gil and Kirk ran for the broken garage door and aimed their guns at the car racing down the driveway, but they were too late. Darth ran after the car regardless, unaware that he'd never be able to catch the speeding sports car. Gil groaned and ran down the driveway after Darth. Kirk shook his head, muttered a curse, and returned to the garage to search for any remaining henchmen.

†

*H*olden stood alongside another federal SUV across the road from Romano's mansion and talked with the agent behind the wheel. Holden's cell phone rang. He removed his phone and answered the call in his usual, gruff manner.

"Falcone," he announced then listened. He appeared relieved to the news. "Great. We're standing by." He disconnected the call and returned his phone to his pocket. "They're on their way with the search warrant."

Both men heard a loud engine along with the repetitive barking of a dog. They looked to the front gate of the mansion near Holden's parked SUV. The sports car, containing a blonde haired driver, suddenly crashed through the gate, sideswiped Holden's SUV, burned out in the road, and sped away. A few seconds later, Darth ran after the car.

"Son-of-a-bitch!" Holden exclaimed while indicating the sports car. "There was a blonde woman behind the wheel!" Holden slammed his hand on the driver's side door. "Go, go, go!"

The SUV burned out onto the road and chased after the sports car. Holden ran for his damaged SUV, jumped inside, and turned on the flashing lights. Gil jumped into the passenger seat just as he was about to step on the gas. Holden reached for his gun, saw it was only Gil, and relaxed his hand on the grip.

"Follow that dog!" Gil shouted while pointing out the windshield.

Holden put the SUV into gear and burned out onto the road before jetting after the other SUV, which was steadily gaining on the dog. The first SUV passed the running dog, still determined to catch the car. Holden's SUV drove alongside the German shepherd. Gil opened the car door and whistled. Without slowing, Darth leaped into the passenger seat nearly on top of Gil. Gil caught the dog and closed the door. Holden eyed the large, panting dog sitting on Gil's lap. Darth stared intently out the windshield and barked at the cars in front of them, slinging saliva over the dashboard.

"What the hell--?" Holden demanded.

Gil glared at Holden while clinging to the dog on his lap. "Technically, that's his collar up there."

Holden eyed Gil, refrained from commenting, and concentrated on his high-speed driving.

t

*A*t the rear gate of the mansion grounds, a white catering van left through the back gate with one of the caterers behind the wheel. The agent sitting within the SUV outside the back gate suspiciously eyed the catering van as it passed. His radio crackled with word of the chase happening on the other side of the mansion. He flipped his flashing lights on and sped away in the opposite direction. Within the catering van, Tonya removed her baseball cap and allowed her long, blonde hair to spill onto her shoulders. She grinned while staring through the rearview mirror at the fading vehicle.

†

*S*everal minutes later, at the office building, the catering van pulled into the parking garage near the entrance and stopped just behind the parked police car with its lights still flashing. Tonya jumped out of the van and hurried toward the back entrance. As she passed, she took a second to stare at the two dead officers and the third body not far from them. Large amounts of blood surrounded the three dead men, soaking into the concrete. She didn't look nearly as confident now. Tonya was about to run the special access key through the lock when she noticed that the alarm hadn't been set. The door wasn't even locked. She hurried into the building and stopped short of another dead man just beyond the door. Someone suddenly appeared in front of her. Tonya jumped with alarm and looked at the man near the steps. Jericho's man saw her and lowered his gun.

"Do you have it?" he asked.

She nodded and regained her confidence. "Make sure I'm not being followed," Tonya informed him then ran for the nearby elevator.

Jericho's henchman approached the door, opened it, and stood just inside, keeping watch over the blood-strewn garage. Despite the earlier carnage, the parking garage was quiet. Tonya paused before the elevator and vigorously pressed the button. It arrived almost immediately, since the building was empty. She hurried inside and pressed the button for the nineteenth floor. The elevator ride was quicker than usual, without the nuisance of other stops. She hurried from the elevator and jogged along the hallway for the computer closet. She threw open the door and stared at the massive computer a moment. Tonya nervously ran her fingers through her hair then took a deep breath and removed the side panel. Upon looking inside, she saw the CPU, main power connector, and IDE cables were disconnected. Although not much of a computer genius, she was able to connect the cables without any trouble.

Tonya didn't appear completely confident in her assembly of the motherboard, but she seemed willing to risk it. She hurried from the computer closet and back toward Wiley's office. Despite the door being shut, it wasn't locked. She darted inside, being certain to shut and lock the door behind her, then sprang into the chair behind the desk. She frantically typed on the keyboard and entered the password. The password was denied. She tried several times and got the same 'denied' message. Tonya screamed aloud and beat her palms on the desk. She hesitated a moment, composed herself, and tried the same password again, this time capitalizing the first letter. 'Access granted' appeared. She clapped her hands together and grinned.

†

*J*ericho's man remained in the partially open parking garage doorway and kept watch on the surrounding area. Everything seemed quiet except for the distant sound of traffic beyond the parking garage entrance. A car was then heard approaching. He allowed the door to close just enough so he could see the approaching vehicle, but so the driver wouldn't see him until it was too late. The expensive Town Car parked near the catering van. Mac slowly got out of the car, cautiously assessed the situation while removing her gun, and approached the fallen police officers. Jericho's man aimed his gun at Mac as she paused by the first dead officer and tightened his finger on the trigger.

"Is that really wise?" Zack asked from behind him.

Jericho's man appeared alarmed then determined as he spun with his gun aimed.

Back within the parking garage, the entrance door was heard softy clicking shut. Mac looked at the door as she took cover behind the first car. When nothing moved, she slowly approached the door, keeping her gun leveled in front of her. She tried the door and discovered it was unlocked. Mac slowly pushed the door open with her free hand while keeping her gun aimed at the opening with the other. As the door opened, she saw two dead men lying on the floor just inside the doorway. The first man was shot and appeared to have been dead for more than an hour. The second man lay in an unnatural position as if his neck had been broken. Mac appeared bewildered and looked around the narrow corridor. When she didn't see anyone around, she headed toward the elevator.

t

*P*into sat behind her father's desk in the study and frantically typed on the computer. Beck and Lee hung over her shoulder while Monroe and Bogart paced the office and watched helplessly. Both men stopped pacing when they saw Pinto's expression suddenly turn enthusiastic.

"Are you in?" Monroe suddenly asked.

"Yes, someone fixed the computer," Pinto informed him. "I was able to bypass the firewall, but someone else is accessing the server." Pinto leaped out of the chair. "You're up," she announced to Lee.

Lee jumped into the chair and wildly typed on the keyboard. Files and folders seemed to open and close at a startling rate. Lee softly said aloud Wiley's children and wife's name. There were several files.

"I found the files," Lee announced as she frantically typed without looking at them. "It looks like nearly a dozen different files, although I could be mistaken."

Sal and Ross entered the study with the bound Jericho. They stopped to see Lee behind the computer, working feverishly and not even looking up from her speed typing.

"What files?" Sal suddenly asked.

Beck straightened and looked at Sal across the desk. "The files containing the fifty million Wiley hid from Tonya and that one," he announced while indicating Jericho.

Sal hurried to the desk to join them. Ross shoved Jericho into the nearby chair and headed across the study past Bogart. He indicated the man to Bogart.

"Watch him. If he so much as moves, I want you to rip his nuts off," Ross ordered then approached the desk with the others.

Despite Bogart not being the 'rip off their nuts' type, Jericho didn't know that. Bogart folded his arms across his chest and glared at the bound man with his best, intimidating look.

Lee stopped typing and stared at the screen with alarm. "Oh, hell, someone's accessing the files. If that's Tonya, she's already transferring the money from one of the files into a private account."

"Can you stop her?" Sal asked.

"Can we access the account she's using?" Beck countered.

"No," Lee replied and began typing even faster. "Once the transfer is complete, the money is gone."

Jericho chuckled softly from where he sat. Bogart sneered at the man. Lee continued to type.

"What are you doing?" Ross asked.

"I'm transferring money into another account as well," Lee informed them without looking up. "I may not be able to stop her from transferring some of the money, but I can keep her from getting all of it. It's spread out over several files, and I'm faster on a computer than she is."

"What account are you transferring it to?" Sal asked with a curious look on his face.

"Sorry," she announced without looking up. "I only know one account number by memory. My savings account." She briefly glanced up at him. "Relax; I'll transfer it back to you."

"I wasn't worried," Sal replied while fidgeting. "Just stop her. Stop her!"

Once she accessed the last file, Lee slowly sat back in the leather chair and watched the monetary amount climb in her personal savings account as the money was transferred.

"Come on, come on," she muttered softly then subconsciously chewed on her finger.

Beck and Pinto stood over her shoulder and watched the number as it continued to climb. The numbers clicked off so fast, it was almost impossible to read the amount.

"Damn it," Ross growled and straightened. "I thought Holden was watching the exits. How did she slip past him? Where the hell is he?"

𝑓

𝑇he first agent's SUV chased after the speeding, swerving sports car. The sports car took a sharp curve, skidding the entire way. The first SUV struck a parked car, smashing both vehicles together in a mass of twisted metal and fiberglass. Holden's SUV flew past the disabled vehicle and chased after the sports car, taking the sharp curve with a little more skill. Within the SUV, Holden kept his eyes locked on the sports car as he closed in. Gil held the German shepherd on his lap while the dog continued to bark and steam up the

220

windshield. He now clawed at the dashboard as if prepared to leap through the glass. The sports car swerved to miss another car and slid into a telephone pole on the passenger side. As Holden's SUV skidded to a stop, the driver of the wrecked sports car jumped out and ran for a nearby abandoned building. His blonde wig flew onto the ground behind him.

"Son-of-a-bitch," Holden yelled out. "It's not Tonya."

"I've got this," Gil announced and opened the car door. "You call it in."

Darth jumped from Gil's lap and ran for the building with Gil chasing after him. Darth barely stopped for the mostly closed door, bounding against it, and knocking it open. The dog ran into the abandoned building after the man. Gil entered behind him with his gun firmly in his hand. Although he didn't see the man, he saw Darth running across the large, open area scattered with debris from a collapsing ceiling. Darth rounded the corner. By the time Gil reached the corner, Darth was gone. He heard the dog barking. Gil ran toward the sound of the barking dog. He passed through another doorway and saw Darth chasing after the running man.

The man turned and fired at the dog gaining on him. Darth suddenly yelped and tumbled to the floor. Gil stopped near the motionless dog, aimed his gun at the man, clenched his jaw, and, without mercy, fired several shots into the man as he attempted to shoot back. Jericho's henchman took all four hits to his chest before falling to the floor. Gil's hardened expression dropped to concern as he fell to his knees near the lying, bleeding dog. He tenderly petted the dog's head and gently attempted to assess the bullet wound beneath the blood-soaked fur on his shoulder. Darth lifted his head and licked Gil's face. As he parted the bloodied fur, he saw the bullet had only grazed his shoulder. Gil sighed with relief and hugged the dog.

"Don't ever do that again," he announced while almost down to tears. "You stupid, stupid dog."

Darth again licked his face and whined softy. As Gil stood, Darth sprang to his feet, whimpered softly with discomfort, and limped alongside Gil as they left the building.

Chapter Forty

$\mathcal{B}$ack at the mansion, the others were still within the study. Bogart leaned against the study door with his arms folded across his chest while glaring at Jericho, who stared across the room at the group who had gathered behind the desk. Jericho's expression matched that of those behind the desk as they stared at the monitor with nervous anticipation. Ross had his cell phone to his ear and talked to someone on the other end while watching the computer screen. Lee remained sitting behind the computer while Pinto and the others either stood behind the chair or leaned on the desk and watched the climbing dollar amount. Sal slammed his palm against the top of the chair, jolting Lee, as he watched the number climbing to nearly forty million dollars.

"Go, go!" Sal cried out excitedly.

The amount came to a grinding halt. Everyone held his or her breath then straightened. Sal groaned and turned away from the computer. Ross turned to Beck and Monroe.

"I need the two of you to go after the others to the office building," Ross informed his men. "Holden and Gil are on their way, and Kirk is a few minutes behind them. I want her caught."

Both men nodded. Ross stopped them with a simple 'hey' and gave them a serious look.

"Try to take her alive," Ross remarked. "We need that account number if we want to get that nine million back."

They started to leave when Sal spun to face the men. "Ten percent," he announced boldly. "Ten percent finder's fee to whoever captures her and gets my money back."

Beck and Monroe exchanged looks then glanced at Ross. He barely flinched and shrugged. Beck and Monroe grinned and slapped hands in the air before heading for the study door with Bogart standing just before it. Bogart stared blankly at Ross.

"I hope you don't intend to keep me here," Bogart suddenly announced. "You can babysit this one."

Ross waved him off. "Just go."

Bogart grinned then politely opened the door for Monroe and Beck. Once they left the study, he hurried after them.

✝

*T*onya stared at the computer screen with a stunned look on her face. The message read, 'transfer complete' at only nine million dollars.

"No," she cried out in a high-pitched squeal and leaped from her chair, causing it to roll back and hit the table behind it. "No!" She suddenly hesitated and looked around the office with a horrible realization. "Oh, hell no."

Tonya ran across the office, fumbled with the lock, and pulled the door open. Mac stood before the door and smiled sweetly. Tonya gasped with surprise. Mac punched Tonya in the face, tossing her several feet into the room and onto the floor. Mac casually entered the room while Tonya scrambled to her feet, holding her reddened cheek. Tonya's eyes were wide with fear as she stared at the approaching woman.

"You know," Mac announced casually, "you and I never did get a chance to have that talk."

Tonya placed her hands in front of her and frantically waved them. "Why don't we come up with a workable deal? We split the money and both of us can disappear forever."

"You're offering me twenty-five million dollars to screw over my boss?" Mac suddenly asked then smiled sweetly while cocking her head to the side. "I'm listening."

"It's only nine million," Tonya quickly announced then slowly straightened. "Someone downloaded the rest out from under me." She suddenly frowned. "Lee, no doubt."

Mac snorted a laugh. "You want me to betray my boss for a mere four and a half million dollars?" She sneered her annoyance. "I'm no longer listening."

Tonya again held her hands up as Mac approached. "I'll give you five."

223

She stopped her approach. "I'll take seven," Mac remarked sternly.

"Seven?" Tonya exploded.

"Or I could just take you to Sal and let him shake that account number from you," Mac replied casually.

Tonya sneered with disgust, huffed, and folded her arms across her chest. "Fine, you can have seven, but we have to get out of here. If they accessed the server, they must know I'm here. Get me out of here, and I'll transfer the seven million to an account of your choosing."

"You want out of here?" Mac demanded. "Then you better give me that account number now."

"I'll give you half of the account number," Tonya bargained. "That way you won't screw me over."

Mac offered a pleased smile. "You're smarter than I gave you credit. What are the numbers?"

Tonya approached the desk and wrote several numbers on a piece of paper then handed it to Mac. Mac glanced at the number. When she looked back at Tonya, Tonya thrust a stun gun against her side. Mac cried out, jerked, and collapsed to the floor. Tonya ran from the office, into the hallway, and headed for the stairs. As she rounded the corner, she saw Zack casually leaning against the wall near the stairs while holding a magazine in one hand and a business card in the other. He tossed the magazine aside then turned the card over to reveal some handwritten numbers. He grinned with an almost humored expression.

"Please tell me you weren't stupid enough to leave your offshore bank account number on this card I found tucked in the pages of a magazine," he announced.

Tonya stared at the card in his hand. Her surprise turned to anger. "Give that to me."

She took a step toward him. Zack grinned and slipped the card down the front of his pants. He suddenly jumped and grimaced his discomfort.

"Ouch, paper cut!" He then looked at her with satisfaction and held up his hands. "Come and get it."

Tonya stared at him and appeared to reconsider her options. She turned and ran down the hall in the opposite direction. Zack casually headed for the elevator. Mac appeared in the hallway and saw Zack leaning against the wall while waiting for the elevator. She stared at him with surprise.

"Where'd she go?" she demanded.

He casually indicated the opposite direction. "Let Holden deal with her," Zack announced. "I have what we came for."

Mac's mouth fell open as she stared at him. "You have the account number?"

Zack grinned and patted his crotch. "Safe and sound."

"Just in case--" Mac announced then ran for the stairs after Tonya.

When the elevator door opened, Zack casually entered and pressed the bottom floor. As the doors closed, he grimaced and scratched his crotch. He then casually clasped his hands in front of him and waited for the doors to close as he whistled a soft tune.

✝

Tonya ran down the last few steps, having run down all nineteen flights, leaped over first dead man near the doorway, and then stopped to grab his discarded gun. She hurried out the door and into the parking garage to her awaiting catering van. She opened the driver's side door to be greeted by a foot striking her chest. She was roughly thrown from the van and to the concrete floor. Tonya groaned softly and slowly pulled herself to her hands and knees. She looked back at the van as Zack jumped out while maintaining his sly grin. He stood over her while casually folding his arms across his chest.

"Would you care to wave the white flag now?" he asked almost cheerfully.

Tonya glanced at the gun only six inches from her hand and appeared to consider reaching for it. The sound of a gun firing echoed through the parking garage, surprising Zack. Tonya's head exploded blood and flesh. As she fell limp to the concrete floor, Zack removed his gun and aimed it at Mac, who stood several feet away with a gun in her hand. Zack appeared angered but mostly stunned. Mac smiled sweetly and tossed her gun aside.

"You're welcome."

Zack remained stunned as he slowly lowered his gun. "What the hell was that?" he demanded.

"She was reaching for that gun," Mac replied casually.

"She didn't reach for the gun," he insisted.

"She was going to," Mac announced firmly. "If I had hesitated, she could have killed you."

"I wasn't in any danger," he snarled.

Mac rolled her eyes and groaned. "Stop being so dramatic," she snapped and headed for her nearby car. "Let's get that account number to Sal."

Zack replaced his gun, muttered something under his breath, and followed her. She glanced at him as they approached her borrowed Town Car. She looked around then appeared puzzled.

"How did you get here so fast?"

"Superpowers," he snapped coldly then climbed into the passenger seat. Zack removed his cell phone and pressed a button. He only waited a moment for a response. "Ross, we have the account number. We're on our way back to the mansion," he announced. "Tell Holden we left some wet stuff for him to clean up."

Ross's voice shouted through the phone.

Zack casually disconnected the call and glared at Mac. "You've created a lot of trouble for me," he remarked. "Ross is going to rip me a new one for *your* kill."

"So tell him I pulled the trigger."

Zack groaned and lacked enthusiasm as he looked out the side window. "He'll never believe that," he muttered. "I have a few marks against me for similar bad behavior."

She glanced at him, smiled sweetly, and held back her chuckle. "Well, maybe there's something I could do to make it up to you," she announced while lustfully raising her brow.

Zack glanced at her with little emotion, yet there was a tiny spark in his eyes. "What did you have in mind?"

Mac grinned.

†

*T*he motel room door flew open as Mac and Zack fell through the doorway while kissing and groping each other. Mac kicked the door shut with her foot without breaking off the aggressive kiss. She threw her legs around Zack's waist as he half tackled her to the bed. They kissed wildly and passionately while shedding clothing without missing a beat. Within moments, both were naked and entangled in each other's arms. Mac cried out with ecstasy loud enough to alert the entire motel of their sexual encounter, prompting Zack's aggression to escalate further. She dragged her fingernails along his back, momentarily startling him, but the action soon increased his aggression.

226

✝

Zack collapsed to the mattress while panting and breathing heavily. Mac panted alongside him. Her hair was mussed and she wore a devious grin on her face. She leaned across his chest and kissed him quickly but passionately on the lips. She pulled back and met his gaze.

"Skilled fighters make the best lovers," she proclaimed then kissed him again with more passion. She broke off the kiss, ran her fingers seductively along his chest, and smiled sweetly. "Since we're pressed for time, you have twenty minutes to recover before round two."

Mac rolled over him and off the opposite side of the bed. She snatched his discarded shirt and headed into the bathroom. Zack watched her naked backside as he attempted to catch his breath. He grinned until she disappeared into the bathroom. When the door shut, he grimaced, turned on his side, and gingerly touched the bleeding scratches on his back. He groaned, fell onto his back, and stared at the ceiling.

"Kitty needs her claws cut," he muttered then shut his eyes.

✝

Mac appeared from the bathroom a few minutes later wearing Zack's dress shirt. Within the dimly lit room, she approached the bed and the mass sleeping peacefully beneath the covers. Mac stopped two feet before the bed, smiled lustfully while gently tilting her head, possibly reflecting back on their lovemaking, and then raised the gun affixed with a silencer. Without hesitation, she fired two shots into the mass on the bed.

"Sorry, Zack," she announced sweetly while lowering the gun. "It's nothing personal. Just greed."

Chapter Forty-one

Ross, Sal, and Lee had gathered in the foyer to await Zack and Mac's return with the account number containing the remaining nine million dollars. Holden and several other federal agents had scattered throughout the mansion, investigating the deaths of Jericho's men, who had once worked for Sal but switched sides in the name of greed. While their investigation continued, Beck sat alongside Pinto on the grand staircase, almost oblivious to the conversation by the others within the foyer. With his chin in his hand, Beck listened intently as Pinto explained her decision to reunite with her father. The love-struck look in Beck's eyes made it difficult to tell if he heard a word she'd said.

"When you and your friends showed up at the lounge, you said you had information on my father and needed my help getting into his computer files," Pinto announced then appeared curious. "You didn't really have anything, did you?"

Beck snapped out of his love-induced trance and shifted slightly. "Oh, we had information," he remarked then clasped his hands between his knees. "I just wasn't sure what we had. Gil had sent some files to our secured server. I didn't have a chance to look over them until later that night." He fidgeted and turned serious. "I hate to tell you this, Pinto, but I'm almost positive they were blackmail photos. Either your father had been blackmailing someone or the other way around."

She stared at him and appeared to hold her breath. It was now her turn to fidget.

"Were they pictures of a car accident and a dead woman, possibly taken from a police crime lab?"

He appeared surprised and stared at her. "Yeah, how did you know?"

She frowned and looked at her father, who entered the foyer while talking with several feds. She drew a deep breath then looked back at Beck.

"I found those pictures in my father's computer, which is what started our last fight," she replied gently. "That's the reason I left in the first place." She fidgeted then reluctantly continued. "I was dating this guy, and, naturally, my father didn't approve. Turns out, my new boyfriend was a suspect in the *accidental* death of his girlfriend. I was mad at my father for digging up the photos and police reports. Even though I knew it was the right thing to do, I just needed to get away from both of them."

"So those pictures had nothing to do with criminal activity by your father?"

She smiled timidly and shook her head. "I'm not saying he hasn't done anything illegal in his time, because I've often wondered the same thing myself, but those pictures had nothing to do with him."

"I'm sorry for everything we've put you through," Beck announced gently.

"You did what you had to do to save Lee," Pinto replied then smiled warmly. "I'm just glad I was able to help you and your friends. I mean, after all, you did go out of your way to return my bracelet...two weeks later."

They exchanged looks. Pinto smiled knowingly.

Beck hid his grin and looked away. "I'm a lousy liar."

Across the foyer, Holden talked to the forensics team placing the dead man into a body bag. Once he had his information, he approached Ross and shook his head.

"You left quite a mess for me to clean up," Holden remarked. "There's a trail of dead bodies from here to the office building." He then looked around and seemed agitated. "Where the hell is Zack? I still need details about what happened with Tonya."

"He should have been here by now," Ross announced then took a step closer to Holden to speak confidentially. "Jericho doesn't know Tonya is dead. You may be able to get a confession out of him if he thinks she's about to throw him under the bus."

"That occurred to me," Holden replied. "Can you try calling Zack again?"

"I left two messages," Ross remarked. "Zack can be annoyingly aloof at times. He'll show up."

Sal approached Lee where she leaned against the hall table while studying Ross with Holden. Sal gently cleared his throat, catching her attention, and then smiled timidly.

"Thank you for believing in me, Lee," he announced warmly. "I told you I'd never hurt you."

She tensed slightly, rubbed her chilled arms, and then smiled timidly. "I just wish I could have put a little more faith in Finn. Maybe he wouldn't be dead."

"Finn's death wasn't your fault," he informed her. "Finn had an unsettling way about him, and he was a bit of a risk taker. You know, he was eager to rescue you from Jericho's clutches. It was a risk he was willing to take to bring you back. You were very important to him." Sal hesitated then smiled gently. "You're also very important to me, Lee. I know you've been through a lot, but I want you to come back and work for me once you've recovered from your ordeal."

She knew she needed her job, but she just couldn't bring herself to commit to returning at the moment.

"I think I need some time to recover from all this," she gently informed him.

"I understand," Sal replied. "I'd like to offer you my beach house for as long as you need it. Then, when you're ready, you can come back to work."

"That's very generous of you," she replied. "But I'll need to think about that."

"You just let me know, and I'll have you whisked away in my private helicopter to that beach house," he announced cheerfully.

The door opened, causing everyone to turn toward the main entrance. Gil entered with the limping dog by his side. Darth had a patch on his injured shoulder. Gil seemed curious by the looks he received.

"What did I miss?" Gil asked.

Bogart, Monroe, and Kirk entered behind him. All three looked equally annoyed.

"No sign of Zack," Monroe remarked. "We met a few dozen of Holden's friends at the office building, but Zack wasn't anywhere to be found."

"Is anyone really surprised?" Beck muttered from where he sat on the stairs alongside Pinto.

"As typical as that sounds, Zack should have been back by now," Kirk remarked. "We should probably look for him."

"Where would we even start?" Monroe almost demanded. "You know Zack. He could be in the Amazon by now."

Sal appeared alarmed and looked at Ross and his men. "You don't suppose he took the account information and ran off with the nine million, do you?"

"Not Zack," Ross replied firmly. "He's more into borrowing expensive toys than stealing money." A strange look crossed Ross's face as he studied Sal. "What about your girl, Mac? Is she trustworthy?"

"She's loyal," Sal replied without hesitation. "A little headstrong and flirtatious, but she's definitely loyal."

There was a round of groans. Sal and Bogart eyed the others, not understanding.

"What did I say?" Sal asked.

Kirk snorted a laugh then grinned slyly. "If she so much as winked at Zack, he'd be looking for an excuse to jump her."

"He's a sucker for dangerous women," Beck remarked.

As the men continued to discuss Zack's bizarre taste in women, Gil sat on the floor and played with the affectionate German shepherd. Darth jumped on him despite his injury and licked Gil's face. Sal watched them, hid his grin, and shook his head.

"Some guard dog, huh?" Sal asked.

"He saved my life," Gil remarked in all seriousness. "That makes us comrades."

"You want to keep him?" Sal asked.

Gil eyed Sal and showed little emotion. "I intended to leave with him, if that's what you meant," he announced, seeming unwilling to give Sal much choice.

Sal laughed softly but didn't seem to mind. "Fine, he's yours. Take good care of him."

Gil flipped the dog onto his back and scratched his belly. The dog thumped his hind leg in response.

"Hear that, buddy?" he announced in baby talk. "You're coming home with me. Although, we'll need to fit you for a bulletproof vest."

After another ten minutes had passed, Sal started pacing while watching the door.

"I don't like this," Sal finally announced. "It's been over an hour. Even if they made an *unauthorized* side stop, they should have been here by now." He glared at Ross. "I think your man went AWOL."

"Who went AWOL?" Zack asked from nearby.

Everyone turned and looked at Zack, who leaned casually in the archway with a plate of hors d'oeuvre, eagerly feasting on them. He indicated the pastry in his hand.

"This is fantastic," Zack announced with his mouth full. "I have to have the recipe."

"Where the hell have you been?" Ross demanded.

Zack gave him an innocent look. "In the kitchen fixing myself a plate. I was starving." He then handed Sal a napkin with some numbers written on it. "This is the account number and the bank where your nine million was transferred. Is that your helicopter out back? That's a nice one. You should probably invest in a better lock. I picked that puppy with a paperclip. Mind if I take it out for a spin?"

Ross groaned softly, quickly losing patience. "Zack, where have you been?"

Zack looked at Ross and appeared almost offended. "I told you."

"Before the kitchen," Kirk snarled.

"Oh, that," Zack replied. "Mac and I stopped off at a motel for a quickie. That girl has no morals. Needless to say, it took longer than anticipated. I would have called, but I was busy--"

"Never mind the details," Ross growled then ran his fingers through his graying hair. "I'm sorry I asked."

"Where's Mac?" Sal asked.

"She decided to move on to greener pastures," Zack replied. "I think I heard her mention Costa Rico."

"What?" Sal demanded. "She quit?"

"It was a sound decision," Zack informed him. "She needed time to get her head on straight."

Sal groaned and threw his hands up in the air. "Terrific," he launched. "Half my men betrayed me, and the other half either quit or were shot."

Monroe approached Zack while the others were busy talking. He eyed his friend and gently cleared his throat.

"She double-crossed her boss, didn't she?" Monroe asked in a soft tone.

Zack shrugged.

"Did she try to kill you?" he pressed.

"Well, you know how it is with women," Zack replied casually and popped another pastry into his mouth.

Monroe awaited the other half of the comment that wasn't likely coming. He grew frustrated, pulled Zack aside, and forced him to meet his gaze.

"Come on, give," Monroe again pressed. "What happened? Between us--"

t

*E*arlier at the motel. Mac stopped two feet before the bed in the dimly lit room and smiled lustfully while tilting her head, possibly reflecting back on their lovemaking. She then raised the gun affixed with a silencer and fired two shots into the mass on the bed.

"Sorry, Zack," she announced sweetly as she lowered the gun. "It's nothing personal. Just greed."

Mac turned away from the bed. The gun flew from her hand and across the floor. Zack, wearing only his boxer shorts, stared at her with a displeased look.

"Bad kitty," he growled softly then spun into a roundhouse kick, connecting with her abdomen, and threw her across the bed, scattering the pillows beneath the bullet-riddled sheet.

Mac sprang up on the other side of the bed and sneered at him. "How did you know?" she demanded.

He snorted a laugh. "Every woman I've ever slept with has tried to kill me," he remarked. "I wasn't expecting you to be any different."

"Fine," she snarled. "You want to play? Let's play."

Mac jumped onto the bed and immediately spun into a roundhouse kick for his head. Zack ducked and swept her legs out from beneath her, knocking her back onto the bed. She landed with a bounce. She scrambled to her knees on the bed with a look of hostility across her face. Her look suddenly turned to horror. Zack lowered the lighter while holding the burning business card. He grinned slyly while watching the flame grow larger. Mac screamed and leaped for him, tackling him to the floor. They struggled on the floor a moment while Mac attempted to reach the burning card, but it was too late, the card was already destroyed. She cried out with anger, straddled his waist while sitting up, and punched him in the face. Zack tossed her onto the floor, landing on top of her, and held her down with his body while putting out the tiny fire with his free hand. She fought against him, attempting to get him off her and injure him at the same time. He pinned her to the floor and appeared curious.

"Are we still on for round two?" he asked slyly.

She cried out with anger then screamed, "You bastard!"

Zack chuckled softly in his throat and pulled her up into a sitting position by her wrists. She was only inches from his face and stared at his twisted, mocking smile.

"Your boss is expecting us," he informed her. "You may want to put some clothes on."

She sneered at him and pulled her wrists free from his clutches. There was an odd silence as she stared at him. Without warning, she threw one arm around his neck, grabbed his face with her other hand, and kissed him aggressively. Zack returned the kiss, pulled her leg up to his hip, and lowered her to the floor.

Chapter Forty-two

*L*ater that evening, just a little after dusk, the garden party had cleared out and the caterers were cleaning up while the rental company busily removed chairs and tables. The gang of Whiskey Tango Foxtrot along with Bogart, Lee, Pinto, and Sal sat at one of the terrace tables with full trays of leftover hors d'oeuvre in front of them. They laughed and had a good time drinking expensive brandy and filling up on party leftovers. Sal finally looked at Zack and grinned.

"I promised a ten percent finder's fee for the return of my stolen nine million dollars," Sal announced then cocked his head slightly. "I guess you're the beneficiary. Where would you like your finder's fee sent?"

"I'd rather play with some of those shiny toys you have out back--" Zack suddenly yelped, jumped in his chair, and looked at his comrades around the table. "Who the hell kicked me?" he demanded.

All five glared at Zack. Beck looked at Sal, fidgeted, and then smiled charmingly.

"What my friend meant to say," Beck announced then turned somewhat serious. "You can write a cashier's check to WTF, Incorporated."

Kirk glared at Zack and snarled lowly in response, "Yeah, considering we have a war-torn lodge to repair."

"And a beach house blown to bits," Monroe remarked with the same look.

Zack looked back at Sal sitting at the head of the table and frowned like a lost, disappointed schoolboy. "I think I've been outvoted," he muttered softly.

Sal chuckled softly. "I'll get that check for you before you leave," he replied then smiled. "And we'll see about letting you play with some of those toys."

Zack's enthusiasm quickly returned. "Well, this has been a fun day."

"I'm glad someone enjoyed themselves," Lee muttered into her glass.

Holden stepped out of the house while replacing his cell phone to his jacket pocket. He joined the others at the table and helped himself to some leftovers. Ross poured him a drink and pushed it in front of him. He reluctantly accepted.

"The team has finished their investigation," Holden announced to Sal. "You're free to return to your home."

"Thank you, Agent Falcone," Sal replied pleasantly. "I assume you've cleared me of any wrongdoing, and I'm officially not out to kill my lovely, young employee?"

"It was an honest mistake," Holden replied.

"I agree," Sal replied. "No hard feelings?" he asked while extending his hand.

Holden forced a tiny smile and firmly shook his hand. "None at all."

Sal casually leaned back in his chair, studied Holden's expression, and chuckled softly. "You still think I'm some sort of mob boss, don't you?"

"Time will tell," Holden replied.

Sal shrugged while maintaining his grin. Holden glanced around the table at the others.

"It's late," Holden announced to the table of men and women. "Jackie agreed to fly you wherever you want to go in the morning. Can I give her a heads up?"

The team exchanged looks then focused their attention back on Holden.

"I have a beach house to rebuild," Monroe informed him. "Back to Florida for me."

Gil fed leftovers to Darth, who sat by his side. He then looked at Monroe with little emotion.

"I'll help you rebuild," Gil remarked then looked back at the dog. "I think Darth would like to chill on the beach while recovering from his first mission."

"Got room for one more?" Bogart eagerly asked while leaning forward in his chair.

Monroe tensed then fidgeted in his seat. "Sorry, man, the trailer I'm renting isn't that big. Gil's going to be sleeping on the sofa as it is."

"Yeah, right," Gil snorted then laughed while scratching the dog's neck. He leaned his face closer to the dog's nose and talked baby talk to Darth. "There are two of us," he announced. "We need more room, don't we?" The dog eagerly licked his face. "Oh, yes, we do."

Bogart frowned and sank back in his chair. He then looked at Holden.

"I guess it's you and me, bro," Bogart announced.

Holden suddenly laughed. "If I bring you home, Jackie will kill us both." He then grinned and looked at Sal. "But I think Sal could use a few good men on his team."

"Yeah, sure," Sal announced without hesitation and glanced at Bogart. "You can settle into one of the rooms in the staff wing until you find your own place. I have a few positions that have recently opened up."

Bogart reluctantly nodded, but he was obviously feeling left out by the team.

"And I'm heading back to Colorado," Beck announced then sighed softly while shaking his head. "The lodge was in bad shape even before it fell under enemy fire. There are a lot of repairs to be made."

"Count me in," Kirk announced then glanced at Zack, who leaned his chin on the table while toasting a piece of shrimp on a toothpick over the candle centerpiece.

Kirk slapped Zack's thigh, alerting him to the conversation to which he appeared oblivious.

"Huh? What did I miss?" Zack suddenly asked while lifting his head.

"Beck needs help fixing up the lodge," Kirk remarked. "What are your plans?"

"Oh, yeah," Zack announced and casually waved him off. "Whatever. I'm in." He returned to toasting his shrimp over the flame.

"I'd like to get in on that flight back to Colorado," Pinto announced.

Sal turned toward her with surprise and disappointment on his face. "You're leaving so soon?"

She gently patted his arm and smiled affectionately. "I have other commitments at the club," she replied. "But I promise I won't stay away so long next time. I'll come back to visit, and you can come to Colorado and visit me."

He gently nodded and forced a tiny smile. "I'd like that. Are you still at the same address?"

Pinto grinned and glanced at Beck, who hid his smile while looking away. She looked back at her father.

"I'll probably be spending a lot of my free time at the lodge," she replied.

The guys looked from Pinto to Beck and appeared surprised. Beck placed his hand to his mouth to keep them from seeing his grin then looked away from the table. Beck fidgeted slightly, gently cleared his throat, and looked at Bogart in an attempt to change the subject.

"We could always use another pair of hands at the lodge," Beck announced, "if you're interested."

Bogart stared at Beck with surprise and could barely contain his enthusiasm. "Really? Ah, man, that's fantastic," he suddenly announced while gesturing excitedly with his hands. "Yes, of course. I'm one of the team now, right?" He looked around the table. "This means I'm one of you guys, right?"

There were several groans around the table. Bogart leaned back in his chair, hid his smile, and waved his hands.

"One step at a time. I understand," Bogart announced. "I'm willing to prove myself."

Sal glanced at Lee and smiled warmly. "If you want that beach house for a few weeks, it's just a quick flight to Bermuda from Florida."

"If I say 'yes' to the beach house that doesn't mean I'm agreeing to return to my old position," she informed him.

"I understand," Sal informed her and waved his hands. "No strings attached."

Lee smiled and nodded her appreciation. "Thank you," she replied. "That sounds wonderful."

Ross glanced at Holden. "You can put me down for transport back to Colorado as well. I've been away from home too long as it is."

"You've got it," Holden announced. He finished his drink and stood. "I'll pick you up here at seven sharp."

"O-seven-hundred," Ross announced. "Got it."

Holden finished his drink, gave a general wave, and then headed back inside through the terrace doors. Lee finished her drink and stood as well. All the men made a motion to stand respectfully, causing her to blush slightly. Bogart was the only one who remained seated and looked around with a baffled look.

"I'm exhausted," Lee announced. "I'll meet you guys in the morning."

"I'll make sure the cook has breakfast ready early," Sal announced pleasantly.

"Why don't I show you to your room," Pinto announced and also stood. "I could lend you something to sleep in."

All the men stood again. Bogart eyed the others, sprang to his feet as well, and then grinned.

"I get it," Bogart announced cheerfully. "It's that gentleman bullshit, right?"

The guys cast looks at him. Pinto joined Lee. They were sent off with a round of 'goodnights'.

†

*O*nce Pinto returned to her room, Lee changed into the moderately revealing, satin nightgown Pinto had lent her. Her bedroom had a balcony overlooking the garden, which contained an amazing view. She opened the balcony doors to allow the warm breeze to enter the room. The moonlight and garden lights provided a romantic glow into her room. She could hear the men joking and laughing while they shared a few more drinks. She leaned against the doorframe near the balcony and listened to them talk. She let her head fall back, inhaled deeply, and then groaned. Oddly enough, she found herself already missing them. Maybe even Zack too. As she listened to the familiar voices, although a bit cruder in conversation now that the women were gone, she wondered what her new life would be like.

Tonya had betrayed her, and she was the only friend she really connected with in recent years. As she listened to Ross's smooth, pleasant voice, she already felt sad. She enjoyed having him as her protector. For the first time in a long time, she felt desire. As much as she hated to admit it, she wondered if Tonya had the right idea regarding men. She no longer wanted to be alone and without male companionship, but she didn't know if she wanted to get over Ross either.

A soft knock on the bedroom door across the hall from hers snapped her out of her fantasy. She couldn't resist taking a peek.

Lee hurried across the room and looked out the dainty peek hole. Beck stood outside the door across the hall. The door opened to reveal Pinto. She grinned, took his hand, and guided him into her bedroom. He casually shut the door behind him. Lee groaned softly and leaned against the door. Why couldn't she be *that* girl just once? Would a one-night stand with Ross be enough, or would it just make it that much harder to say goodbye? She struggled with her emotions and morals a moment longer, groaned with disgust, and flung herself onto the bed. She could still hear Ross and the guys beneath her balcony through the open door. Lee pulled the covers over her head and attempted to forget about him.

Chapter Forty-three

Lee tossed restlessly beneath the covers within the elegant bedroom. The mansion and estate were almost as quiet as the lodge in Colorado. She looked at the bedside clock. It was a little after two in the morning. There were no more voices coming from the terrace below, and with good reason. They would be leaving for the private airfield in less than five hours. She was certain sleep wasn't coming anymore tonight. Light from the garden still filtered into her bedroom, although she was positive that wasn't the reason for her inability to sleep. She finally got out of bed, approached the open balcony door, and stepped outside into the warm night. The garden looked so peaceful; she couldn't even tell that there had been two-hundred guests just a few hours earlier. She heard the sound of a glass clinking against the table below. Lee leaned on the balcony railing and looked to the terrace beneath her. Ross slouched in his chair with his feet comfortably crossed and propped on the nearby chair. His hands were clasped over his abdomen and his eyes were shut, although she was certain he wasn't asleep, since he had just set down his glass.

She studied him, staring helplessly at the distinguished man. Although far from a cowboy, she couldn't help the desire she felt for him. She leaned heavily on the concrete half wall, shut her eyes, and ran her fingers through her mussed hair.

"Trouble sleeping?" Ross asked from below.

Lee opened her eyes and stared at the man who now stared up at her. She straightened, aware of the revealing nightgown she wore, but she didn't care what he saw. For once, she wanted a man to look at her *that* way.

"No," she replied gently. "It's just been a, uh, weird sort of day."

Ross laughed softly then casually replied, "Just another day at the office for me."

Lee managed a throaty laugh. "And yet you're unable to sleep as well. Unless Sal ran out of guestrooms."

"I'm steerage," Ross teased with a grin.

"I sincerely doubt that," she replied almost more to herself.

He placed his feet on the stone terrace, straightened, and held up the bottle of brandy.

"Perhaps a little nightcap will take the edge off," he announced cheerfully.

"I'm a little underdressed for the occasion," she informed him, although she was toying with the thought of joining him.

"Well, you're in luck," he announced. "A first-class joint like this has balcony service."

She considered his comment. Was he actually asking permission to come up to her room? As her mind raced for a response, a dozen scenarios rushed through her subconscious. He returned the cork to the bottle and stood.

"I'll warn you," he announced. "If you miss, it's going to wake the entire house."

She then realized he intended to toss the bottle up to her. Lee's expression dropped, but before she could protest, he was already swinging the bottle for an underhand toss. As the bottle flew up to her, she let out a startled gasp, and caught the flying projectile. Her heart was pounding as she held the bottle. She let out a relieved laugh and shook her head while staring down at him and the cheap grin on his face.

"I actually thought you meant you were coming up," she remarked while attempting to hide her panic from the potential of missing the bottle and having it shatter on the balcony.

"Oh," he replied while giving her an innocent look. "That was rude of me. Women should never drink alone."

Ross took a short running start, half ran up the wall, and caught onto the bottom edge of the balcony. Lee suddenly gasped while watching him dangle a moment. He swung his legs upward onto the ledge, grabbed onto the half wall, and sprang over it, appearing alongside her where she stood. Lee stared at him with her mouth hanging open. She looked over the balcony to the terrace below then looked back at him.

"Holy hell," she gasped softly.

"I still have a few surprises left in me," he informed her while grinning. "Just for the record, the odds of getting back down the same way without breaking my neck are not nearly as good."

"You can use the door," she replied with a soft laugh.

He took the bottle of brandy from her and removed the cork. "I'm also not going back down for glasses, so it's going to be the Navy way."

Ross took a swig from the bottle and handed it to her. Lee laughed and accepted the bottle. She took a small sip then glanced at him as he casually leaned over the railing. She couldn't deny how sexy he looked standing on her balcony. Moreover, she couldn't deny how turned on she was by how he got up to the balcony in the first place. Lee tore her eyes away from him and took a large swallow from the bottle then returned it to him. Ross accepted the bottle, turned his back to the half wall, and leaned against it while facing her. He stared at her a moment then became tense.

"So you're staying at Sal's beach house in Bermuda, huh?"

She stared into his blue eyes and felt her heart pound. She wanted to throw herself at him and beg him to stay with her tonight. Lee cleared the inappropriate thoughts from her mind and smiled weakly.

"It's certainly a better option than returning to my apartment and staring at the four walls," she replied. "If I'm sitting alone in my apartment, there's a greater chance I'll give in and go back to work for Sal. I'd rather have a clear head before making that decision."

Ross casually set the bottle on the half wall and looked back at her.

"There are other options, you know," he announced gently. "When people aren't trying to kill you, Colorado can be very peaceful."

"If the guys wanted me to crash their little lodge renovation party, I'm sure they would have asked," she replied.

"I didn't mean the lodge," he announced gently. "My place offers similar scenery with less cursing."

There was an awkward silence between them. Lee stared at him as she attempted to make sense of what he was actually saying. Ross suddenly fidgeted and offered an embarrassed smile.

"That wasn't meant to sound like a proposition," he quickly announced. "I didn't mean any disrespect. I just meant, well, you could stay at my place while you figure out what you want to do next." He offered a warm smile. "I'm very much a gentleman, I promise."

She continued to stare at him as a thousand thoughts flooded her mind. She wasn't even sure how to respond, but she needed to say something.

"What if I didn't want you to be such a gentleman?" she almost whispered while staring at him as her heart pounded to her own words.

It was his turn to stare at her. She'd successfully rendered him speechless and immediately wondered if it was a mistake coming on so strong.

"I'm sure we could come up with some sort of arrangement," he replied softly.

Despite her pounding heart and the slight dizziness she suddenly felt, she smiled warmly.

"I'd like that."

Ross appeared relieved, although neither moved. He suddenly pulled her into his arms and kissed her briefly but passionately. He broke off the kiss as quickly as he'd engaged and smiled with some embarrassment.

"I'm sorry," he announced. "My brain shut off for a minute there. I don't want you to think any less--"

Lee threw her arms around his neck and kissed him with desire and urgency. She wasn't about to let the moment pass. Ross immediately returned the kiss with added aggression while pulling her against him. His hands firmly traveled her back and hip, pressing her against the half wall for additional support. She felt the brandy bottle as she hit it. The bottle fell from the wall and shattered on the terrace floor below, startling both. Ross jumped away from her to the loud crash that surely woke everyone. He grabbed her hand and pulled her into her room, shutting the balcony doors behind him. He peered out through the part in the sheer curtains. When other lights on the second floor came on, he let the sheer curtains fall back into place.

t

*L*ee nuzzled Ross's chest as they lie together beneath the slightly mussed covers. He held her against him, his eyes closed and a permanent grin on his face. Lee ran her hand along his chest and shoulder and sank into her own thoughts. She didn't know what would happen with her and Ross, but she decided it was time to live in the moment for a change. And she was enjoying this moment. Ross chuckled softly in his throat, catching her attention. She lifted her head and met his gaze. He saw her look and maintained his smile.

"My brother-in-law and niece are going to be shocked that I'm actually bringing a girlfriend home," he informed her. "Since my sister died, it's just been the three of us."

"You live with your brother-in-law and niece?"

"Well, not technically," he replied. "They live in the guesthouse, although my niece spends more time in the main house. After my sister died, my brother-in-law needed someone to help raise his daughter, and I needed help with the ranch."

Lee's expression dropped slightly as she stared at him through the dim lighting. "Ranch? As in horses and cattle?"

"Not really a ranch. More of a gentleman's farm. Less than one hundred acres," he corrected. "I have a few head of steer, half a dozen horses, some pigs, chickens, and a few dogs and cats."

She stared at him as her mind reeled with the new information. He stared back at her and appeared concerned.

"Does the idea of a ranch bother you?" he suddenly asked as his body tensed. "It's really just a hobby. I keep the farm animals as lawn ornaments. I wouldn't dream of butchering them, if that's what's worrying you."

Lee suddenly laughed and clung to him. "No, I actually like the sound of a ranch," she remarked and held back her pleased smile. "I'm just trying to imagine you in a cowboy hat and boots." It was true; she was trying very hard to imagine that.

"Wait until you see me at the annual barn dance," he announced cheerfully. "Nothing more amusing than a former Navy SEAL doing a drunken hoedown."

She grinned and kissed him quickly on the lips. "I'm looking forward to it. I, uh, sort of have a thing for cowboys."

"I'm glad to hear," he announced. "Being a cowboy was a dream of mine since I was a boy. Of course, I'll have to teach you the hoedown."

"Deal," she replied happily.

t

Seven o'clock the following morning. Ross and Lee hurried down the stairs to join the others already waiting in the foyer. They received strange looks from his men, although Whiskey Tango Foxtrot appeared to be short two men. Holden glanced at his watch then looked around.

"Where's Zack?" Holden demanded hotly. "And why is he always missing?"

Ross glanced around the foyer and appeared curious. "Kirk's not here either," he announced then glanced at Sal. "Which rooms are theirs?"

"Oh, you don't need to worry about them," Sal announced while casually waving. "I made a deal with your friend last night."

All eyes were suddenly on Sal with shared concern.

"What deal?" Ross asked sternly.

"I cut a check for eight hundred thousand and threw the helicopter in," Sal announced cheerfully. "He really wanted that helicopter. Seeing how Finn was my pilot--"

The men stared blankly at Sal, alarming him with their looks. He eyed each man in silent question.

"Please tell me they're still out back," Ross muttered.

"No, they left half an hour ago. Zack said they'd meet you in Colorado," Sal remarked and stared back. "Why? What's the problem?"

"The idiot doesn't know how to fly a helicopter," Monroe snapped. "Although he has mastered the art of crashing one."

Sal stared at them with his mouth hanging open and appeared at a loss for words. "Oh--"

Holden groaned and removed his cell phone. "I'll tell Jackie to contact them and talk him down."

†

*T*he helicopter teetered while flying through the air at high speeds, scraping the tops of trees as it passed over them. Zack sat before the controls with his headset on while hooting and hollering like a deranged lunatic. Kirk clung to the side and seat while staring frozen out the windshield, screaming in terror. The helicopter flew into the horizon.

The End

Other books by Holly Copella!
Reviews left on Amazon are appreciated!

"The Battle for Andrea Maria"

A cruise ship attack turns six survivors into overnight celebrities after they take credit for the heroic act of a stowaway who died saving them.

The cruise is just what Jess needed--a bit of harmless fun far from her daily grind. But what begins as a relaxing vacation turns into a desperate fight for her life when terrorists take over the ship and start piling up bodies. Teaming up with a mysterious stowaway, Jess attempts to send out a distress call but knows they cannot wait for help to come. If she or the few remaining passengers have any hope for survival, Jess must act now. The papers dub it "The Battle for *Andrea Maria*," but to Jess it is the moment she fought side-by-side with her enigmatic Romeo, saving the ship--and losing him. She thinks the story ends there, but really, the nightmare is just beginning...

"Insanely Deadly"

When the dead return to life, it's up to an admiral's daughter and a mildly insane, former war hero to save their small town.

Jetta Cross, a Navy Admiral's daughter, is tasked with keeping her father's comrade, a former war hero turned town crazy, grounded in the real world. Capt. John Hunter is still fighting the war in his head, where imaginary dead people are part of his world. When a viral outbreak brings about a zombie uprising, Hunter is left to his own devices. He must resume his role as a one-man commando unit in order to destroy the ravenous undead. With Hunter still fighting his own inner demons as well as the undead, the townspeople fear their zombie neighbors may not be the only threat. Stranded at the island's luxurious resort with a handful of workers, Jetta is forced to live up to her father's reputation and take charge of the deteriorating situation at the hotel. She must wage her own war against the infected before the government declares her hometown a total loss.

"Deadly Institution"

A town recluse suspected of killing his wife teams up with a young woman in order to stop a killer.

After being accused of murdering his wife, Konrad Asher turns his back on the town that once adored him. Ten years later, he still holds his grudge and the title of the most feared man in town. With the reopening of the burned mental institution, where his wife had died, former employees are now murdered one-by-one, throwing suspicion back on Asher. A young local reporter, Jacey, is forced to reveal her long-time friendship with the infamous recluse in order to clear his name not only in the recent murders but to exonerate him in the death of his wife as well. Will Jacey's relationship with Asher invite the killer closer to her? Or is the killer already in her life?

"Screenplays: The Island Collection" *"Jungle Princess", "A.L.F. Resort", "Brighton Island"*

Discover how romance and fun in the sun can be downright *chilling*!

"Jungle Princess" is a romantic/thriller that leaves a teenage girl stranded on an island with two male shipmates and a creature of "unknown" origin. She soon discovers the island is home to an abandoned prison with several prisoners roaming free. What really killed over one hundred prisoners? And is it still out there--?

"A.L.F. Resort" is a romantic/thriller set on an island resort with Artificial Life Forms as the main draw. At this resort, all your fantasies come true...until a malfunction removes safety inhibitors on the A.L.F.'s. Zombies, biker gangs, and mobsters run amuck, turning fantasies into nightmares. A young reporter gets more of a story than she anticipates, but will she survive long enough to write the story?

"Brighton Island" is a romantic/thriller set on a private island. When the owner's niece brings her psychic friend to the mansion, his presence awakens the spirits' tortured souls. As the psychic attempts to solve the old murders, the niece is confronted with the possibility that she's next to join the mansion ghosts. Stranded on the island with a crazed killer, her uncle wages his own war to save them. Will his "shock and awe" tactics actually save them or get them killed?

"Reaper of Souls" A fantasy short story

A young woman must outwit an evil sorcerer in order to save her brother or become one of his minions forever.

Unwilling to believe her brother is dead, Reggie discovers an underhanded deal made with Kahn, a less than ethical sorcerer, who collects humans to serve as slaves in his kingdom. In order to rescue her brother from his horrible fate, she must complete his failed task or be forced to serve Kahn forever. After being transported to his world, Reggie realizes that even if she beats Kahn at his own game, she's at his mercy for him to uphold his end of the deal. All seems lost until Kahn's discontented, self-serving brother, Helsing, arrives. Can Reggie convince Helsing to help her? And at what cost?

"Death Displacement"

A grief-stricken man travels back in time to seek revenge on the woman who murdered his girlfriend but inadvertently falls in love with her.

Kane is about to marry the woman he loves. His life is perfect. A few weeks before the wedding, a vindictive woman from his girlfriend's past mysteriously arrives and kills her. He learns of a traumatic accident that happened five years earlier, which triggers Riley's hatred for his girlfriend. Distraught over his girlfriend's death, Kane uses an antique time machine to travel into the past in order to find and destroy the woman responsible. When he runs into Riley's younger self, he realizes she's not the monster she later becomes, and he can't bring himself to destroy her. With a little help from his oddball friend from the past, they formulate a plan to prevent the accident that sends Riley down her destructive path. Kane's plan backfires when he falls for the younger Riley. His new tortured existence is further complicated when future Riley, his girlfriend's killer, shows up with her own devious agenda that doesn't include him. Will he be able to stop the time ripple, which ultimately ends with his girlfriend's death? Or will future Riley take him out of the timeline forever--

"Dead Village"

After strange happenings isolate a small resort town from the rest of the world, nearly one hundred residents seek refuge at the closed hotel. Only eight survive the night. And that's just the beginning...

One day after the entire population of Fox Ridge Village disappears, a car wreck forces several unsuspecting crash victims to seek help at the closed summer hotel. Within the hotel, they discover the grisly aftermath of a brutal slaughter. Crash victims Vander and Devon, a reluctant clairvoyant, team up to solve the riddle of the "haunted hotel" and the mass hysteria plaguing the remaining survivors. By the time they discover the hotel's secret, they're already drawn into the hysteria. As the body count continues to climb, it's a race to isolate the source and bring everyone back to reality before they kill one another. Will Devon be able to communicate with the traumatized spirits before their fate becomes her own?

"Misfits, Inc."

A seemingly ordinary, young woman meets four misfits who claim she has given them supernatural powers.

While on a business trip to a remote island paradise, a bored secretary, Hailey, has her world turned upside down when her path collides with a psychic freak, Skyler. He attempts to convince her that they had met in his dreams, and she had chosen him as one of her four mystic warriors. After Skyler foresees a woman's death, they discover an unidentified creature has killed one of the guests. They are joined by a lounge pianist and a rich playboy, who also claim they had met her in their dreams. If Skyler's prophecies are genuine, the evil entity controlling the ravenous creatures needs to destroy Hailey to ensure its survival. Reluctantly accepting her fate, Hailey has to locate the last and most powerful of her chosen warriors, The Guardian. Their fate is in doubt when The Guardian turns out to be a self-absorbed, former cat burglar with a bad attitude. Can Hailey turn her company of misfits into an elite team of mystic warriors? Or will The Guardian's secret agenda destroy them all?

"Basement Dwellers"

A viral outbreak at a hospital leaves a mortician, sheriff, and coroner fighting for their lives against a horde of undead and the CDC.

After a massive car wreck leaves several survivors in critical condition at the local hospital, a surgeon uses experimental drugs on his critical patients and accidentally causes a zombie outbreak. When local mortician, Lexx, receives an infected corpse as her client, she becomes stranded in the hospital basement during CDC quarantine along with the local sheriff and the coroner. The infamous surgeon struggles to find a cure for his infectious blunder by using the other survivors as test subjects. Meanwhile, Lexx and the sheriff attempt to locate his missing sister, who's stranded somewhere in the battle zone that once was the emergency room. It's a race against time and the ravenous undead. Can they survive the undead before CDC sanitizes the hospital of all infection?

"Witness Protection"

After witnessing an execution, a resourceful young woman attempts to disappear while being pursued by a hitman and a handsome federal agent.

A helicopter pilot, Jackie Remus, reluctantly agrees to go on a date with one of her clients, but her date is unexpectedly cut short when she witnesses a man being murdered. After narrowly escaping with her life, she is placed into protective custody. When the safe house is breached, Jackie makes a daring escape from both the hired killers and the handsome FBI agent, who wants to return her to protective custody. With a little help from her sly and crafty friend, Monroe, Jackie is convinced she can disappear until the trial. While on her journey to meet with her friend, she solicits help from a few shady but lovable characters along the way. Although she manages to stay one-step ahead of the hired killers, the federal agent remains in hot pursuit. Will Jackie reach Monroe before she's captured by the FBI and returned to protective custody? Or will the hired killers silence her first?

"Town Darling"

After surviving a brutal attack that claims the lives of those she loves, a young woman seeks revenge on a corrupt town.

Going back home is never easy, but for Casey, it means returning to her corrupt hometown where she barely survived a brutal attack. Accompanied by two family friends, she seeks justice for the night that destroyed her life. Her physical scars are nothing compared to her emotional ones, forcing the local sheriff to believe that the town darling is back for revenge. As the conspiracy for her revenge appears to be leading up to the coveted town fair, the sheriff is determined to stop her from fulfilling her vengeful scheme...but guilt over his role on that fateful night continues to haunt him. Will his desperate need for Casey's forgiveness be his undoing? Or will Casey's desire for revenge destroy them both?

"Unconditional"

A young woman puts her life on hold to care for an unstable, highly skilled combat soldier, who believes someone is trying to kill him.

A botched military coup leaves a team of elite fighters injured with one clinging to life in a coma. When Harlan wakes from his coma, he's left with no memory of his past life. His commander's daughter, Indy, takes it upon herself to care for the fallen war hero. She's challenged with more than just his physical care as she combats with not only his memory loss but also his newly found desire for her. His infatuation with her becomes the least of her worries when he sinks back into his role of a combat soldier. Believing his life is in danger, his fighting skills surface, turning him into an unpredictable and dangerous man. Will his memory return to him before Indy is forced to commit him? Or will he finally find his nemesis, "the coyote", and possibly claim the life of an innocent person?

Coming Fall 2016!
"Deadly Institution 2"

ABOUT THE AUTHOR

Holly Copella has been writing since the age of twelve when her frustration at a book's poor plot drove her to author her own story. Over the last decade, she's written a number of screenplays, some of which she's now adapting into novels. Her fascination with zombies and other darker material lends an edge to her writing, which tends to lean toward horror. As a fan of Agatha Christie, she appreciates the craft of a good plot and the importance of creating significant characters.

Hailing from Pennsylvania, Copella lives in the Endless Mountains on a farm with her rescue horses and other animals. In addition to writing and reading fiction, she enjoys riding horses and traveling to Las Vegas and Disney World.

www.ingramcontent.com/pod-product-compliance
Lightning Source LLC
Chambersburg PA
CBHW071247210626
46818CB00013B/274